Miss Ellicott cleared her throat and intoned, "'Speak the words that Haywith spoke, and keep the vow that Haywith broke.'"

"I beg your pardon," said Chantel. "I was wondering what the second part meant."

"It does not matter what it means. Recite!" said Miss Ellicott.

Chantel obediently repeated the couplet. She was good at memorizing things. All Miss Ellicott's students were.

"Very well. Do not forget. The meaning will become clear in time."

Chantel wanted to shrug, but her deportment wouldn't let her. And Japheth couldn't do it for her. Snakes are ill-equipped for shrugging.

"Remember what I have told you," said Miss Ellicott. "A great destiny awaits you, and the entire kingdom will depend on you. You may go, and tell no one."

SAGE BLACKWOOD

MISS ELLICOTT'S SCHOOL
for the
Magically Minded

KATHERINE TEGEN BOOKS
An Imprint of HarperCollins Publishers

ALSO BY SAGE BLACKWOOD

Jinx

Jinx's Magic

Jinx's Fire

Katherine Tegen Books is an imprint of HarperCollins Publishers.

Miss Ellicott's School for the Magically Minded
Copyright © 2017 by Karen Schwabach
All rights reserved. Printed in the United States of America.
No part of this book may be used or reproduced in any manner whatsoever
without written permission except in the case of brief quotations embodied in critical
articles and reviews. For information address HarperCollins Children's Books, a
division of HarperCollins Publishers, 195 Broadway, New York, NY 10007.
www.harpercollinschildrens.com

Library of Congress Control Number: 2016935939
ISBN 978-0-06-240264-6

Typography by Carla Weise
19 20 21 22 23   PC/BRR   10 9 8 7 6 5 4 3 2 1
❖
First paperback edition, 2019

To
Gaby

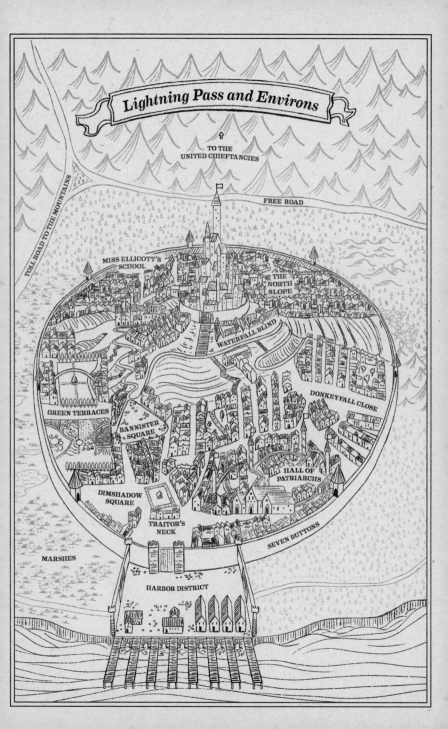

1

CHANTEL

A secret nearly cost Chantel her life, on a dark summer morning when the rains ran down the stairstepped stone streets of Lightning Pass.

And Chantel didn't even know, at first, that there was a secret, let alone that she had been part of it for seven years. But there was, and she had, and it was a secret that had the power to destroy the Kingdom of Lightning Pass and everyone in it.

She found that out later, after disaster had struck Miss Ellicott's School, and just after the bit of trouble with the snake. Let us begin a little closer to the beginning.

Miss Ellicott's School stood like a candle trembling in a dark storm, perched on a steep, twisting street in the peak-built city of Lightning Pass. The school was an unlikely-looking brick building crammed in between two other buildings, almost sitting on the roof of the house just below it. Fate's Turning was the name of the street, and some of the twists in it were actually old stone stairways. Carts couldn't come up the street, and only the most determined of horses.

A brass plate on the door read

MISS ELLICOTT'S SCHOOL FOR MAGICAL MAIDENS
SPELLS, POTIONS, WARDS, SUMMONINGS
AND DEPORTMENT
TAUGHT TO DESERVING SURPLUS FEMALES

Inside lived a dozen or so girls, and one boy. The boy was not a Surplus Female. His name was Bowser, and he had been left there by mistake. Miss Ellicott kept him as a pot-scrubber and general factotum.

Chantel was the brightest of the students. There was no doubt about that. While most of them spent years learning to summon their familiars, and ended up with dust bunnies and catnip mice for their efforts, Chantel had already summoned a snake named Japheth by the time she was six. Japheth was small and green, though he had a habit of turning gold in certain lights. He often wrapped himself around her neck, and visitors thought he was jewelry until he flicked his tongue. Much of the time, however, he was off on business of his own.

As for her spells, potions and wards, they were coming along nicely. Chantel privately thought her magic was good enough that she ought to have been sent to strengthen the city wall with the grown-up sorceresses, but she didn't mention this to Miss Ellicott. Miss Ellicott was not the sort of person to whom one mentioned things.

Deportment was more of a problem.

The fact was, Chantel did not like to deport. Oh, she was good at it, on the outside. She stood up straight, and she curtseyed demurely, and she sat and listened to adults with her slim brown hands folded neatly on the lap of her green school robe. She spoke only when spoken to, although sometimes this involved gritting her teeth so hard they ached for hours afterward.

The trouble was, sometimes she couldn't help giving people a Look. Because sometimes, people deserved it.

And she *thought* things. More and more often, as she got older, she wanted to *say* them. Sometimes she barely managed to stop herself.

Thinking things and having a Look were not good deportment. Good deportment, as one learned at Miss Ellicott's School, meant being shamefast and biddable.

One of Chantel's most famous failures of deportment happened the year she was ten. It happened on an icy night

3

when a long cold rain froze the streets of Lightning Pass.

Chantel and her best friend Anna were up on the roof, where they were not supposed to be. An ocean-scented wind slapped their school robes against their legs. Pellets of ice stung their faces. These were things that let you know you were alive.

The moon crept out from behind a cloud. It lit the city, from the castle at the top, its dragon flag snapping in the wind, all the way down to the high wall at the bottom. The wall was called Seven Buttons. It surrounded the city, encircled it, protected it. It kept the outside out and the inside in. It stopped untoward things and strange people from happening to the city of Lightning Pass.

The moon shone on ice-coated streets, which just begged to be slid down. And Chantel loved her city, even if she wasn't allowed out in it very much. She couldn't let it beg in vain.

"If we took a big pot lid from the kitchen—" she said.

"Don't," said Anna. "You'll get in *so* much trouble."

But Chantel always wanted to know what was going to *happen*.

So she sneaked downstairs, with Anna in her wake exhorting her not to do it. She tiptoed past where Bowser the pot-boy was dozing by the fireplace (not waking him, because she didn't want to get him in trouble) and she found the biggest pot lid there was. Then, with Anna beside her

4

imploring her not to, Chantel took the enormous brass key from its hook and opened the front door.

The steps were so icy she slipped and went right down them, and landed painfully in the street. She had to scramble to get onto the pot lid, because she was already sliding, gliding, rattling and flying—down Fate's Turning, thump-thump-thump over the steps, and then out into Rosewood Walk. She zoomed through streets and twisting alleys— this was being alive! She zipped over a high bridge that arched across the Green Terraces, and—

And off it.

Chantel flew through the air.

But in a generally downward direction. The fact is, she fell.

She might have had time to think, just then, about whether she could have deported herself better and whether Anna was perhaps occasionally sometimes right. But she didn't think about either of those things. She was too busy scrambling for a spell, any spell! Everything she had been taught, almost, was meant to protect against something: fleas, winter fever, moldy cheese. But there was absolutely nothing that protected against—

SPLUNCH.

Chantel landed on a stone bench, set in one of the Wednesday lawns on the Green Terraces. And it ought to have been her that went SPLUNCH, but instead the bench did. It turned all soft, as if it had been made of pudding.

Chantel picked herself up, feeling rather stunned. The bench, which had become gray blobs on the ice-spiked lawn, gathered itself up and turned into a bench again. She looked around for the pot lid.

It came down on her head with a painful clang. And then another, and another. Raising her arms to protect herself, Chantel looked up at the tall, robed figure of Miss Ellicott herself. Miss Ellicott, standing in the dark garden in the middle of an ice storm. Miss Ellicott, wielding a pot lid.

"Miss Ellicott, what are you doing here?" Chantel was startled into asking, as she dodged the next descent of the pot lid.

"You," said Miss Ellicott, in tones icier than the night, "are in a GREAT deal of trouble."

⁂

Chantel wasn't *really* afraid she would be expelled. That didn't happen to girls like her, girls to whom spells came easily, girls who had summoned a familiar.

She told herself that.

Still, she was extremely nervous when she was called into Miss Ellicott's study the following day.

The room smelled of magic and furniture polish. Miss Ellicott herself smelled of soap and magic potions. Chantel sat where Miss Ellicott told her to sit, tucked her robe neatly around her, and folded her hands in her lap. Japheth the snake was looped around her neck.

Miss Ellicott straightened her steel-rimmed spectacles on her nose and directed a grim gaze at Chantel. "To say that I am displeased with your deportment, Chantle, would be greatly understating the case."

Chantel did not say *It's pronounced shahn-TELL*. Miss Ellicott was a force of nature, like a thunderstorm. You didn't correct thunderstorms.

"Do you understand why it is particularly important for you to comport yourself in such a way as to frighten no one?"

Chantel looked up in surprise. The idea of her frightening anyone was ridiculous. She was, at the time, only ten. And she was only Chantel.

Miss Ellicott was waiting for an answer.

"Er, because I'm a girl?" Chantel ventured.

"Because you are a *magical maiden*. And this frightens people, Chantle. The city needs sorceresses, but it fears them."

Miss Ellicott looked at Chantel to see if she was taking this in.

"Er, doesn't the city kind of fear everything?" said Chantel.

"Chantle!" Miss Ellicott's eyebrows drew down like twin lightning bolts. "What a thing to say. With Seven Buttons and all our soldiers to protect us, we have no need to fear!"

But we do, Chantel wisely didn't say. That's why we *have* Seven Buttons, isn't it? That's why we have soldiers. And all the spells we learn, they're all about things we're afraid of, aren't they? We don't learn to fly. We learn to hide.

"A magical maiden must be shamefast and biddable," Miss Ellicott went on, "so that she can learn magic without anyone being unduly upset. A magical maiden must show promise of growing into a proper and correct sorceress. If a sorceress were not proper and correct, she—"

Japheth gave a mighty wriggle on Chantel's neck, and Chantel reached up and grabbed him.

"—would not survive," said Miss Ellicott.

Chantel froze in surprise, her fingers around the snake. "Miss Ellicott, has somebody . . . not survived before?"

"I have warned you," said Miss Ellicott. "There is nothing further you need to know."

She stared at Chantel through those steel-rimmed spectacles until Chantel looked down and said, "Yes, Miss Ellicott. Thank you, Miss Ellicott."

"Very well." Miss Ellicott sat back perhaps a fraction of an inch in her chair. "Now, there is something else I must discuss with you, Chantle."

Chantel waited.

"When you came to us from the orphanage, they told us how you arrived there. I waited until you were old enough, but now I feel you are ready to hear."

Chantel knew how she had arrived at the orphanage: the same way nearly everyone did, in a basket balanced on the narrow, uneven orphanage steps. These baskets happened often, because babies were in excess supply in Lightning Pass. At the age of five, children outgrew the orphanage and were moved on to something else . . . being a servant, or working in a factory, or sweeping the streets. Chantel knew she was extremely fortunate to have ended up at Miss Ellicott's School instead.

The important thing was, it didn't sound like she was being expelled. So she kept her hands neatly folded in her lap even though her nose was beginning to itch.

"You were left in a basket, Chantle, on the night of—" Miss Ellicott stopped and peered in the registry book open on her desk—"July 3rd, in the seventh year of the reign of King Wiley the Warmonger, of blessed memory."

Chantel knew this. She'd been told it at the orphanage. The basket had a hole in it, and she herself had been wrapped in a very worn but reasonably clean dishrag. Both items had then been used around the orphanage until they fell apart.

"Perched on the edge of the basket was a small golden dragon," said Miss Ellicott, in the same tone in which she'd stated the date. "And when the orphanage matron came to

9

the door, the dragon breathed letters of fire that spelled out 'Behold the Chosen One.'"

Chantel had not heard this part before, and she was surprised into speaking. "I didn't know the orphanage matron could read."

Miss Ellicott turned a hard glare on her student. "That remark was impertinent, Chantle."

"I beg your pardon." Chantel spoke politely. But Japheth, who had never been taught deportment, reared his small green head and flicked his tiny forked tongue. Chantel was pretty sure the matron *couldn't* read, and this seemed to her a real hole in Miss Ellicott's story. And there was another. Chantel stroked Japheth's smooth, scaly skin. "My familiar is a snake, not a dragon."

"A snake is merely an immature form of dragon. That is neither here nor there," said Miss Ellicott haughtily. "Do you not want to know what the message meant?"

"Yes please," said Chantel.

"Chosen to save the realm," said Miss Ellicott. "Chosen for a great destiny. Without you, the Kingdom of Lightning Pass cannot survive. Without you, Seven Buttons will crumble, and evil will rush in."

This was the first time anyone had spoken to Chantel of her future.

"You mean," she said eagerly, "I'll go into battle and—"

"Certainly not! Magical maidens do not go into battle."

"So will I cast a great spell that—"

"I sincerely hope you will have no reason to do anything of the kind."

"Then what—"

"You will do as the king and the patriarchs tell you," said Miss Ellicott. "You will grow from a shamefast and biddable maiden into a proper and correct sorceress, and you will do your duty. That is how you will save the realm."

"Oh," said Chantel. As destinies went, it sounded rather dull.

"I am sure you must feel overwhelmed by this news," said Miss Ellicott. "Keep it to yourself, and consider it. Do not tell the other students, as they would naturally be jealous."

"Yes, Miss Ellicott." Chantel refolded her hands neatly on her lap.

"You have years to go in your education," said Miss Ellicott. "Now that you know the great future that awaits you, I trust you will apply yourself to your lessons, and take very seriously everything your instructresses try to convey to you."

Chantel thought this was unfair. She always *had*. Miss Ellicott, of course, hadn't noticed. Miss Ellicott was an important sorceress, and did little of the actual teaching herself. Most of it was done by the underteacher, Miss Flivvers, who was not magical at all, and by jobbing

11

sorceresses who lived elsewhere. The jobbing sorceresses taught the students to do small protective and household spells, and to bring light into the darkness, and to summon lost things.

She waited to see if Miss Ellicott was going to say anything else. Once she would have asked "Can I go now?" but that sort of question was smacked out of Miss Ellicott's students in the first year. Chantel let Japheth do the impatient squirming for her, sliding ticklishly along her collarbone.

"There were more words that the dragon flamed," said Miss Ellicott. "A mysterious couplet. Do you wish to hear it?"

"Yes please," said Chantel.

Miss Ellicott cleared her throat and intoned, "'Speak the words that Haywith spoke, and keep the vow that Haywith broke.'"

"What does that mean?" asked Chantel.

"Do not tell me you are unaware of the treachery of wicked Queen Haywith. Has Miss Flivvers taught you nothing?"

Chantel's face burned at the accusation. Even if Miss Flivvers *had* taught her nothing, Chantel would still know that, five hundred years ago, Queen Haywith had opened a breach in Seven Buttons and let evil Marauders into the city. *Everyone* knew that. It was the reason for the saying

"She's about as trustworthy as Queen Haywith." Which meant not trustworthy at all. Or, likewise, "I wouldn't trust her any further than I could throw Queen Haywith."

"I beg your pardon," said Chantel. "I was wondering what the second part meant."

"It does not matter what it means. Recite!" said Miss Ellicott.

Chantel obediently repeated the couplet. She was good at memorizing things. All Miss Ellicott's students were.

"Very well. Do not forget. The meaning will become clear in time."

Chantel wanted to shrug, but her deportment wouldn't let her. And Japheth couldn't do it for her. Snakes are ill-equipped for shrugging.

"Remember what I have told you," said Miss Ellicott. "A great destiny awaits you, and the entire kingdom will depend on you. You may go, and tell no one."

<hr>

Chantel did tell no one, of course, except her friend Anna, and Bowser the pot-boy. And when a year later Miss Ellicott called Anna into her study and said that *Anna* was the Chosen One, Anna of course told Chantel.

The three of them puzzled over it in the skullery at the back of the high, twisty brick house, which was their refuge from things Ellicott. (In most houses it would be called a scullery, but in Miss Ellicott's School it was a skullery, for reasons that may be explained later.) This was where Bowser worked. Much of his life was spent scrubbing out burned pots with sand, and that was what he was doing at the moment.

"Well, we can't both be the Chosen One," said Chantel, feeling a little miffed.

"Maybe she thought I was you," said Anna. "Bowser, we could do a scouring spell—"

"Frenetica doesn't want any magic in the pots," said Bowser. "Because of those frogs that one time."

Frenetica was the cook.

Chantel did not think Miss Ellicott had mistaken her for Anna. Anna had yellow hair, and skin the color of raw chicken. "What did she tell you about being the Chosen One?"

"She said I was left in a basket made from oily grasses that don't grow in Lightning Pass," said Anna. "And woven into the basket were the words THE CHOSEN ONE, in red-dyed reeds."

"Hmph," said Chantel. Anna's story had a nicer basket in it.

"I don't think I'm the Chosen One," said Anna. "The only thing I'm much good at is brewing potions."

"Maybe she was trying to encourage you both," said Bowser, his voice ringing from deep inside an iron kettle. "You know, give you something to shoot for."

Chantel and Anna looked at each other. They shook their heads.

"I don't think so," said Chantel. "She doesn't encourage people exactly."

"No," said Anna. "I wonder if she means we're going to be two of the Six?"

Six sorceresses—the very best in the city—were tasked with the Buttoning, the spell that kept the wall called Seven Buttons strong. Miss Ellicott was one of the Six.

Most of the girls from Miss Ellicott's School would grow up to be jobbing sorceresses. They would keep the Green Terraces growing, and they would mind shops that sold potions, small protections, and conjurings. But Chantel had hoped—and sometimes rather confidently expected—to become one of the Six.

She had to admit she hadn't really thought about Anna.

"If she was talking about you being part of the Six, she wouldn't have said the Chosen *One*," said Bowser, inside the kettle.

Chantel and Anna and Bowser more or less forgot about Chosen Ones after that, up until the day a mysterious stranger appeared at the door, uttered the word "Dimswitch," and changed everything.

2

The Will-Be

Chantel grew tall and thoughtful. She excelled in summonings, spells, wards, and, as time went by, deportment, at least until the day the snake crawled into her ear. But that comes later.

Her life began to change one ordinary day when she was thirteen, and enduring an unnecessary magic lesson from the utterly unmagical Miss Flivvers.

There were many kinds of magic it would have been quite useful to learn, Chantel thought. Like flying. Or turning into something—a cat, for example. Or turning invisible. Chantel could do a self-abnegation, of course; most of the older girls could. But that didn't make you invisible, just hard to notice.

Instead, the magical maidens were learning to summon small and useful household objects. And Chantel had been able to do that since she was five.

Nonetheless, there they all were, a dozen magical maidens, lined up in front of Miss Flivvers—the little girls like Holly and Daisy, who hadn't even learned to make light-globes yet, and big girls like Chantel and Anna. Only Leila, the oldest student in the school, was missing.

"First," said Miss Flivvers, "recite for me the two principle rules of summoning objects."

"One," chorused the girls. "Do not summon anything that does not belong either to you, or to the person for whom you are performing the summoning. Two—"

At this point Holly faltered, forgot her lines, and burst into tears. Anna took her hand and led her from the room.

"Two?" Miss Flivvers demanded.

"Two," the girls said. "Do not summon anything likely to frighten, upset, or offend any of those present."

"Correct," said Miss Flivvers. "Now, for this spell we use what signs?"

"Sixth, fourth, and nineteenth," chanted the girls.

"Very well. First, you will show me your sixth sign. Left arms up, and—if Chantel will deign to join us?"

Chantel curtseyed quickly by way of apology and raised her left hand with the others. The fact was she had already summoned the scrub-brushes and sponges that were waiting at the other end of the room several times while Miss Flivvers's back was turned. Then she'd sent them back again. She would be asked to summon them again, of course, after the little girls failed to do the spell the first time. Which was very—

Leila stuck her head in the door. "I beg your pardon," she said in a deportment-y tone. "Miss Ellicott wishes to see Chantel and Anna. And me."

Leila swept out.

"You may go, Chantel," said Miss Flivvers. She looked worried. Maybe because she would have to finish teaching the lesson without Chantel's help, or maybe because worried was just an expression that sat naturally on Miss Flivvers's face.

⁂

Chantel knocked on the tall, stern door of Miss Ellicott's office.

"Enter," said Miss Ellicott.

Anna and Leila were already there, sitting in severe, straight-backed chairs, with their faces to Miss Ellicott and their backs to the shelves that held jars of useful magical supplies. Chantel curtseyed and took a seat beside them.

Miss Ellicott stood and surveyed them somberly. "Circumstances change."

This was a surprise. One of the fundamental lessons of life in Miss Ellicott's School was that circumstances did *not* change.

"Regrettably, the future may not be like the glorious present. The present is a pinnacle that man has achieved by overcoming the trials of the terrible past."

Miss Ellicott looked at her students to see how they would react to this pronouncement. Her students looked back and blinked.

"Although, in general, a girl is best off memorizing the wisdom of her elders and seeking to be worthy of it, there are times when originality and creativity may be unavoidable," Miss Ellicott went on. "We find ourselves now in difficult times, interesting times, times when what *is* may change. Perhaps for the better, perhaps . . . not. Therefore, it becomes necessary to teach a few of my more advanced pupils the more difficult branches of magic.

"Later, I will teach you the spells by which you can help the patriarchs and the king. The Gleam, with which you can make a man feel and appear ten feet tall. The Contentedness spell, which brings peace to our city. But we will begin with principles of prognostication. We will see if any of you has the least aptitude for seeing the Will-Be or the Ago."

Her tone conveyed that she did not expect they would.

"Prognosticatory magic is slippery stuff," Miss Ellicott went on. "It is difficult to see the Will-Be, and even the Ago can be wavery and uncertain."

Chantel was surprised by this, as she had always assumed that once something happened, it was done and was known. Miss Ellicott now told them this was not the case. It all came down to missing information, lost perspectives, and points of view.

Points of view are funny things.

Miss Ellicott showed them the spell for seeing the Will-Be.

It was important, Miss Ellicott said, to burn the right herbs, and then put the fire out suddenly with blood from a mortal wound.

They did this. There was a terrible burned-blood smell. Eye-watering purple smoke rose from the ashes, glowing, and formed itself into . . .

"Well?" said Miss Ellicott, looking from the smoke to the girls with eyes as sharp as a toothache.

Well, Anna said the smoke formed into a dog digging its way under a fence to escape from its yard. And Leila said there was indeed a fence, but a fearsome beast (possibly a dragon) was burrowing under it to attack the city.

Chantel was embarrassed to say that she didn't see any animal at all, though she did see a fence. The fence was made of iron palings. A girl was walking along, pushing them over, one by one.

The other students looked at her in confusion. "So the girl's the monster?" said Leila. "That's stupid."

"The girl's trying to escape," said Anna, clearly trying to be supportive.

"If she's trying to escape, she should run as soon as

she's knocked down enough palings," said Leila. "The girl's stupid."

Miss Ellicott looked at all of them and shook her head. "I expected better."

She didn't say what she'd seen, and naturally no one dared to ask.

For the next spell, they looked at the Ago. They peered into a mist made by boiling seven herbs and then dashing the hot brew onto ice cut from a pond in which seven maidens had drowned, tragically, while washing out their socks.

"Well?" said Miss Ellicott.

"I see a king sitting on a throne, bestowing justice on everyone," said Anna.

Leila gave her a pitying look. "I see a mighty king leading men into battle. With each swipe of his sword, he knocks off two enemies' heads."

"Which king?" Miss Ellicott demanded.

"King Mergaunt the Meticulous," said Anna.

"King Wiley the Warmonger," said Leila.

"Hm." Miss Ellicott turned to Chantel and waited.

Chantel was embarrassed to say. "I just saw, um, a crown. And it was, um, bleeding."

Leila rolled her eyes expressively.

"Which king wore the crown?" said Miss Ellicott.

"Nobody wore it," said Chantel. "It was just sitting there. Bleeding."

She felt like a hideous failure. She was the one who was supposed to be *good* at things. If it was the Ago, she ought to have seen a king from the past. Leila and Anna had. Leila's king had been fairly recent.

The year Chantel was eight, King Wiley the Warmonger had died of a sudden case of daggers in the back. Two years later, his successor died of a surfeit of lettuce, and was replaced by King Rathfest the Restless. It was soon after this that Miss Ellicott had been visited by a royal messenger.

"The king wishes prognostications," said the messenger. "He wishes to know if he is likely to fall victim to the same sort of misfortune as his predecessors."

Chantel thought it extremely likely, but nobody asked her.

So Miss Ellicott went to the palace to prognosticate. And when she returned, Chantel heard her talking to Miss Flivvers.

Miss Ellicott clearly approved of the new king. "This is a new era for sorceresses. King Rathfest doesn't blame women for the treachery of Queen Haywith five centuries ago. King Rathfest puts women on a pedestal."

"It seems to me," said Miss Flivvers, who had been in a sour mood, "that once you're up on a pedestal, you can't take a step in any direction without falling."

"It is better than the alternative," said Miss Ellicott. "Mark my words."

I give you now Chantel Goldenrod, magician, age thirteen.

Dangerous?

Yes, of course. All people are dangerous, especially when they think and act for themselves.

And does she?

Not yet.

Not _entirely._

But there are signs.

And the girl is certainly magical, and she is training to be a sorceress.

Therefore, there are dangers. She is carefully watched.

We have seen nothing to alarm us yet. She is a model of deportment. She speaks when spoken to and otherwise maintains a proper silence in the presence of her elders and betters.

She can't possibly be planning anything.

Nonetheless, she is thirteen, and she is a magician, and she is female.

We will keep an eye on her.

3

The Hall of Patriarchs

Considering how badly she'd done in her first prognostication lesson, Chantel was not exactly happy when Miss Ellicott decided to tutor her alone. She went into the close, candlelit study at the appointed time, feeling nervous.

"Now then," said Miss Ellicott. "Describe to me exactly what you saw last week. First, the Ago."

"I saw a bloody crown. But I've been thinking about it," said Chantel. "And I don't think the crown was empty. I think there was a king in it. I think it was one of the ancient kings, and that I just didn't recognize him."

A stony silence followed this remark. Chantel shifted uncomfortably, and Japheth the snake flicked his tongue. It occurred to Chantel suddenly that she had never seen Miss Ellicott's familiar.

"You do not think that," said Miss Ellicott.

Chantel was reluctant to contradict, because of her deportment. "I beg your pardon. I think it was King Fustian the First."

"Oh? And what did King Fustian the First look like?"

"Uh, square," said Chantel. "His face was kind of square, and his ears were kind of square, and his eyes were kind of—"

"Square, because the sculptor who carved the bas-relief on his tomb was incapable of curves," said Miss Ellicott. "Do not lie to me, Chantle. It is useless, annoying, and a waste of time."

Japheth gave an angry twitch. "I *thought* it *might* have been King Fustian," said Chantel, controlling her temper.

"You mean, you thought that was what I wanted to hear," said Miss Ellicott. "That is *not* how prognostication works. You see what you see. You make yourself an empty vessel into which the vision pours."

"Well, I guess I can't do it, then," said Chantel.

"Not with that attitude, certainly," said Miss Ellicott. "If you wish to be of service to your king, so that he may defend our country from the evil Marauders Without the Walls, you must put aside these adolescent vaporings. *You* do not matter. But at least your vision sounds like a real one. Tell me again exactly what you saw."

"A crown with blood coming out of it," said Chantel, her neatly folded hands clenching angrily. "That's all."

"Good. You must never let anyone convince you that you have seen something other than what you have seen," said Miss Ellicott. "And that means you must never convince *yourself* that—"

There came a tapping at the chamber door.

"I am engaged!" said Miss Ellicott, to the closed door. "Never convince yourself that—"

The knock came again, timid but determined.

"Whoever is at the door had better think very seriously about whether she wishes to remain within my household!" said Miss Ellicott. "Chantle, you must never—"

The knock came a third time.

Miss Ellicott stalked to the door and tore it open.

Bowser stood trembling in the doorway. He looked, Chantel thought, as if he'd been staring into his own open grave.

"M-Miss, there's somethi—someone to see you."

Miss Ellicott fixed on him the look that students got when they should not have dared to speak. "I am engaged." She turned back to Chantel.

"I told him that," said Bowser. "He said you'd want to see him."

"He was mistaken."

"The man said—"

"If he must see me, he may come back tomorrow at nine o'clock," said Miss Ellicott.

Bowser looked as if he was caught between two terrifying things. "M-Miss. He said to tell you 'Dimswitch.'"

Miss Ellicott stared.

Then she turned to Chantel. "Chantle—" She opened her mouth, and closed it again. She did this three times, as if she was thinking of things to say and then discarding them.

"Chantle," she said finally. "Whatever happens, I expect you to do your duty."

Chantel was startled. "Do my—?"

Miss Ellicott swept out of the office. Chantel and Bowser heard her hurrying down the stairs.

They looked at each other in confusion.

Chantel took Japheth from her neck and let him slither from one of her hands to another. "Why did you almost call him a 'something'?"

"Because he was." Bowser was looking at the jars of magical ingredients on the shelves. "What are all these things?"

"Stuff for spells," said Chantel. "What did he—"

"What's this?" Bowser picked up a jar.

"Screeching mandrake roots harvested on the night of a blood-red moon," said Chantel. "Never mind them. What did he look like?"

Bowser put the jar back. "Like death, I guess. He looked . . ." Bowser frowned. "Like something that was going to happen no matter what, and nobody was going to be happy about it."

Chantel looped Japheth back onto her neck and went out into the hall. She looked down the stairs. The front door was shut, and the hall was empty.

Up above they could hear the chatter of the other girls, reciting rules for spells or sweeping the dormitory. Down in the kitchen, they could hear Frenetica clattering pots.

"Did he say what that meant?" Chantel asked. "Dimswitch?"

"No," said Bowser. "He just said 'Dimswitch.'"

"Hm," said Chantel. "Maybe we'll find out more when she comes back."

But Miss Ellicott did not come back.

It was only late that evening that it began to become clear that something was wrong. And when she was still not back the following morning, it was clear that the something was very wrong indeed.

❦

The day after the mysterious stranger spirited Miss Ellicott away, none of the jobbing sorceresses showed up to teach. There was only the non-magical Miss Flivvers. And Miss Flivvers went into a tizzy.

Chantel had always thought of Miss Flivvers as a

grown up, and she'd expected her to behave in a grown up way, which up to now she always had. But it seemed that without Miss Ellicott to tell her what to do, Miss Flivvers had no idea. She gathered all the girls into an upstairs classroom. And she gave them lists to memorize, and that was that.

Chantel and Anna slipped away. No one said anything. They were suddenly freer than they had ever been. Chantel and all the other girls could have sledded down the streets on pot lids; there was no one to stop them.

But it was late spring, and anyway the situation was too serious for sledding. Chantel and Anna went down to the skullery to confer with Bowser.

"Could Miss Ellicott have gone to do the Buttoning spell?" said Anna, without much hope.

"That's done every second Thursday," said Bowser. "And she always goes really early in the morning—more like night, actually."

"Maybe she just went away on a visit . . ." said Anna.

She trailed off as the others shook their heads. You could walk anywhere in Lightning Pass in an hour. There was no need for overnight visits. And she couldn't have gone outside the wall. People didn't.

Frenetica the cook stuck her large head around the doorway. "If you're through solving the world's problems," she said, "you can go round to the shop and get me some cinnamon, and two dozen eggs. And place an order for another hundred pounds of potatoes."

She meant Bowser, of course. Magical maidens didn't run errands. But on this strange, unsettled day, it didn't seem to matter. Chantel, Anna and Bowser slipped out the skullery door, down the alley, and around the corner to Mr. Whelk's grocery on Fate's Turning.

Where there were only three eggs, and no cinnamon.

"Can I have the eggs, then, please," said Bowser, setting his basket on the counter.

"I suppose so." Mr. Whelk spoke in tones Chantel imagined a mournful walrus might use. "Somebody has to."

He reached for the box behind him and drew out the credit slip for Miss Ellicott's School. He wrote on it, and pushed it across for Bowser to sign.

"What?" said Bowser. "Fifteen dollars? For three eggs?"

"Is that a lot?" said Anna. Magical maidens didn't handle money.

"It's highway robbery!" said Bowser.

Japheth gave a wriggle on Chantel's neck, perhaps in surprise at this lack of deportment. But Bowser, after all, was not a magical maiden.

"That," said Mr. Whelk, in heavy, hollow tones, "is a matter of opinion. Prices"—he pushed the card forward again—"have risen."

"Fine." Bowser signed. It wasn't his money, after all. "And we want to order a hundred pounds of potatoes."

"Please," Anna added.

Mr. Whelk blinked sorrowfully. "I doubt, young people, that there are a hundred pounds of potatoes in the entire city at this moment."

"Why?" said Chantel.

"Some sort of trouble." Mr. Whelk took the card back, and picked his teeth with the corner of it.

A woman came into the shop, balancing a baby on her hip.

"An ounce of butter, please," she said. "And two eggs."

Mr. Whelk took the card out of his mouth and regarded her sadly. "There is no butter," he intoned. "There are no eggs."

Without saying anything, Bowser took one of the eggs out of his basket and handed it to the woman. And without demur, she thanked him for it and left.

Because that was Lightning Pass, Chantel thought with a surge of pride. People relied on each other. They were usually kind and they expected kindness.

From each other, that is. Not from anyone outside the walls. But people outside the walls hardly counted. You never saw them.

They went back to the school, with two eggs and no hope of future potatoes.

"Do we have any potatoes now?" said Chantel.

"Nope," said Bowser.

This was dismal news. It was bad enough to have strange things suddenly happening to your safe and comfortable world. But to have them happening without potatoes was worse. It was Chantel's opinion that baked potatoes were one of the best things in the world. When you held a hot baked potato in your hands, grown in the Green Terraces under the sorceresses' cultivation spells, you knew you were safe and you knew you were home.

And if there was butter, so much the better.

There wasn't any butter now.

"Also, there's no milk, and no cheese," Bowser said, as they climbed the stairs of Fate's Turning. "And no leeks, and—"

"I don't like leeks," said Chantel.

"And I don't like cheese," said Anna.

"I bet you'd rather eat them than nothing," said Bowser. "We have enough food through lunchtime tomorrow, and that's it."

"Can't you go somewhere else besides Mr. Whelk's?" said Chantel.

"Not without money," said Bowser. "And Frenetica asked Miss Flivvers for money, and Miss Flivvers burst into tears."

Chantel didn't know what to say. It was a horribly

insecure feeling when grown ups burst into tears, because it more or less left you in charge.

"Where does the money come from?" said Chantel.

Anna knew this. "From the patriarchs."

Chantel had seen the patriarchs. On important occasions they paraded in velvet robes. The king paraded too, but the patriarchs had nicer robes and people cheered more loudly for them.

Anna said that the patriarch in charge of the money for the school was named Sir Wolfgang. And Bowser said that they might try looking for him in the Hall of Patriarchs at the bottom of the city hill.

So they left the eggs in the kitchen, and went down the steep, uneven stairs of Fate's Turning, and through the crooked, narrow alleys that wound back and forth, toward the sound of the sea. They climbed tortuous trails to bridges that spanned streets and squares, topped by tall towers upon which the dragon flag of Lightning Pass rippled in the wind. And they went down staircases, and up more staircases, and through arched alleys, and at last they reached the grand, imposing Hall of Patriarchs, in the shadow of the wall called Seven Buttons.

⟨≡✤≡⟩

The Hall of Patriarchs was part cemetery, part government building, with a tower stuck onto the side. When you first entered, you were in the dank and windowless Hall of the

33

Dead, where footsteps echoed like books dropped in silent libraries.

Chantel and her friends made their way among rows of sarcophagi. Some had carvings of dead patriarchs and kings, staring stonily at the vaulted ceiling.

Chantel felt the breath of cold, musty air as they passed the dark hole of a stairway that led down to the catacombs.

Beyond the Hall of the Dead was the sudden warmth of a sunlit office. A round-eyed clerk with a mustache waxed into two curlicues sat at a severely-sloped desk. He smiled—the kind of smile that welcomes any interruption to a dull day.

"Yes?" He drew the word out slowly.

"We want to see Sir Wolfgang, please," said Bowser.

"Indeed? And yet I highly doubt Sir Wolfgang wants to see you," said the clerk, still smiling.

"We could come back—" said Anna uncertainly.

"No need for that," said the clerk. "Why shouldn't Sir Wolfgang do things he doesn't want? Third doorway on the left."

He waved toward a high arched hallway. Chantel wasn't at all sure they should go in. It was hardly good deportment to bother a patriarch who didn't want to see you.

On the other hand, Miss Ellicott was missing and there was nothing for dinner tomorrow.

They walked down the passage, between fluted stone

columns, past arches that led to chambers great and small. They found Sir Wolfgang sitting at a broad table, reading a scroll.

Sir Wolfgang was dressed in a long black coat, red velvet pantaloons and a waistcoat embroidered with golden lions.

The girls curtseyed perfectly, and Bowser bowed.

"What are you doing here?" Sir Wolfgang barked. Apparently no one had made him learn deportment.

"We're from Miss Ellicott's School," said Chantel. "And I'm afraid it seems that . . ." She trailed off. Money was not a polite matter to discuss.

"We can't buy food past lunchtime tomorrow," said Anna bluntly.

The patriarch said nothing, but looked questioningly at Bowser.

"We can't buy dinner," Bowser said.

"Why should you need to?" said the patriarch. "Surely you are supplied with it on a quotidian basis."

"Miss Ellicott's gone," said Anna. "And there's no—" Chantel watched her swallow the unmentionable word. "There's no way to buy any food."

This elicited no response but a glare, which was directed not at Anna but at Bowser.

"She's gone," Bowser echoed.

"Who?" said Sir Wolfgang.

The girls and Bowser looked at each other in consternation. Could the patriarch actually not *hear* girls?

"Miss *Ellicott*," said Bowser. "Miss Ellicott is gone from the school, and there's no money for food."

"What do you mean, gone?" said the patriarch. "She has no business to be gone. The school is her station in life, and there she must remain."

Anna looked at Chantel, and Chantel looked at Bowser, and Bowser told the patriarch about the mysterious stranger.

"Eloped, has she?" said the patriarch.

"We think she's been kidnapped," said Chantel, curtseying to cover the rudeness of contradicting him.

The patriarch ignored her. "What did this mysterious stranger, so called, look like?"

Chantel did her best to translate Bowser's odd description into something sensible. Bowser dutifully repeated Chantel's description so that the patriarch could hear it. The effect of this was alarming. Sir Wolfgang's eyebrows shot up, and then they dove down into a deep V shape. His jaw clenched and he leaned forward across his desk.

"Did he say who had sent him?"

"No," said Bowser.

"Did he make any signs?"

"I . . . I don't think so."

"Did he leave any marks or ciphers on the house? On the doorjamb, on the step?"

"Um, I didn't see any," said Bowser.

"I'll send searchers to look for signs," said the patriarch. "There may be magic involved. Now run along. I have important things to do."

"But what about the"—desperation made Chantel use the terrible word—"money?"

"What about the money?" Bowser repeated.

"Money is not for the likes of you," said Sir Wolfgang. "You'll be looked after. I'll send someone. Now be off."

"Are you going to send another sorceress to look after the school?"

"No," said the patriarch. "The other sorceresses are busy. Now, go!"

So the three of them had no choice but to retreat.

"Put him in a wretched mood, have you?" asked the clerk.

"Yes, sir," said Chantel. "Thank you for letting us in."

"No no, thank *you*," said the clerk, nodding them out. "Come back any time. My name is Less."

They climbed back through the winding streets between the leaning buildings in the twilight. They took a detour through the gardenlands, where vegetables, vineyards and orchards grew in terraced green beds that scaled the south side of the mountain.

Then they climbed Fate's Turning, and returned to the school, no better off than when they started.

In fact, they had only made things worse.

The patriarch *did* send someone. He sent a number of someones. First he sent quick-eyed men with magnifying glasses to search the steps and the bricks and the door for marks and ciphers. Then he sent swift-fingered men with crowbars and hammers, who searched the school thoroughly, tearing into the walls and ripping up the floorboards. Miss Flivvers gathered all of the girls into the upstairs classroom and set them all to reciting frantically. The more the school was pulled to pieces around them, the more loudly Miss Flivvers, rigid with terror, made them recite. They recited the 29 reasons to say *excuse me*, and the 19 best forms of apology, and the 174 reasons to be grateful for the way things are, and the 423 situations in which a magical maiden must never find herself.

"If *I* ran the school—" Anna muttered in between recitations.

The only people who didn't have to recite were Frenetica and Bowser, who were doing their best to defend the kitchen as cauldrons were banged with hammers and drawers were split open to see if they had false bottoms.

Oh, the men were searching for something, all right.

Meanwhile the patriarch, instead of sending money, sent a manageress.

The manageress was named Mrs. Warthall, and the first thing she did was to go down to Mr. Whelk's store and place new orders. Not very nice orders. Meals had never exactly been grand at Miss Ellicott's School, but since Chantel didn't know anything about grand meals she had been happy enough with them. Now they were largely composed of gruel and offal, or as Chantel called it in her head, Cruel and Awful.

Mrs. Warthall didn't believe in schooling, not having had any herself, and so she put the girls and Miss Flivvers to work cleaning instead. In practice this actually meant using adhesion spells to stick the school back together, as best they could, after the searchers' depredations.

But, Chantel kept wondering, what had they been searching *for*?

4

In Search of Sorceresses

Chantel was helping Bowser with his work. She very much wished she could help him scrub potatoes, as she had in the past. But there were no potatoes. Or rather, there was just one potato, every night, baked for Mrs. Warthall, and served with a pat of butter. The smell of it was very hard to bear when you were eating watery gruel or a scrambled mess of boiled animal organs.

Chantel was cleaning the kitchen fireplace. Mrs. Warthall said that it should never show a speck of soot, inside or out. This was rather a tall order for a fireplace. But Mrs. Warthall would run her handkerchief along the inside, and if it came away black, or even gray, Bowser would be beaten and miss dinner.

Mrs. Warthall had also told Bowser to scrub all the other fireplaces in the school, which meant he didn't have time to scrub this one.

So Chantel scrubbed.

Meanwhile, she could hear Mrs. Warthall talking to her friend Mrs. Snickens out in the hall.

"It's only until they find the spells, and the gentlemen figure out how to do them," Mrs. Warthall was saying. "After that the school will be closed."

Chantel froze and listened.

Mrs. Snickens said something. Chantel couldn't make out the words.

"Oh, no, men can't generally do magic," said Mrs. Warthall. "But I figure that's because they hain't tried. After all, if women can be magicians, it stands to reason men can be better ones."

Mrs. Snickens asked something.

"Because the children themselves might know something," said Mrs. Warthall. "*I* don't know what—they're as silly a bunch of misses as you ever did see. But they may have overheard something."

Mrs. Snickens said something else, a soft insinuating murmur.

"I think it's just so those sorceresses don't suspect anything," said Mrs. Warthall. "This pack of brats can't know much that the great patriarchs themselves don't know, can they? But as long as the school stays here, no one will suspect—"

The other woman interrupted, said something, and chuckled.

"The children will be sold to the factories, of course," said Mrs. Warthall. "Once the foremen beat some sense into them, they may be worth something."

A query from Mrs. Snickens.

"Oh, *I* won't have the selling of them," said Mrs. Warthall. "Still—"

She stopped suddenly, as if she'd noticed the silence in the kitchen. Chantel began scrubbing frantically, just as Mrs. Warthall surged into the room, wielding a ladle. Chantel ducked into the fireplace as the ladle caught her a clanging blow.

"So you're spying on me, are you?" Mrs. Warthall stood before the fireplace, hands on hips. "Heard what I said? So what if I do sell you? You're going to be sold anyway. You belong in some respectable establishment where you can be given enough work to keep you out of trouble."

Chantel's neck hurt from crouching over, and her eyes stung from the soot. Japheth didn't like the fireplace at all. Chantel felt his scales sliding over her neck. He wriggled over her shoulder, down her arm, and away.

"You can be sure the patriarchs intend to get what they

can for you. And I might help them out," Mrs. Warthall went on. "I might just sell the little ones first, who'll be easiest to train, and—"

She broke off with a squawk as Japheth slid past, a golden streak of life on the cold brick floor. She raised her ladle to strike.

"Don't you dare!" cried Chantel, forgetting her deport- ment entirely. She burst out of the fireplace and gave Mrs. Warthall a shove in the stomach.

Blows from the ladle rained down on her. Chantel ducked and tried to cover her head with her arms. At least she was saving Japheth.

She didn't know where Japheth went during the times he disappeared. She only knew that he always came back.

⁂

Chantel told Anna and Bowser what she'd heard.

"She can't sell us!" said Anna. "We don't belong to her."

"So what do we do?" said Bowser.

"Tell the patriarchs," said Anna.

"Then they'll just sell us before she does," said Chantel.

"I don't think so," said Anna. "They let the school exist. They *need* sorceresses. To strengthen the wall, and make plants grow, and—"

"Mrs. Warthall said she thought the patriarchs could do magic if they tried," said Chantel.

"They can't," said Bowser flatly. "Only girls can do magic."

They looked at him. He looked embarrassed. "Well, I've tried. And I can't."

Chantel was struck with a flurry of memories: Bowser looking longingly at the jar of dried mandrake root. Bowser surreptitiously making signs over a particularly badly burnt cauldron, Bowser casting herbs into a bubbling pot of soup, Bowser trying to get the skulls at the back of the skullery to talk.

She felt bad for never having noticed how much he wanted to do magic. She wanted to say that after all, no one had taught him. But he clearly didn't want to discuss it.

"I think we should ask one of the other sorceresses for help," Chantel decided.

So they went in search of sorceresses. They wended their way through twisting streets, and into arched alleys and up certain staircases that wound around watchtowers, and over various bridges.

"A couple of them live in a house up on Turnkey Crescent," said Bowser. He knew the city better than they did.

Turnkey Crescent was a street that curved gradually around the hill on which the city was built. Beech trees grew thickly and joined overhead, their branches meshing. It was like walking through a green leafy tunnel, loud with birdsong. The sorceresses' house was number 526, a thin, tall building with a narrow green door topped by a stained-glass transom, depicting a sorceress stirring a cauldron. They knocked.

A servant answered. She was about nine years old, and had pale skin, red pigtails, and a frightened expression. "How-may-I-be-of-service?" she demanded.

"We're looking for Miss Tripes," said Bowser.

"You're too late," said the girl. "They got her already, and Miss Davidson too. And they got Miss Faranoko up on Waterfall Blind, so don't bother looking there."

Chantel had a terrible feeling of foreboding. "Who?"

"Some man," said the girl. "Came and said 'Wayswitch.'"

"Did he look like death?" Chantel asked.

"Pretty much."

"Who's looking after you?" said Anna.

"I'm looking after myself," said the girl. "Now if there's nothing else—" She started to close the door.

Chantel felt like there was something else. "Wait!"

The girl stopped closing the door.

"You should come home with us—" Anna began.

"What about all the other sorceresses?" said Chantel. "Are they gone too?"

"How would I know?" The girl shut the door with a clunk.

"We should make her come home with us," said Anna.

"She's too young to look after herself."

"She's better off here than with Mrs. Warthall," said Bowser.

Chantel felt torn. They ought to try to help the girl, but . . . Bowser was right. They had no help to offer.

They wound their way back around the hill, bypassed Waterfall Blind, and then followed Rosewood Walk down to Bannister Square. The square was actually a triangle, a cobblestoned wedge that projected far enough over the city that you could see the sea. Chantel spared the ocean a glance—it was a distant, iron-gray band at the bottom of the sky—and hurried with her friends to the sorcery shop kept by Miss Waterstone and Miss Baako.

Chantel was vaguely aware of an abnegation spell beside the shop . . . something hidden, but she had no time to think about that now.

The shop door hung open. Everything inside had been removed, even the curtains.

"Miss Baako?" Chantel called. "Miss Waterstone?"

Her voice rang through the empty shop.

They went up the corkscrew staircase to the little apartment above. That was empty too. A single broken chair was all that remained.

No one questioned them when they came out of the shop. Everyone they saw looked the other way.

"Shall we ask them?" said Anna.

"No," said Chantel. "They're not going to tell us any-thing. I think they stole the sorceresses' stuff."

She was horrified to hear herself say this. One might *think* such a thing, but to say it aloud . . . !

"There's an abnegation spell here," she added.

She twitched her fingers in the signs to undo it. It was hiding nothing interesting—just a slab of rock, behind which was darkness and cold, dank air.

They went on searching for sorceresses. They climbed steep alleys and they followed dizzying walkways that spi-raled out over open space. They plodded through the wide streets at the bottom of the hill, in the very shadow of Seven Buttons, and they followed the tightly wound pas-sageways of the High Peak neighborhood, just below the castle. But it was the same in High Peak, and Buttonside, and Donkeyfall Close.

There were no sorceresses anywhere. They'd all van-ished. The few people who would talk all told some version of the same story. The sorceress in question had been vis-ited by a stranger who looked like death, and had gone off in a hurry, and that was all anyone knew, and wasn't it time the girls got home?

In the end they had no choice but to do just that.

⟨⁘⟩

"All of the sorceresses are gone," said Anna.

It was late at night, and they were sitting in the kitchen.

Chantel stretched her bare feet out on the brick floor. Japheth, who had been exploring the kitchen in search of someone to eat and had found the place far too well scrubbed for his taste, slithered smoothly between her toes and snaked his way up to his favorite place around her neck.

"Sir Wolfgang says they're busy with other things," said Bowser.

"I think he knows they're missing," said Chantel. "He just doesn't want other people to know. Because people might panic if they knew there was no one to do the Buttoning."

The other two looked at her in surprise.

"You're right!" said Anna. "There's no one to protect the walls, and—"

"And there are Marauders out there," Bowser finished. "You girls are going to have to do the Buttoning yourselves."

"We don't know how," said Anna. "And anyway we have more important things to worry about. Mrs. Warthall is going to *sell* everyone!"

Chantel stroked Japheth and thought. "I wonder . . . Those searchers who came here. Mrs. Warthall said they were looking for a spell."

"You think they were looking for the Buttoning?"

"If they were, and if we could find it—" said Chantel.

There was a sound of bare feet pattering along the hall. Chantel looked up to see Daisy, a little girl with beetle-black eyes and hair that hung over her ears in two shaggy braids.

Daisy reached out a finger to stroke Japheth, who flicked his tongue at her. "Chantel, when is Miss Ellicott coming back?"

"I don't know," said Chantel.

"Are you going to go look for her?"

"I—"

Chantel thought how frightened the younger girls would be if they knew that *all* the sorceresses were missing. They must already be scared. They still had Miss Flivvers, of course, but Miss Flivvers was proving woefully inadequate, no protection at all from Mrs. Warthall and her ladle.

Daisy was looking up at Chantel trustingly, big eyes in a hungry face. Miss Ellicott was not exactly loving, but there had always been a certain *thereness* to her. With Miss Ellicott around, you never doubted that someone was in charge, and that any bad thing that was going to happen was going to have to get through Miss Ellicott first.

Well, now it had gotten through Miss Ellicott.

"Yes. We're going to look for her," said Chantel. "Don't worry."

"Come on, Daisy," said Anna, and led the child away. Chantel heard them going up the stairs.

"We'll find the spell for the patriarchs," Chantel told Bowser. "And when we do—we're going to ask them to take Mrs. Warthall away before we give it to them."

5

In Which Chantel Considers Guts As Garters

The searchers had already torn the school apart looking for the Buttoning. But the searchers couldn't do magic.

Chantel and Anna did summoning spells. They did them up in the attic, away from Mrs. Warthall's suspicious gaze. For Chantel this was easy; summonings were her thing.

They did the spell again and again, holding in their minds pictures of things the Buttoning spell might be written on. Clean white sheets of paper, and yellowed old parchment scrolls, and much-blurred palimpsests of sheepskin. All sorts of documents came flying through the air: recipes, and bills, and homework, and something that appeared to be a death-bed confession, although to what, Chantel couldn't tell.

Then the spells stopped working. They had summoned every loose bit of paper in the school. So Chantel, Anna, Bowser, and the younger girls searched the school by hand. (Leila couldn't be bothered.)

They looked under the carpet of the wide mahogany front stairs, and in every corner of the dark twisty back stairs. They climbed on chairs and felt behind the carved dragons atop the doors and windows, and they scaled bookshelves and peered at the dusty tops. They poked into the oddly-shaped closets and cupboards that filled in the crooked corners of the school. They searched the ceilings.

Anna and Chantel took a hammer and pried up the attic steps, one by one, to see if there was anything written on the back of them.

They searched the sloped attic walls where the nails from the slates stuck through. Bats hung in ranks from the rough wood, and opened their tiny pink mouths and squeaked in protest at the intrusion.

"Maybe it's hidden under the bats," said Chantel.

"I'm sure those searchers looked under the bats already," said Anna.

Nonetheless the girls went back in the night, when the bats were gone, and searched the walls again.

They looked through all the trunks and boxes in the attic. Old school robes. Winter coats. Dishes. There had been books, but the searchers had pried them to pieces looking for messages hidden in the bindings. They had burned most of the pages looking for invisible ink. Chantel felt no particular sadness about this, because she had never found any secrets or mysteries in books. She had never in her life read a book that hadn't been sniffed over carefully by others, checked and rechecked, and stamped with approval as perfectly safe and unlikely to give her ideas.

There was a sudden storm of mad flapping all around them. Chantel and Anna hit the floor—the bats were coming home. The girls clamped their hands protectively over their hair. They both knew, in their brains, that bats have a spell that keeps them from bumping into people or getting tangled in anyone's hair. But their hair refused to believe it.

The bats hung themselves up on the sloping wall. There were a few more rustlings and flappings, then quiet.

The girls stood up, cautiously.

Chantel looked at the bats. She looked around the attic. There was nowhere else to search.

"It's almost dawn," said Anna. "I have to go up to the roof."

"Why?" said Chantel.

"I always do."

Chantel had been Anna's friend for years and years, and she had never known this. "I thought you were just an early riser."

"Yes. Because I have to get to the roof."

If you knew Anna well, you knew she had a rock-solid firmness that she hid from most people. You could see it now. Chantel followed her up the ladder.

The girls emerged into the cold gray dawn. There was a small platform on top, surrounded by an ornamental paling. Below that were the steep slated sides of the roof.

Birds were twittering and screeching in the trees down below.

Anna fixed her gaze to the east, where the sky was brightening into splashes of pink and orange.

"What—" Chantel began.

"Shh. Wait." Anna's mouth was a thin hard line. The sun appeared, a sliver of red on the horizon that grew to an arc and then a semicircle. Abruptly Anna spun on her heel and faced west. "You should turn too."

Chantel obeyed. "Why are we doing this?"

"Because Miss Ellicott told us to," said Anna. "Or at least, she told me. I'm surprised she didn't tell you."

"Well, she didn't," said Chantel, feeling annoyed. She'd been up all night and she was tired, stiff, and no closer to finding the spell than before. "And it seems pretty silly."

"I have to do it because I'm the Chosen One," said Anna. "It's what she told me."

"She told me I was the Chosen One too," Chantel reminded her. "But she never said anything about coming up on the roof and spinning around."

"She told me always to remember," said Anna. "'At the dawning of the day/Face the sun and turn away.'"

"Why?" Chantel said.

"How should I know? She just did," said Anna. "Maybe it's some kind of spell."

They looked at each other in surprise.

"What she told me," said Chantel, "was 'Speak the words that Haywith spoke/And keep the vow that Haywith broke.'"

Around them, in the city, bells rang and trumpets sounded to announce the new day.

"'At the dawning of the day/Face the sun and turn away. Speak the words that Haywith spoke/And keep the vow that Haywith broke,'" said Anna. "Wait . . . you think she hid the spell inside our heads?"

"Not just ours," said Chantel. "I bet she told other girls that they were the Chosen One, too."

They hurried downstairs to the dormitory. The girls were still asleep, but Chantel and Anna rousted them out of bed and assembled them into two frowsy, yawning, eye-rubbing rows seated along the edges of two beds.

"How many of you," Chantel asked, "have been told by Miss Ellicott that you are the Chosen One?"

The girls looked startled. Several hands went up. One of them was Daisy's, and one was Holly's.

"If Miss Ellicott gave you something to memorize, we need it," said Chantel.

Most of the girls didn't have couplets, as Anna and Chantel did. They just had single lines.

The lines came out of order. Daisy's was: "And touch the wall, and make it whole." Which sounded like it ought to come near the end.

Holly's was: "Write the third sign with your feet." That was easy enough. The third sign was a bit like a circle and a bit like an eagle that had swallowed an anchor.

Anna wrote each line on a separate scrap of paper, and she and Chantel set them down on the floor and shuffled them around. Each line was part of a rhymed couplet. The trick was to get the couplets in the right order.

"There's something missing," Chantel said.

"Before the writing-with-your-feet bit," Anna agreed.

"Right," said Chantel. "Do you write in the dust? Or—"

"Maybe you cut your feet and write in blood," said Leila.

She looked smug.

"Do you have a line, Leila?" Chantel asked.

Leila just smirked.

"If you do," said Anna, "I think you'd better tell us, please."

"I don't see why I should," said Leila. "I really *am* the Chosen One. Miss Ellicott said so."

"She said it to a lot of us," said Anna patiently. "It was probably just her way of making sure we didn't forget."

Leila continued to look smug.

"I don't think she has one," said Chantel. "I don't think Miss Ellicott ever told her she was the Chosen One."

"Think what you want," said Leila.

That tactic obviously wasn't going to work. "If you don't tell us," said Chantel, "I'll have Japheth bite you."

The snake obligingly reared its head and bared its tiny fangs.

"That snake doesn't scare me," said Leila.

And then an odd thing happened. Japheth reared his head higher. And higher yet. His weight on Chantel's shoulders was very much increased. Chantel cricked her neck and saw a mighty cobra rising above her head, its hood spread, its curved fangs gleaming, its forked tongue flicking in and out.

One or two girls let out a squawk of terror. The rest gazed, awestruck.

"Fine," said Leila, in an I-don't-care tone which nevertheless quavered a bit. "It's just some stupid thing about tombs."

She gave them a single line. Japheth, to Chantel's simultaneous relief and disappointment, turned back into a little green-gold snake.

Once they had Leila's line, they had this:

At the dawning of the day
Face the sun and turn away.
When the bells and trumpets sound
Cast dust from seven tombs around.
Standing barefoot in the street
Write the third sign with your feet.
Speak the words that Haywith spoke
And keep the vow that Haywith broke.
Bring the peace that Haywith stole
And touch the wall, and make it whole.
This remains from long lost lore.
The rest is gone. We know no more.

The girls read it over several times. They tried mixing the bits of paper around some more, but they decided this must be how it was supposed to go.

"And nobody's got anything else?" said Chantel.

No one did.

"It's not exactly a spell, is it?" said Anna.

Leila looked amused and superior. "It's instructions for how to *do* the spell."

"I guess," Chantel agreed reluctantly. "Part of it. But it says there's something's missing. And it doesn't tell us what words Haywith—"

There was a knock on the door.

"Sorry," said Bowser, sticking his head in. "Mrs.

Warthall said if you don't come down to breakfast right now she's going to tell Frenetica to pour it into the gutter."

"Small loss," said Leila.

"What do you think of this, Bowser?" said Anna.

Bowser came over and looked. "Is it a spell?"

"Almost," said Chantel. "I think it's instructions for the Buttoning. The spell to strengthen Seven Buttons."

"What are the seven buttons, anyway?" asked Holly.

But none of the girls knew this, because none of their teachers had ever told them. And it certainly wasn't in books.

Anna frowned at the assembled rhyme. "Even with what's here, it doesn't say where to stand to do it—"

"Somewhere on the west side of the city," said Bowser. "Because you have to face the rising sun, which is in the east, and then turn around, and then you're going to touch the wall, so the wall must be to the west. Could you all kind of get dressed and come down right away? Mrs. Warthall's really not in a very good mood. I mean compared to what she usually is," he added meaningfully.

⟨E✦S⟩

Mrs. Warthall was furious, and distributed smacks, threats, and extra chores.

"You girls may think you have it made," she said grimly. "Lying late in bed and swanning in for breakfast when you're good and ready. But you just wait. You won't be living this easy life for long."

Chantel and Anna were assigned to help Bowser scrub down the walls in the kitchen. It was nasty work, involving a vile-smelling paste that burned Chantel's hands.

"I'm almost sure it matters where you stand," said Chantel. "When you do the spell, I mean."

"Somewhere west," said Bowser.

"But where?" said Chantel, reaching into a tub of the nasty-smelling glop and quickly slapping the stuff onto the wall. "Seven Buttons is fourteen miles long."

"So there's a button every two miles?" said Bowser.

Chantel had never thought about it like this before. "You think it has actual buttons?"

"Maybe a button is a place where the wall can be breached," said Anna. "Like treacherous Queen Haywith did?"

"I bet there's nothing you can actually see," said Chantel. "I mean, it's all just stone the whole way around, isn't it?"

"There are the guard towers. But it mostly just looks like wall," said Bowser. "I walked all around it that time I ran away from home. They don't let you out, you know? If you go to the gate, the guards stop you."

Chantel grabbed a brush and scrubbed vigorously. "Someone must know where the buttons are. If there *are* buttons."

"I suppose the patriarchs know," said Bowser.

"What about 'Keep the vow that Haywith broke'?" said Anna. "What's that mean? And what are the words that Haywith spoke?"

"I don't know," said Chantel. "In history books, she doesn't speak at all. The books just say things *about* her."

"The patriarchs might know the words," said Bowser.

"They wouldn't tell us," said Chantel irritably. The smell of the wall-scrubbing glop was really overpowering. It disturbed Japheth too; the snake had hidden his head inside the collar of her robe.

"Anna! Chantel!" Holly ran into the room, trembling.

Anna reached out to catch her, then stopped, apparently remembering she had evil-smelling muck all over her hands.

"What's the matter?" said Chantel.

"Mrs.—" Holly swallowed a sob. "I just heard her talking. In the parlor. To a man. She was—" Holly burst into tears.

Bowser looked uncomfortable. "Can't you just tell us what the problem is?"

Chantel knelt and tried to look into Holly's eyes, but Holly had her face buried in Anna's shoulder. "Tell us what happened, Holly."

Holly unburied her face. "I heard her. Mrs. Warthall. Bargaining. To sell us. To a factory. To make glue."

"If he wants us for glue," said Chantel, "then he wants

us to *work* at *making* glue. He doesn't want to make glue *out* of us."

Holly was not mollified. "My sister worked in a factory and she burned all up into nothing!"

"We have to go see the patriarchs *now*," said Bowser. "Before Mrs. Warthall can—"

"Right," said Chantel. "Holly, stay close to Miss Flivvers. Tell the other girls. Don't be alone anywhere where Mrs. Warthall can catch you. We're going to go talk to the patriarchs and—and put a stop to this."

Holly brushed tears out of her eyes with her sleeve.

"Go on," said Anna. "Go tell them. We'll be back very soon."

Holly hurried away.

They quickly washed their hands and slipped out the kitchen door into the alley that sloped down the hill beside Fate's Turning.

⁂

Seven Buttons didn't *look* unprotected. It was forty feet high, looming over Chantel and her friends as they hurried toward the Hall of Patriarchs. It was faced with polished marble, inside and—Chantel assumed—outside. It was unclimbable, unbreachable. Nobody could ever get out . . . er, *in*, Chantel corrected herself.

It was also not her concern. She was here to strike a bargain with Sir Wolfgang.

Trying to look more confident than she felt, she led Anna and Bowser up the steps. They passed through the deep shades of the tombs. In the gloom they could just make out the carvings of dead kings, lying with stone swords clutched across their chests. They passed the dank stairway to the catacombs, and went into the bright office of the bored clerk.

Mr. Less smiled. "Here to see Sir Wolfgang again? He was furious last time. Ooh, he was mad. He told me if I ever let you in again he'd have my guts for garters."

"Oh dear," said Anna. "We're so sorry we—"

"Could we at least send in a message?" asked Chantel.

"All the patriarchs are meeting in council," the clerk said. "A terribly official occasion. If I interrupted them, I'd never hear the end of it."

"Maybe we could come back another time," said Chantel.

"No need," said the clerk. "Go right in. End of the hall."

"But—" said Anna.

"He won't really have my guts for garters," said the clerk. "I'm the only one who understands the filing system."

"Oh," said Chantel.

It occurred to her that the clerk's guts were not the only ones that could conceivably be had for garters.

But the younger girls back at the school were depending

on her. So she mustered her courage.

They heard voices and followed the sound, down the columned hall, past Sir Wolfgang's empty office. A carved wooden door stood open. Chantel and her friends looked into a high-ceilinged chamber, where nine velvet-clad men sat around a polished table. Chantel recognized some of them, from processions and ceremonies.

The patriarchs' talk died away, and they stared.

"What is the meaning of this?" one of them asked. "Who dares to interrupt the patriarchs in council?"

This was not a promising beginning.

Chantel and Anna curtseyed. Bowser bowed. Japheth poked his head up thoughtfully and flicked his tongue, tasting the air.

"Pardon us, sirs," said Bowser. "We've come about the missing sorceresses."

"And what do you have to do with sorceresses, eh, boy?" said the patriarch at the head of the table.

He was tall and thick, with a mighty mane of hair and a beard like a hibernating badger. He had the most gold embroidery on his waistcoat and the thickest gold chain. Chantel had seen him at the annual ceremony celebrating the sealing of Seven Buttons, and at the yearly commemoration of the treachery of Queen Haywith, when all the patriarchs wore black. She thought his name was Lord Rudolph.

"I'm the pot-boy at Miss Ellicott's School," Bowser explained. "And Miss Ellicott is missing."

"We know that, boy," said Lord Rudolph. "Have you found her?"

"No sir," said Bowser. "But we've found—well, we think we've found something that might have to do with the Buttoning."

That got the patriarchs' attention. They leaned forward eagerly.

"You found the spell?" Lord Rudolph demanded. "You, a mere pot-boy?"

Bowser didn't seem to mind being called "mere," but Chantel minded for him. Japheth gave an angry squirm.

"No sir," said Bowser. "The girls found it."

"Then why in the name of the Seven Buttons don't the girls speak?" Lord Rudolph demanded.

"Um," said Bowser, taken aback. He turned to Chantel in distress.

"We found something," said Chantel firmly. "Not the whole spell, but a clue. But we want—" She took a deep breath and went on. "There's something we want in return."

It seemed that Lord Rudolph, unlike Sir Wolfgang, actually could hear girls. "You found a clue? What's your name, girl?"

"Chantel. I . . . we . . . We've got a clue but we want to ask—"

"Supposing you just hand that clue over," said Lord Rudolph, "and run along and let the men worry about important matters."

Chantel swallowed. Her deportment made it very hard to keep going when she'd been told not to. "I don't think we can do that, sir."

Lord Rudolph leaned back in his chair and turned a speculative, assessing gaze on Chantel. "Oh? Why not?"

"Because we need you to do something for us," said Chantel, amazed at her own temerity. "We need you to get rid of Mrs. Warthall. We'll give you these words if you send her away, and let Miss Flivvers be in charge of the school, and . . . and . . ." She steeled herself. "And give Miss Flivvers *money* so we can buy real food."

There was an angry rustle of velvet around the table. Chairs were shoved back, muscles tensed as if the patriarchs were ready to spring. Japheth raised his head and switched it from side to side, tickling her ear.

Chantel wished Japheth would turn huge and cobra-like, as he had before. That would be useful right now. She had nothing to defend herself with except her deportment. Anna and Bowser weren't much help. They were looking at her as the person in charge.

Chantel took a deep breath. "And I think you need to tell us what happened to Miss Ellicott. And to the other sorceresses. If you know."

Angry cries and murmurs from around the table.

Alone among the patriarchs, Lord Rudolph remained calm. "We're aware of the situation, young Chantel."

To her utter horror, Chantel heard herself say, "So what are you doing about it?"

"She dares!" cried one of the patriarchs.

"She questions us!"

"A mere girl!"

All the patriarchs were on their feet now. Hands flew to sword hilts. Lord Rudolph made a gesture, and the men's hands dropped to their sides.

"What we are doing is no concern of yours, Chantel," said Lord Rudolph. "All *you* need to know is that we have the matter well in hand—and indeed, you do not even need to be told that. You should assume it. The only thing you should be wondering is what you can do to help us. And the answer is you can hand over that clue, now, like a good girl."

He held out his hand.

It was really difficult to believe you had a right to argue when you were confronted by wise-looking men telling you that you did not. Chantel looked at Anna and Bowser. They looked back, clearly waiting to see what Chantel would decide.

Chantel took a deep breath. "If I hand over the words, then I would like to know that in return you're going to take away Mrs. Warthall, who beats us and doesn't let us learn anything and makes us eat cruel and—gruel and offal."

"You have no right to ask anything in return," said Lord Rudolph.

Fury rose up in Chantel. She and Anna had searched all night for the spell. They and the other girls had found it. She and Anna and Bowser had risked the wrath of Mrs. Warthall, which was no small thing, to come down here. And for all their trouble, they were being treated as if they had done something *wrong*.

She could feel her face burning with anger. Her hands clenched. Her deportment was slipping away fast. Japheth reared up high on her shoulder, switching his head around furiously. He should have made himself ten feet tall. He should have grown a hood and fangs. He should have sprouted wings from his back and flown at the patriarchs, spouting flame.

Instead, the snake did the most useless thing he could possibly have done.

He crawled into Chantel's ear.

6

Which Is, on the Whole, Fiendish

It was a horrible sensation. Chantel could feel the snake inside her head, squirming about. But she hardly had time to think about it, because immediately she heard herself shouting.

"Well, that's not the only thing I want!" she said. "I want to know what happened, because I think you know more than you're telling us! And I want to know why sorceresses who can do magic have to listen to you, if you can't do any! And I want to know what—"

"Chantel, shut up," said Bowser urgently, grabbing her arm.

Chantel shrugged him off. "—what you're doing to get them back!"

"Fie!" cried one of the patriarchs.

Even Lord Rudolph looked angry. "For your information, the sorceresses have been taken by the Marauders Without the Walls, who have offered to exchange them on condition that we tear down the wall."

"How did any Marauders get into the city to take them?" Chantel demanded.

"She has no right to speak to us like that!" said a patriarch.

Lord Rudolph waved him to silence. "We do not know," he told Chantel. "We suspect a weakness in the walls. A breach of the buttons. That is why *you* must hand over your clue to *us* immediately."

"How would you even do the spell if you had it?" A part of Chantel was horrified at her behavior, but the snake in her head made it impossible to recover her deportment. "None of you is a sorceress."

"Some of us feel we may have some magical talent," said Lord Rudolph. "The sorceresses have monopolized the field of magic for long enough. Now really, Chantel, I have been quite patient with your impertinent questions. Be a good girl and hand over the clue."

The snake wriggled against Chantel's brain, interfering with thirteen years of careful training. "I am not a good girl," she heard herself say. "Sorry."

"Chantel—" said Anna nervously.

"In fact," said Chantel. It was hard to think with a snake in her brain, but the pieces were falling into place. "If the Marauders want the wall taken down, or they won't give the sorceresses back, and you want the spell, so that you can strengthen the wall . . . you don't intend to get the sorceresses back, do you?"

"Why are we even listening to this fool girl?" cried a patriarch. "She must obey!"

"Seize them!" roared another. And Lord Rudolph said something in protest, but it wasn't heard as the chairs were overturned and the patriarchs came charging around and over the table in an angry wave.

Chantel, Anna, and Bowser fled.

They ran down the hall, the patriarchs thundering after them. They dodged through the clerk's office—Mr. Less jumped hastily aside—and out into the gloom of the Hall of the Dead, a dark maze of tombs.

"Bar the door!" It was Sir Wolfgang's voice, panting. "Don't let them get out!"

And Chantel saw the patriarchs moving through the darkness, running to block the exit.

Chantel, Anna, and Bowser ducked down in the black shadow of the tomb of King Fustian the First, whose square face Chantel had described to Miss Ellicott. The patriarchs' voices rang out as they called to each other, searching among the tombs in the darkness.

In a story, Chantel thought wildly, we'd lie on top of the tombs and pretend to be statues, and in a story that would actually work.

In real life it wouldn't. Chantel could see two of the patriarchs moving closer. They were going around each tomb, kicking at the shadows with their heavy boots.

Bowser twitched at Chantel's sleeve and pointed with his nose. Staying low, the three of them slipped over to the next row of tombs.

"I heard something!" called a patriarch. "All of you be still."

The patriarchs fell silent, and Chantel and her friends froze, not breathing. Chantel could hear blood pounding in her ears. (The snake had calmed down for the moment.)

"Think they're inside a tomb?" called one of the patriarchs.

"No, we'd have heard them lift the lid." It was Lord Rudolph's voice. "We'll find them. Circle around. Surround the tombs, then move in. Swords out, gentlemen."

Chantel heard the rasp of swords being unsheathed. Heavy footfalls echoed through the great stone hall as the patriarchs circled, closing in.

She looked around frantically. In the gray gloom it was hard to see anything. A cold draft hit her face. It came from somewhere off to the left.

"The crypt," she whispered. "Now!"

And she ran, praying the others would follow.

"There they go!" roared a patriarch.

Chantel could hear Anna and Bowser close behind her. The patriarchs rushed toward them. The gaping mouth of the crypt was just ahead.

A patriarch made a grab at Chantel and she ducked out of his way. She, Bowser, and Anna stumbled onto the stairs and hurtled, half-falling, down them.

They scrambled away from the staircase, crawling, staggering to their feet, running. It was only when Chantel smacked into a wall—a bumpy, not-quite-right feeling wall which rattled when she hit it—that she stopped.

Anna and Bowser were beside her, panting.

The darkness down here was total. The feeling was damp and small and made Chantel want to scream. There was a smell of mold. The walls felt oppressively close. The one Chantel was pressed against shifted and clanked.

Why aren't they following us? Chantel wondered.

"Chantel!" Lord Rudolph's voice boomed down from above. "Chantel, and, er, company. Come back! There are things down there that you don't want to meet."

Chantel could well believe it. But there were things up there she didn't want to meet either.

"Come up here and cooperate," said Lord Rudolph. "No one will hurt you."

That, Chantel did not believe. *Swords out, gentlemen.*

"Can we get anyone to go down there after them?" said Sir Wolfgang.

"Any volunteers?" said Lord Rudolph sardonically.

Silence from the patriarchs.

"No one should go down there without a strong protection spell," said Lord Rudolph. "We'll post a guard, in case they come out alive."

Chantel tried to convince herself that this exchange was merely meant to frighten her and her companions.

It was working.

Something gripped her arm, and she stifled a yelp. It was only Bowser. "Can't you girls make a light or something?" he whispered.

"It . . . yes," said Chantel. "Wait."

This spell was not as easy for her as summoning. She moved away from the not-quite-right wall. She traced the fourth sign in the air. Carefully, she took four steps backward, turned twice, put her hands on her shoulders, and then reached out her right hand. A globe of white light appeared in her hand.

Thousands of empty eye sockets stared down at her.

The narrow corridor was formed of bones and skulls, stacked. Rows of bones were topped by rows of skulls. Then more rows of bones and more rows of skulls, all the way to the ceiling. No wonder the wall had felt not-quite right.

"They can't hurt us," Anna whispered. "They're dead."

"Right, I know," said Chantel firmly. "Let's walk fast."

They walked away from the stairs and the patriarchs. Chantel held her light out before her. The rows of skulls interspersed with rows of bones went on and on and on. Lightning Pass had been a very big city for a very long time, and millions of people had died in it. And now those millions were underneath it, separated, sorted, stacked, and staring.

"There is another way out of here, isn't there?" said Anna, speaking aloud. They were well away from the Hall of Patriarchs now.

"Of course," said Chantel. "There has to be, because of the air flow. Otherwise people couldn't breathe."

"The kind of people who are down here aren't the breathing kind," Bowser pointed out.

They walked on in uneasy silence.

After what seemed like a very long time, they reached a place where the walls were no longer fitted out with floor-to-ceiling bones. Instead, there were shelves scooped from the stone. Waiting for the people who aren't dead yet, Chantel thought.

The snake in her head had settled down a bit, but every now and then he gave an uncomfortable squirm that made it hard to focus her thoughts.

Which was probably just as well.

"Chantel, you gave Lord Rudolph a *Look*," said Anna.

"He deserved it," said Chantel.

"Do you think we should try to get Japheth out of your head?" said Anna.

"Not right now," Chantel snapped. "Let's just get out of here."

"He really went into your head?" said Bowser. "It wasn't just magic?"

"Of course it was magic," said Chantel. "But he's in my head, all right?"

Bowser shrugged and looked hurt, and Chantel was annoyed at him for being hurt, annoyed at herself for hurting him, annoyed at him for pretending *not* to be hurt, and just generally extremely annoyed.

The narrow catacomb ended abruptly, and there was a passage leading off to the left and two leading to the right.

"Which way do we turn here?" said Bowser.

"Let's go left," said Anna. "If we turn left whenever we come to a split—"

"Then we'll go in a circle," said Chantel.

"Maybe we should take this one. I think it goes up a little bit," said Bowser.

"What's that noise?" said Anna.

There was a scraping sound somewhere behind them.

They took the passage Bowser suggested, and quickly. The scraping came again, followed by an almost imperceptible sound like cloth brushing over stone. It was closer this time.

They broke into a run. Their shadows were huge black shapes sliding along the walls. The thing chasing them sped up, too.

"Left!" Bowser called, and that was how Chantel knew there was another split. She followed the others. The thing was closer still, and now she heard its breathing, in-out-in-out, impossibly regular for any living thing. It sounded like a bellows with pneumonia.

"Right! And then left!" yelled Bowser.

The sound was closer, and Chantel felt ice-cold breath against her neck. Inside her head Japheth squiggled. "Faster!" Chantel yelled. "It's almost—"

Something grabbed at her shoulder. The light-globe rolled off her hand and went out. She felt cold slime soak through her robe, and there was an algae smell, like a flooded grave. She tore away and put on a burst of speed, shoving Anna forward.

"It's a fiend!" Chantel yelled.

The fiend screeched, and they all ran faster than Chantel would ever have thought possible.

"Daylight!" Bowser gasped.

And Chantel saw it too, a tiny yellow-white scrap of light up ahead. She felt hope for a second, then two slimy clawlike hands gripped her.

"It's got—" she yelled, and then the hands were on her neck.

She turned and fought, hard. She hit and kicked. She clawed at the fiend's horrible green face as its slimy fingers tightened around her throat. Then Bowser and Anna were climbing over her to get at the fiend, grabbing it, dragging it forward, why—?

Chantel understood, just as Anna yelled, "Get it into daylight!"

The three of them fell, got up, and stumbled onward, Anna and Bowser pulling Chantel and all three of them dragging the fiend. Everything was going black at the edges as the fiend strangled her.

Then they reached the sunlight.

Suddenly the horrible hands were gone, and Chantel lay gasping in the patch of daylight on the floor of the catacomb.

"Get up, Chantel, quick!" said Anna.

Chantel got to her feet with difficulty. She and the others staggered up a narrow, uneven set of steps. They squeezed through a gap between two rocks, and out into the bright, bright sunlight. Chantel collapsed on the ground.

Her throat hurt. She still had a snake in her head. She was overwhelmed by the horror of what had happened underground. If the others hadn't turned back for her, if they'd run to save themselves . . .

She owed them her life. She thought of saying this, and then she thought of how uncomfortable that would make everybody. While she was thinking this, her eyes gradually got accustomed to the light.

She saw her two friends. First they looked gray and indistinct. Then, as her eyes adjusted, she saw that they were staring around them in amazement. Finally, she saw what they were looking at.

Land. More open space than Chantel had ever seen. Rolling, broken hills and bluffs. Ravines and woodlands. A mesa above them with a still-standing dead tree sketched against the sky. A heap of boulders at the base. Faraway mountains climbing the horizon. And when Chantel turned around—

A wall. A high, imposing wall, marble-white, smooth as sheet steel, tall and implacable. A wall that was the only interruption of the forever-space around them.

For the first time in her life, she was looking at Seven Buttons from the outside.

7

WITHOUT WALLS

It was at the same time wonderful and terrifying . . . so much space with nothing being done to it. In Lightning Pass, there were the Green Terraces, carefully planned, painstakingly arranged. So much space for growing fruit, so much for vines, so much for vegetables. Gardens for people to sit in, or stroll in, at such and such hours of such and such days.

Here the land was alive. Things were growing wherever they wanted to, with no plan at all. You could probably walk right up to the trees and touch them—though then again, Chantel wasn't sure if that was safe.

She took an unsteady step, dizzy and uncertain. It was hard to stand upright with no walls closing you in, hard to walk with no doors or gates ahead of you.

They turned around and stared at Seven Buttons, out-lined by the setting sun.

"Well, there has to be a gate in it somewhere," said Anna.

"We could go back the way we came," said Bowser, without enthusiasm.

Chantel could still feel the cold grip of the fiend's slimy hands on her neck. "No."

"If we follow the wall we'll come to the gate," said Anna.

Chantel looked over her shoulder. She didn't feel safe turning her back on the vast, open land where anything could happen.

"The gate's at the port," said Bowser.

"And which way is that?" said Chantel.

Bowser frowned up at the sun. "Well, it's in the south part of the city."

"We know *that*," said Chantel impatiently. The snake in her head was making it hard to be polite.

"Which is this way," said Bowser, with a firmness that communicated quite clearly that he didn't know.

Chantel didn't have a better suggestion. They started walking.

It was difficult. They were used to cobblestone streets and flag-paved steps. They weren't used to uneven ground, and weeds that came up to their waists, and then to their necks. Thistles and teasels snagged at Chantel's robe, combining with the snake wriggling in her head to make her crankier and crankier. She tripped over something and fell headlong.

"Owl's bowels!" she yelled.

She'd never sworn before in her life, and she found it worked.

"Shouldn't we try to get the snake out of your head?" said Anna, helping her up and pulling a burr off her robe.

"Not now," Chantel snapped. "We have to get out of here before we meet any Marauders. And besides, there's the little kids at the school."

"Right," said Bowser, pushing his way through a tangle of plants higher than his head. "We don't know what that woman is doing to them. She might . . ."

He let out a squawk, said a much worse word than *owl's bowels*, and disappeared.

Chantel and Anna hurried through the broken weeds, and stopped short at the edge of a ravine.

"Bowser?" Chantel called.

"Down here."

All Chantel could see down there was more weeds.

"Are you all right?" said Anna.

"Yeah." There was a rustling, and his head appeared above the scrub. "Look, we can't get through this stuff.

We're going to have to find a street or something."

"Are there streets out here?" said Anna.

"Who knows?" said Chantel.

Bowser looked around. "It looks easier to walk down here."

The girls started to climb into the gully. They slid, crashing through undergrowth and grabbing at nettles. They landed jarringly at the bottom.

Chantel swore again. Anna gave her a shocked look, but Chantel and the snake in her head didn't care.

It *was* easier walking down here. The weeds didn't grow quite as high and there weren't as many thistles. And the closeness of the gully walls was reassuring. They heard things scurrying away from them, and once Chantel trod suddenly into an ice-cold hidden stream. She worried because they were heading away from the wall. Away from the little girls at the school.

"How much further is it to the street?" Anna asked.

"Oh, not much further at all," said Bowser.

"He doesn't know," said Chantel irritably. "Why are you asking him?"

Anna looked hurt, and so did Bowser. Chantel felt bad, but Japheth's scales were tickling the inside of her head.

She couldn't bring herself to actually apologize for being in a bad mood. After all, other people were in bad moods all the time—Miss Ellicott, Miss Flivvers, and as for that manageress woman, Mrs. Warthall, she was all bad mood. Why shouldn't Chantel be in one for once? She was sick to death of deportment.

She grumbled to herself as she pushed through the brush. The gully smelled of mud and dirty water. There had been no sign of civilization anywhere, except for the blank glaring face of Seven Buttons, and there was no way to know whether they were getting closer or further away from this street that the Marauders might or might not have, and anyway, who knew *what* Marauders had? They probably all rode around on warhorses all the time, and maybe the warhorses didn't need—

"The gully stops here," said Bowser, turning to look at them. His face was covered with scratches and dirt, and he had a stinging-nettle welt on his neck. His shirt was torn. Chantel expected she didn't look any better.

"I guess we have to climb up, then," said Anna. She, too, was covered with scratches and nettle stings, and her clothes were even more of a mess than Bowser's.

"Stay right where you are," said a voice from above. "We have you surrounded."

8

MARAUDERS

Chantel looked frantically up and all around. The rim high above them was covered with thick growth. She couldn't even be sure which side the voice had come from. The Marauders surely had weapons aimed at them.

"We should have gone back to the catacombs," said Anna.

"We couldn't," said Chantel. "The fiend."

"Lay down your weapons!" The voice was deep and booming. It had an annoying twangy drawl that made the snake in Chantel's head twitch.

"We haven't got any weapons, fool," she heard herself say. "Do we look like we have weapons?"

Bowser took his knife out of his pocket and laid it on the ground at his feet.

"Good," said the voice. "Now don't make any sudden moves, and—"

"If we were going to make any, we would have made them while we still had the knife," Chantel pointed out.

"—*And*," said the voice, "take all your money and tie it in a handkerchief, and toss it up here."

"We haven't got any money," said Bowser.

"I left my handkerchief at home," said Anna.

"I don't know if we could throw that high, anyway," said Chantel. "And we don't know which side of the gully you're on."

"Both sides! I told you," said the voice, still with that awful twang. "We have you surrounded. However, you should throw it on this—I mean, on the north side."

There had been a high squeak at the end of *surrounded*.

"I think it's just kids," Chantel told Anna and Bowser.

"No whispering!" drawled the voice.

It was hard to be circumspect when you had a snake in your head. "I'm not afraid of you," she called up at the weeds. "I think you're just kids."

A crossbow bolt zipped past her ear and buried itself in the ground.

"I think you shouldn't have said that," Anna remarked unnecessarily.

Chantel shivered. Not because of the crossbow bolt. It was getting dark, and a chill had begun to settle in.

Shadows filled the bottom of the gully.

"It's cold down here," she said. "We're going to come out."

"Chantel, they've got crossbows," said Anna.

"And we don't," said Chantel, loudly. "We're unarmed. They have nothing to fear from us."

"Can we climb up?" Bowser called. "Without you shooting us?"

"Wait!" said the voice above. "Let me—us—let us consult our comrades at arms. Each other, I mean."

There was a sound of murmuring from above. It all seemed to come from one side of the gully, and from the same spot.

"All right," said the voice. "But leave your knife down there."

It was nearly dark now. Chantel started climbing. Bowser picked up the crossbow bolt and stuck it in his belt. Chantel had the impression that he also picked up his knife at the same time.

It was much harder climbing up the slope than falling down it. Chantel kept stepping on her robe. Most of the plants she grabbed to pull herself up were prickly. She uprooted one by mistake and nearly fell. Finally she arrived at the top, even dirtier and more beprickled than before, and having uttered even more dire swearwords. Despite the sheer misery of the situation, she couldn't help but notice that nothing bad had happened when she swore. Somehow she'd always assumed that, at the very least, the sky would fall.

It was dark up here, too. Twilight was edging toward night.

Chantel reached down and pulled Anna up the last couple feet, and they futilely brushed dirt off each other's robes. Bowser scrambled up after them.

"Right," said the voice, now much closer and definitely cracking. "So put your hands on top of your head and—"

"You're the ones with the crossbows," said Chantel. "Why are you scared of us?"

"I'm not scared!" the voice snapped, from deep in the night-shrouded thicket.

"All right, you're not scared," said Chantel. "Are you going to come out and let us see you?"

"Chantel," said Anna warningly.

"They've got crossbows," Bowser said.

There was a rustling sound, and a Marauder emerged from the brush.

As best as Chantel could see in the darkness, the Marauder, just one Marauder, was about five feet tall and had red hair that stuck up, and front teeth that stuck out. His nose was slightly crooked, as if someone had broken it for him sideways. His eyes had an amused look that was doing its best to conceal a hunted look . . . he'd been running from things, Chantel thought. He held the cross-bow so casually in front of him that Chantel was afraid it might go off by accident.

"Who're you?" said Chantel.

"Pardon her," said Anna. "She's got a snake in her head." She curtseyed. "I'm Anna Bellringer, of Miss Elli-cott's School, and this is Chantel Goldenrod, and Bowser Stepmonger."

Bowser appeared to consider bowing and then discard the idea as ridiculous. The Marauder was no older than they were.

"Who're you?" Chantel repeated.

"Franklin," said the Marauder. "Are you from the walled city?"

"Yes, Lightning Pass," said Anna, managing to stop herself from curtseying again. "And we're lost. We came through the catacombs and we ended up out here, and now we need to know how to get back again."

"Catacombs?" Franklin looked interested. "You can get into the city that way?"

"Absolutely not," said Chantel, recognizing the dan-ger. "There are hordes of bloodthirsty fiends, plus some vampires and a really grumpy zombie. And a dragon," she added for good measure.

"Wow. You got away from all of that?" said Franklin.

"We're very fast runners," said Anna.

"Plus they're sorceresses," said Bowser.

Franklin had lowered the crossbow, but now he raised it again. "Good ones or evil ones?"

"Good," said Bowser at the same time that Chantel said, "Evil."

"Can you tell us how to get to the city gates?" said Chantel.

"Do you really need gates, sorceress?" Franklin looked skeptical. "Don't you have magical ways to get through the wall?"

"No magic can get you through Seven Buttons," said Chantel firmly.

Franklin shrugged. "The only gate is down to the south, at the harborside. That's where you Lightning Pass folks trade with the outside world, without letting anybody actually come into your precious city. Don't you even know that?"

"Of course we know it," said Chantel. "But we don't know how to get there. So if you could show us—"

"Wait a minute." The Marauder boy raised his crossbow again. "You're forgetting that I've captured you. You're not going anywhere unless I say so."

Chantel had never seen a crossbow pointed straight at her before. She found the experience rather exhilarating. It cut through all the usual nonsense of life, the veiled threats and the worries about the future and about people not liking you and about not being good enough. A crossbow was immediate and real.

Besides, she had a snake in her head. Chantel took a step toward the boy.

"Chantel!" said Bowser urgently.

"Don't move again or I'll shoot," said Franklin. The crossbow didn't waver. "I've shot people before."

The look in his eye said he meant it. Chantel had to admit she'd assumed he hadn't. But she found she still wasn't frightened.

"Fine," she said. "I won't move. So now that you've captured us, what are you going to do with us? We don't have any money. We don't have anything worth stealing."

Franklin looked nonplussed.

"And you're all alone," she went on. "How long can you keep that crossbow pointed at us?"

"Chantel—" said Anna.

"Look." The crossbow wavered. "You can't go around telling people you're a sorceress. There are people who would kill you for it."

"Is sorcery illegal in the Roughlands?"

"The what?" said Franklin.

"The Roughlands." Chantel gestured broadly. "This place."

Franklin looked amused. "'This place'? What exactly do you mean by 'this place'? You're in the kingdom of

West Pharsalia, near the southern border of the United Chieftancies."

"I've heard of those," said Anna.

"I'd think so," said Franklin. "Since you can't possibly live more than a few miles from them. Wow, you people are really shut off from the world, aren't you?"

"I read a book about the Chieftancies, for your information," said Chantel.

"That's nice," said Franklin. "Stay out of them. They'd probably eat you for breakfast."

He lowered the crossbow, and Chantel felt rather insulted by this. Apparently he no longer considered her a threat.

"The worst chieftain is the warrior Karl the Bloody," Franklin added. "They *say* he lines the road to his fort with the heads of his enemies, and when he captures you, he lets you choose the stake he's going to impale you on."

Chantel shrugged. Everyone in the Roughlands was more or less a barbarian. She'd learned that in school.

"I only mention this because he's looking for me," Franklin added. "If you can hide me with your magic, I might show you the way to the gate."

Franklin lived in a cave. It wasn't a very big cave, and the floor was rocky and not at all comfortable, but at least he had food. He gave them soup made from eggs and green stuff. He told them the green stuff was nettles. It tasted pleasantly salty. He baked some potatoes, too, in the embers of the fire. He said he'd scavenged them from a farm.

The snake in Chantel's head wanted her to say, "You mean you *stole* them." But she wanted a baked potato very much, so she resisted.

"Is there a street that goes to the port?" Anna asked.

"A street? There's a road," said Franklin.

"What'd you do to get a guy called Karl the Bloody chasing you?" Bowser sounded slightly jealous.

"Doesn't matter," said Franklin. "What can you do to hide me from him?"

Chantel thought it did matter. "Nothing," she said, at the same moment that Anna said, "We can do an abnegation."

"A what?" said Franklin.

"It's a thing where you make people think you're not important enough to notice," said Anna.

Franklin huffed impatiently. "I can do that myself."

"You can do magic?" Bowser looked even more jealous.

"No, but making people not notice you—that's *basic*." He turned back to Anna. "You can't make me invisible?"

"No," said Anna. Then she went on, despite Chantel's frantic gestures: "We need a lot of supplies and things to do most of our spells."

"So get supplies and things! What kinds of things?"

"Magical ingredients," said Anna. "Water from certain wells, blood shed in certain ways. And then for wards—"

"Wards? What do those do?"

"Strengthen walls," said Anna. "They can be used to seal doors and windows, too. Chantel's really good at them. But we couldn't do anything here, because there's nothing to seal."

They were sitting in the open mouth of the cave, around a crackling campfire. The soup pot was balanced on rocks over the fire, and the baked potatoes were beginning to smell nearly done.

"It's the sorceresses that strengthen Seven Buttons," said Bowser. He'd been watching the stranger in silence, summing him up, Chantel thought.

"Seven what?"

"The wall around the city," said Bowser. "But now that—"

Chantel made a shut-up gesture at Bowser, and to her relief, he trailed off. The Marauders had kidnapped Miss Ellicott and the other sorceresses. Lord Rudolph had said so. The Marauders mustn't find out how much the sorceresses' absence endangered the city.

"The wall is impenetrable," said Chantel firmly.

"I'd think it would be that even without magic." Franklin poked a baked potato with his knife, nodded, and flipped it to Bowser.

Bowser caught it, winced, and dropped it. Franklin set potatoes down more gently in front of the girls, and for a while there was silence as they ate. The potatoes were hot and crumbly, and the best thing Chantel had tasted in a long time.

"Right, I've decided," he said when they'd finished. "I'll guide you to the port, and then I want you to take me into the city with you. It's the one place Karl the Bloody will never think of looking for me."

"I think that would be treason," said Anna uncertainly. "I mean, no offense, but you're a Marauder, right?"

She looked to Chantel for support.

"Everyone outside the walls is a Marauder," Chantel explained.

"Take it or leave it," said Franklin. He leaned back against a rock, hands behind his head, and looked like he didn't care.

"We'll discuss it," said Chantel.

They stepped out of the cave. The night sky was a dome of stars, with no walls or towers to block them out. A breeze brushed the land, bringing a smell of green growing things. It suddenly came to Chantel that she might like it out here, once she got used to it.

Of course, that would be only if the place weren't full of Marauders with names like Karl the Bloody.

"We can't take him into the city with us, can we?" said Anna. "It *would* be treason."

"He's only one Marauder," said Chantel. "And he's just a kid. What could he do?"

"Open the Seven Buttons?" said Anna.

"How, without magic?" said Chantel.

"He could open the gates to the Marauders," said Bowser.

"The guards would stop him," said Anna.

"They probably won't even let him inside," said Chantel. "He's got a crossbow. And a horrible Marauder accent. And at least he'll help us find the gate."

They walked back to the cave. Franklin was still lying with his head against the rock. He sat up. "So what did you decide?"

"We decided we'll take you to Lightning Pass," Chantel lied.

9

The Harbor

Franklin said they should wait until the moon rose. So they lay down to rest for a few hours. Chantel couldn't sleep. She was too worried about the little girls. What if Mrs. Warthall had sold them already?

The moon crept over the distant mountains. Franklin jolted awake and said it was time to go. White mist hung heavy over the land, weaving around the tall weeds and reminding Chantel uncomfortably of ghosts and fiends.

Chantel made a light-globe (which impressed Franklin) and they picked their way along a path through bushes and thorns. After an hour or so they stumbled out onto a road.

"Put the light out now," Franklin murmured. "Some-one might see it."

"Who?" said Chantel.

"He means Karl the Bloody," Bowser said. "Just put it out."

Chantel did. "I don't see why Karl the Bloody would come all the way down here from the United Chieftancies, looking for you."

"He might send someone," said Franklin, as they made their way by moonlight along the road.

"What's so important about you anyway?" Chantel demanded.

"Chantel's usually very polite," said Anna. "It's just that she has a snake in her head."

"Is that an expression?" said Franklin.

"Never mind my snake," said Chantel. "What did you do?"

"Keep your voice down," said Franklin.

"I guess he's, um, probably a deserter," said Bowser.

Franklin looked at Bowser through narrowed eyes. "Yeah. I'm a deserter."

But Chantel had a feeling he was lying.

"You mean you're a soldier?" she asked. "Aren't you too young?"

"He's not," said Bowser. "Our soldiers enlist when they're thirteen."

"Can you all just keep your voices down?" said Franklin nervously.

Now and then they saw dark farmhouses, surrounded by

fields. Twice they passed through sleeping villages. There were no lights. Somehow Chantel would have expected these village-dwelling Marauders to be prowling about at night, like cats. But it seemed they preferred to stay in.

"It's not just that he's chasing me," said Franklin. "He's coming this way anyway. The king's given him permission to march through West Pharsalia."

"You mean the king of West Pharsalia?" said Anna.

The snake in Chantel's head gave an unhappy twitch. "Why is he marching?"

"To break the tollgates," said Franklin. "Can't you keep your voice down?"

"I *was* keeping my voice down," said Chantel. "What tollgates?"

"The ones you people use to control the road to the mountains," said Franklin. "Don't you even know *that*?"

"Why would I?" said Chantel. "I've never been in the mountains. Anyway, if they're ours, why—"

"Because everyone is sick of you people controlling the only pass through the mountains and the only decent harbor for three hundred miles," said Franklin. "Shh!"

He froze abruptly, then grabbed Chantel's arm and pulled her off the road. Chantel only struggled for a second, then she heard it too.

They all ducked down in a damp ditch. A trio of men appeared on the road, barely visible in the moonlight.

"Didn't you see something up here?" The speaker had

the same twangy accent as Franklin.

"Just some peasant," twanged another man.

"That farmer said he saw a red-haired boy, though . . ."

Chantel and the others stayed still and silent for a long time after the men tromped past.

"Red-haired boy? Did they mean you?" Anna asked at last.

"Those were scouts," said Franklin. "Karl's men. He always sends three, because he thinks one or two might betray him."

Chantel wondered if having Franklin as a guide was such a good idea after all.

"It's a good thing it's so dark," said Franklin. "You all left a track in the grass like a herd of elephants."

They walked on. It was morning when they reached the port.

❦

Chantel had not known there was a wall around the port as well.

This wall was less formidable than Seven Buttons. It was only twice as tall as a man. There was a wide-open gate, with a sign over it that read

HARBOR DISTRICT
KINGDOM OF LIGHTNING PASS
PERMITS REQUIRED

A seagull perched atop the sign.

There were guards checking papers. But there was some advantage to being young, after all—nobody paid any attention to Chantel and her companions. Adults had to show permits, and argue, and pay. A woman driving an empty oxcart had been pulled off to the side, and her cart was being carefully measured inside and out. She looked frightened.

"What's going to happen to her?" said Anna as they slipped past.

"How should I know?" said Franklin. "They probably think she has a false bottom."

Bowser looked confused, then said "Oh, you mean in the cart. Why?"

"To carry stuff you guys don't let out into the kingdoms and chieftaincies," said Franklin.

"Contraband, you mean?" said Chantel.

Franklin shrugged. "If that's what you want to call it. Spices, silver. Medicine for spotted swamp fever. We can never get as much as we need of that, because you guys control it."

"What's spotted swamp fever?"

"What killed my mother," said Franklin.

Chantel felt a little twist of horror in her stomach. She did not, herself, have a mother. But she understood that those who did were often very attached to them.

"I'm sorry your mother died," she said.

"You might be sorry," said Franklin. "I mean you yourself. But it was your wretched city's fault, so don't tell me you're sorry."

Chantel turned away angrily, fighting the retort that the snake in her head wanted her to make. After all, Franklin (whose twangy drawl was not getting any less annoying) was talking about something that upset him. And he wanted to blame someone for it. Chantel could understand that. So he was blaming the Kingdom, which meant the patriarchs. Nothing to do with her.

Chantel had been taught in school that there were two sides to every issue, and that one of these sides was wrong.

"We're really very sorry to hear about your mother, Franklin," said Anna.

"Yeah, 'cause she's the one you *did* hear about," said Franklin.

Chantel and Anna exchanged a look. Franklin was difficult. But anyway, they would soon be rid of him.

They had reached the harborside. They stopped and stared. Broad wooden docks edged the cobbled street. Wharfs reached out into the sea. Ships bobbed and thumped beside them. The air smelled of salt and fish.

The ships' masts rocked. Looking up at them made Chantel dizzy. Seagulls screeched, coasted down the sky, and landed on the decks. A sailor sent them flapping away with a snap of a rope.

Men and boys were everywhere, shouting, cursing, singing. They rolled barrels that rumbled along the docks. Chantel saw a boy her own age climbing a ship's rigging. He stepped into the crow's nest and trained a spyglass, not out to sea, but into Lightning Pass.

"He's spying on us!" said Chantel, incensed.

"'Course he is," Franklin twanged. "You put up a high wall and don't let anybody in. What do you expect?"

"*I* didn't put up a high wall," said Chantel.

"Look." He took Chantel by the shoulders and turned her around. "Do you see your city? Do you see what it looks like?"

Chantel shrugged away angrily. But she looked. She saw Seven Buttons, and the buildings rising behind it, climbing to the castle at the top.

"It's a fortress," said Franklin. "You see those towers, ready to fight the world? You see the wall?"

They would be rid of him soon, she told the snake in her head. They were leaving him at the gates. "The wall's always been there. It's to protect us."

"Nah. It's been there a couple hundred years, sure," said Franklin. "But you didn't always need 'protecting.'"

"It's been there more than five hundred years," Chantel informed him. "Because it was five hundred years ago that Queen Haywith caused a breach in the wall, and the

Marauders got in, and the city was nearly lost."

"It's been there time out of mind," said Anna, trying to make peace.

"Okay." Franklin exchanged a glance with Bowser and made a *whatever* shrug.

Chantel looked at the ships, and at the open sea beyond. The smells of the harbor were familiar to her—fish and seaweed and salt. They blew into the city when the wind was from the south.

But she'd never seen the ocean up close, rolling in glass-green waves toward the shore, crests of white water breaking slowly, crashing against the stone pier.

And the ships! They could go anywhere. They could sail forever. Across a world without walls. The thought was at once thrilling and frightening.

"There are so *many* ships," said Anna.

"Not really," said Franklin. "About three-fourths of the berths are empty. *Berths* means places for the ships to dock," he added.

"We knew that," said Chantel.

"I didn't," said Bowser.

The snake in Chantel's head twitched. "Do you have to take his side?"

Bowser looked hurt.

"Ships only come to you if they can't sell their goods anywhere else," said Franklin. "The merchants don't like the way they're treated, so they bring their worst goods and charge high prices. To *all* of us."

"Well, anyway," said Bowser, "we need to get through the gate."

Franklin looked around at all of them. "If you tell the guards at the gates that I'm not one of you, that I'm a—Marauder, is it?—then I'll say that you're the same."

"We weren't going to do that!" said Anna, but Bowser ruined everything by looking embarrassed.

"They'll know as soon as you open your mouth," said Chantel.

"So I won't open it," said Franklin. "You'll do the talking."

There was a whole neighborhood between the harbor and the gates. It had warehouses and markets, inns for the sailors and houses. People lived out here, whole families. They must be Marauders, Chantel thought. She couldn't imagine anyone from Lightning Pass wanting to live among the noise and the smells and the loud, rough sailors.

Or being *allowed* to, she thought with a pang.

"Anyway," said Chantel, "they're not going to let you in with that cross . . ."

She trailed off. Franklin was unarmed.

"With what?" said Franklin.

"Where's your crossbow?" said Bowser.

Franklin shrugged. "They wouldn't have let me in the

first gate with it, you know. Let's go."

Chantel frowned. She was sure he'd had the crossbow recently.

The city gates were, in fact, two iron-clad doors in Seven Buttons. They were shut fast. Towers rose on either side of them, bristling with guards. Two ranks of guards stood before them, heavily armed.

Their purple uniforms meant Home. The place where Chantel belonged, and Marauders didn't. Inside the wall, safe from the Roughlands.

She started toward the doors. A guard stepped in front of her, blocking her path.

"No entry," he said.

"I live in there," said Chantel. "And so do my friends."

"Nonsense," said the guard. "Now run along, before you get hurt."

Chantel felt the snake twitch inside her head. "Owl's bowels!" she cursed. "I do live there, blast you. Lightning Pass is my home. It's all of our homes! Now let us in!"

"I don't think so," said the guard, looking amused. "Lightning Pass girls don't talk like you. Lightning Pass girls are shamefast and biddable."

"I beg your pardon, sir," said Anna. "We do live in Lightning Pass. We go to Miss Ellicott's School for Magical Maidens."

"Nice try," said the guard. "But a Lightning Pass girl

would never be outside the walls. Certainly not a nice little schoolgirl. She'd be all shut up inside her school where she belonged, doing as she was told. Now run along."

"Well, I live in Lightning Pass too," said Bowser. "And I want to go home."

The guard eyed him a little more suspiciously than he had the girls. "That's what they all say. No one in Lightning Pass is as ragged and dirty as the lot of you."

"We—" said Bowser.

"Look." The man bent down, while the other guards stared straight ahead and pretended they couldn't hear. "I've got kids at home, myself. I wouldn't want to see anything happen to you. Run along before something does, eh? I don't want to see you dragged off to the dungeons."

Chantel, Bowser, and Anna didn't want to see that either. They backed away from the gate, and turned down a cobblestone lane, out of the guards' line of view. Franklin followed, regarding them all with an amused expression.

"Nice work," he said. "You guys guard that place so carefully."

"But we live there!" said Anna, outraged.

"Looks like you don't anymore," said Franklin. "So what are we going to do now?"

"We *have* to get in," said Chantel. "We have to get back to the school. Mrs. Warthall said she was going to sell the younger girls."

"Sounds like a funny kind of school," said Franklin, raising an eyebrow.

"I heard a story once," said Anna doubtfully, "where some soldiers got through the gate hidden in a wagonload of hay."

"It was the story of the treason of Wendy the Wayward," Chantel snapped. "Ever since then all wagonloads of hay have been pierced with swords and pitchforks at the gate."

"Oh," said Anna, looking hurt.

"Sometimes w— in stories people crawl through a sewer grating in the walls," said Franklin.

"Well, that sounds lovely," said Chantel. "But the sewers in Lightning Pass are underground all the way to the sea. I read that in a book."

"So there's no way to get in," said Franklin. "Oh well. I guess we'll go somewhere else. What about High Round-pot? Or the Stormy Isles?"

Chantel looked longingly at the ships. To sail off on a wind that blew toward places with magical names . . . She sighed. "No, we . . . we can't. You go ahead."

"Too bad you threw the crossbow away," said Bowser glumly.

"No it's not." Franklin looked at Chantel. "You've thought of something. You think there's another way in."

"Oh, Chantel, are you thinking of the but—" Anna stopped, and clapped her hands over her mouth.

"Thinking of the butt?" said Franklin, smiling.

Chantel glared at Anna, and Anna glared back.

"Whatever you're thinking of, you'd better tell me." Franklin sat on a barrel and folded his arms and very plainly wasn't about to go off in search of High Roundpot.

Chantel decided it was better to get her version in before Anna or Bowser told too much. "Fine. There might be a magical way to get through the wall. There are these things called buttons. But we've never seen them, they're probably invisible, and we're not sure where they are."

"Well, that's helpful, then," drawled Franklin.

It was quite possible he was the world's most annoying person.

"We know at least one of them is on the western side of the city," said Bowser.

"An invisible portal and you don't know where it is. Maybe it would be easier to go back and find that place where you all came out," said Franklin.

"Fiends," said Chantel shortly.

"Besides, it's a maze down there," said Anna. "It's only luck we got through it once."

"What about the vampires and zombies? And what *are* fiends, anyway?" said Franklin.

"Spirits of the restless dead who take you with them to wander the wastes between this world and the next," said Chantel.

"Oh," said Franklin. Chantel was pleased to see he looked slightly nonplussed.

Finding a button didn't seem like much of a hope. But treacherous Queen Haywith had once opened a breach in the wall . . . maybe now, with no sorceresses to do the Buttoning, it might be possible to do it again.

They followed the wall. They made their way through the harborside neighborhood. A woman was cooking stew, over an open fire on the cobbles. People were lining up to buy bowlsful of it, and Chantel looked at it longingly. It smelled good and she was very hungry.

The woman said something to a girl next to her and handed her a bowl. The girl took the bowl and, stepping carefully so as not to spill it (the bowl was very full) brought it over to Chantel.

"I don't have any money," said Chantel.

"My mother said to give it to you." The girl's accent was different from Franklin's, but also different from the people in Lightning Pass.

"We're not beggars," Chantel heard herself say, to her horror. It was terrible having a snake in your head.

"But we *are* grateful," said Franklin, taking the bowl from the girl's hands. "Thank you."

The stew was the best thing Chantel had ever tasted. It had things from the sea in it, fish and shellfish and green stuff, and tomatoes and potatoes and a lot of pepper. It was gone too quickly, and the little girl came and took the bowl away. Then she brought it back, full again. Bowser tried to give her his knife in payment, but she wouldn't take it.

They gave the empty bowl back, and walked on, feeling considerably livelier and better about the world.

They passed through another gate, and were out in the Roughlands again, this time to the west of the city. They were, according to Franklin, now in the kingdom of Eastern Karute.

"I know that," said Chantel. "Eastern Karute is known for its—"

Barbaric behavior. Bloody history. Vicious Marauders. Even with a snake in her head, Chantel had to stop and think. Not everything she'd learned in school about the Roughlands seemed to be bearing up.

"Apple trees," said Franklin. "I wonder if we'll see any."

They didn't, though. They saw weeds. The Roughlands seemed to be largely composed of weeds. And then, although they were climbing toward the mountains, they ran into marshes. By the time they were all soaked well past their knees from stepping on what looked like solid ground and turned out to be cold, murky water, Chantel had learned to avoid walking on the greenest bits.

"How far do you think we've come?" said Anna.

"About two miles," said Franklin promptly. "I'm going to climb this tree."

It was a three-quarters-dead tree, drowned, Chantel thought, by the surrounding marsh.

"What good does that do?" Chantel asked, as he hoisted himself into its bare branches.

"He wants to see where we are," said Bowser.

They watched the Marauder boy climb as high as he could, and stare off to the north, shading his eyes. A moment later he was clambering down at great speed. He fell off the bottommost branch and picked himself up, wincing.

"There's an army coming," he said.

"An army?" said Anna.

"I don't believe you," said Chantel. "Why would there be an army?"

"Let me see," said Bowser, grabbing the branch and trying without success to swing himself up as Franklin had done.

Franklin seized him and pulled him down. "There's not *time!* Where's your wretched secret gate?"

Chantel looked at the wall. If they'd come two miles, they ought to have reached one of the seven buttons by now. The wall looked exactly the same everywhere. Flat and shiny and utterly impassable.

"Hurry up!" said Franklin.

Chantel ran to the wall, jumping from tussock to hummock, and occasionally missing and splashing into cold muck. She put her hands on it, feeling for a crack, a line, anything.

"Do some magic or something!" Franklin yelled.

"We're trying," muttered Anna, who had joined Chantel at the wall. "Chantel, can you—"

Chantel wasn't listening. She was trying as hard as she could to *summon* an opening in the Wall. To summon a spell. To summon anything.

It wasn't working.

Consider the girl.

We do. We have considered her for some time. The girl is dangerous.

But is she more dangerous inside the wall, or out?

Outside the wall she cannot cause any harm. At least, not for some time.

But if we lose her?

Inside the wall, we can keep an eye on her.

Inside the wall, she may be of use to us.

Of use? She may be one of us.

I think she summons us.

Summons us? A mere child?

A powerful child.

Why does she not see Dimswitch, then?

She ought to.

If she is as powerful as we think she should see it plainly.

She is upset. She is angry. She is thirteen. It's a difficult age.

Very well.

Show her Dimswitch.

10

DIMSWITCH

Suddenly Chantel saw something—a dark shadow against the vast expanse of smooth stone. "There! See that?"

"I think," said Anna, squinting. "Almost. Yes."

The shadow was the shape of a—well, a coffin, Chantel thought. And it was oddly really there. When Chantel put her hand over it, the shadow didn't cover her hand; it stayed beneath it.

"It's a button. It's—it's called Dimswitch. And it seems like we have to—turn it somehow," said Chantel. Touching it, she felt she could understand how it worked. She could feel that it was connected to the other buttons, and to . . . something else. She couldn't tell what. "We kind of push it a little bit sideways . . . Anna, do the fourth sign and the sixth. Fourth with your right hand and sixth with your left. Together."

"That's impossible," said Anna.

"No it's not," said Chantel distractedly. "I'm sure you can do it." She listened to what the button was telling her. She took two steps backward, and sloshed into water halfway up her shins.

She heard a cry behind her.

She spun around. Bowser was still beside the tree—with a Marauder's arm around his neck and a Marauder's knife at his throat.

The Marauder was tall and thick and utterly diabolical-looking, just like the drawing from the *Girls' First History Book* at school. Chantel desperately wished she'd been taught any kind of magic that would help.

"Let him go." Franklin was halfway between the wall and the tree, his crossbow aimed at the Marauder. "Now."

His crossbow? Chantel wondered, with the tiny portion of her mind that wasn't watching in horror.

"You can't shoot me," said the Marauder. "You'll hit the city boy."

"He's right!" Anna called. "Franklin, don't—"

The crossbow went *kerchunk*.

The bolt struck the Marauder in the arm, an inch from Bowser's head. The Marauder yelped and dropped his knife. Bowser wrestled free and ran. Franklin, meanwhile, was fitting another bolt to the crossbow.

The Marauder fumbled with his own crossbow—it couldn't be easy with the bolt sticking through his arm—and Franklin shot him again. In the other arm.

The Marauder turned and fled.

Bowser reached the wall and collapsed against it, panting.

Franklin was close behind him. "Open the blasted thing! Do your magic! There'll be more coming!" He turned on Anna. "You had to call me 'Franklin,' didn't you?"

"You could have hit Bowser!" said Chantel.

"No. I couldn't have," said Franklin. "Open it!" He raised his crossbow and pointed it at the distant fleeing Marauder. "I should have killed him."

"Why didn't you?" said Chantel.

Franklin spared her a look. "Killed a lot of people, have you?"

"Chantel, let's do the spell," said Anna urgently.

"There. There's the other two," said Franklin. "Karl the Bloody always sends three."

"I don't see anyone," said Bowser, still out of breath.

Chantel didn't either. She saw tussocks and hummocks and space.

"Chantel, start the spell again!" said Anna.

"I'm *not* bringing a Marauder with a crossbow into the city," said Chantel. "Where did you hide it?"

"They're not much use for city fighting anyway."

Franklin had the crossbow aimed straight at something only he could see. "No good at close range."

"Then drop it," said Chantel.

"Chantel, he can't!" said Bowser. "There are more of them out there. Just do the spell!"

"There. They just moved closer," said Franklin, shifting his aim slightly.

"Come on, Chantel," said Anna.

Chantel didn't like it, but she started doing the spell again. Anna, looking relieved, joined her and made signs.

Chantel drew the third sign in the air with one hand, and the ninth and first alternately with the other. Then she switched hands. It was difficult. But not impossible.

And slowly Dimswitch turned, folded itself sideways. A passage opened through the wall.

Seven Buttons was fifteen feet thick. At the end of the passage Chantel could see a cobbled street of Lightning Pass.

"Great. C'mon!" said Bowser.

Franklin gaped.

"Now leave the crossbow," said Chantel.

Still staring through the gate, Franklin began undoing little catches and clasps on the crossbow. It came to bits, which he stuck into various pockets.

Chantel didn't want him armed at all. But just as she opened her mouth to protest, two Marauders sprang up from the swamp and rushed at them.

Bowser shoved Anna into the passage, and then ran back and tried to grab Chantel. Anna ran back too. Chantel dodged them.

"I have to be last! It's part of the spell! Just go!" She grabbed Franklin, pushed him into the passage, shoved Bowser and Anna after him, and then leapt after them as the Marauders reached the wall.

The wall shut, starting from the outside. The children ran, passing solid wall that crunched as it tumbled into place behind them. Then Franklin, the fool, stopped, and just stood there, staring at the inside of the wall as it closed toward him.

Chantel threw all her weight at him and knocked him through the passage and into Lightning Pass. The wall shut so quickly behind them that it caught a shred of her robe.

Franklin picked himself up off the ground, without seeming particularly upset or grateful. "That's odd," he said. "The insides of walls don't usually look like that."

"Why have you seen the insides of walls?" said Bowser.

"Well, we knock them down sometimes. There's usually infill." Franklin stared up, down, and all around. "Everything here is so . . . squashed together!" he said. "All those tunnels and arches and things! Where does that one go to?"

"To a court, probably," said Bowser. "C'mon."

"You mean you don't know?"

"There are hundreds of arched alleys like that," said Bowser. "They all go to courts with houses and shops and stuff, and then there are more alleys off of them to other places."

"Amazing," said Franklin. "And those bridges up there—"

"Yeah. They go places," said Bowser. "But could you stop being amazed? People are staring."

They were, Chantel saw. Not many people, but a few—a woman sweeping a doorstep, a boy carrying a load of firewood, a passerby stopping to open a door for him. Chantel wondered if anyone had seen them come through the wall.

The only sign that Dimswitch had been there at all was the few green threads from Chantel's robe, sprouting from a blank expanse of wall.

"Let's go," she said.

Mrs. Warthall might be selling the girls at this very moment.

They climbed up steep streets, crossed by arched bridges that braced the stacked houses. They climbed a staircase that spiraled around a tower and deposited them on a path that crossed the rooftops. It was funny to see Franklin, the know-it-all of the Roughlands, utterly dazzled by Lightning Pass. Chantel felt a surge of pride. Lightning Pass *was* amazing. And it was a relief to have walls around her again. She was back where she belonged.

Still, she hoped she hadn't seen the Roughlands for the last time. She hoped she'd get a chance someday to see High Roundpot and the Stormy Isles.

They hurried up the narrow alley that ran behind Fate's Turning. The back door to the skullery was guarded by two skulls set into the bricks.

From inside came the sound of thumps, followed by wails of pain.

"What's that?" said Franklin, alarmed.

Chantel grabbed the doorlatch and tugged. The door was locked.

"Hang on." Bowser kicked off his boots and climbed up the brick wall, fitting his toes into small cracks and gaps left by crumbling mortar. He reached behind one of the skulls and retrieved a slim length of metal.

They heard a sharp, angry crack from inside the school—the sort of noise that might be made by a belt hitting someone. Chantel jerked furiously at the locked door.

"Let go." Bowser stuck the length of metal into the crack between the door and the wall and slid it all the way to the top. Something clicked. "Okay, now try it."

Chantel yanked the door open and charged through the skullery, pausing only to grab a frying pan. She could hear the others behind her. The snake inside her head was a mighty hooded cobra, all fangs and venom. She hardly had time to take in the scene—all the girls lined up, except Leila, who was standing before them wielding the ladle. Mrs. Warthall was swinging a belt.

Chantel rushed in and hit Mrs. Warthall with the frying pan.

In a story, the frying pan would have clanged and Mrs. Warthall would have dropped to the floor, unconscious.

In real life, the frying pan hit Mrs. Warthall edge-on in the face, opening a gash. And since Chantel wasn't used to hitting people with frying pans, the momentum made it fly out of her hand. It struck the brick floor with the world's loudest clang. Mrs. Warthall didn't even fall down. She grabbed Chantel by the hair and wrapped the belt tightly around Chantel's neck.

Chantel dug at the belt with her fingers, but it just drew tighter. Everything went gray at the edges. Through the ringing in her ears she heard Mrs. Warthall bellow, "Nobody move, or this brat dies."

And then suddenly Chantel and Mrs. Warthall fell together to the floor. The belt slackened for a moment, and Chantel struggled furiously. Then hands were pulling at her, yanking. She fought back.

"Stop it! It's me!" Anna yelled.

Anna? Fighting? But there was no time to think about that, among all the yells and smacks and clangs. Chantel's part in what came next was not much, because she found she could only sit and hold her throat and gasp. She felt as if she would never get enough air. She watched as the little girls, Anna, Franklin, and Bowser fought back. Mrs. Warthall had seized up the frying pan and was laying about her, but people kept coming at her from behind. Leila's ladle was grabbed away from her.

Leila fled first, out the skullery door, and when Mrs. Warthall saw her lieutenant leaving, she admitted defeat and ran for her life.

"The door!" Chantel rasped. "Lock it! All the doors! Windows. Wards. Anna, wards."

But Anna wasn't as good at wards as Chantel was, so Chantel had to stagger to her feet and help her. Franklin, meanwhile, began tending to the little girls' injuries with surprising expertise. He was ordering Bowser to bring him things.

"When Mrs. Warthall had that belt around your neck, Franklin came up behind and kicked her legs out from under her," Anna explained, as they sealed the roof door.

"I want to know where Miss Flivvers is," said Chantel, when they got back to the kitchen. It still hurt to talk.

"Locked into Miss Ellicott's study," said Daisy. "After Mrs. Warthall sent Frenetica away."

"They locked her in?" said Anna.

"No, she locked herself in," said Holly. "When it started."

"Owl's bowels!" Chantel swore. The little girls stared at her, impressed. "Well, come on," she said. "It's time for her to come out and face us."

They all tromped upstairs and crowded into the hallway. Through the heavy paneled door, they could hear Miss Flivvers reciting, in hushed, desperate tones, the 17 Steps to Curtseying Correctly. Chantel knocked, grimly.

Miss Flivvers stopped reciting, but didn't answer. Chantel felt the snake in her head tense, still and alert, as if it were about to tackle a field mouse.

"Miss Flivvers, open the door," said Chantel. "I know you're in there."

No answer.

"Miss Flivvers, open up. It's me, Chantel."

Silence. Then, timorously: "You don't sound like Chantel."

Chantel looked to the others for help.

"It's true, Miss Flivvers, it is Chantel," said Holly. "And Mrs. Warthall is gone, and so is Leila."

Pattering of feet in thin-soled shoes. The door opened and Miss Flivvers peered out. Dismay paled her face at the sight of everyone waiting for her.

"They're gone," said Chantel. Her throat still hurt; was that why Miss Flivvers had said she didn't sound like herself? "And we've sealed the doors. But that's not going to be the end of it. So we've got to decide what's going to happen next, and we need you to come along and . . . and act your age. Please."

"Chantel, I am absolutely shocked by the state of your hair and your robes," said Miss Flivvers. "Go and repair yourself at once."

"I can't right now," said Chantel. "This is an emergency. And it's an emergency with you in it, Miss Flivvers. Come on."

They gathered in the largest classroom. The snake in Chantel's head seemed to feel that Chantel's place was at the teacher's podium. So she went there, taking a large mug of water that Daisy had fetched for her aching throat. Miss Flivvers made a dismayed little gesture of protest, then went and sat on a student bench.

"The first thing we need to consider is Mrs. Warthall," said Chantel. She took a long gulp of water.

"She's going to go straight to the patriarchs," said Bowser.

"Who are the patriarchs?" said Franklin, in his twangy, Marauder drawl.

Miss Flivvers sat bolt upright and stared. "Chantel! Who is *that!*"

She did not point, because Miss Flivvers was the very model of deportment, but her nose quivered in consternation.

"This is Franklin," said Chantel. "Franklin, Miss Flivvers."

"Nice to meet you," said Franklin distractedly.

"Chantel, that is a boy. You have brought a boy into this school, among all Miss Ellicott's magical maidens. A *boy*."

"Yes, Miss Flivvers," said Chantel. "Bowser's a boy too, and he's always been here. Could we talk about this later, please?"

"This boy has a most unusual manner of speech," said Miss Flivvers. "I fear he may be a savage influence upon poor Bowser."

Bowser looked annoyed. He turned to Franklin. "The patriarchs are a bunch of rich guys who run everything in Lightning Pass."

"Run everything?" Franklin frowned. "I thought you guys had a king."

"We do," said Bowser. "But he doesn't really run things. The patriarchs just let him think he does."

Miss Flivvers had subsided back to looking shocked. Although, Chantel noticed, she also looked rather fascinated. Well, it couldn't be very interesting, being Miss Flivvers on a day-to-day basis. This was at least a change.

Chantel thought about what Bowser had said. She'd seen the king, walking in procession under a velvet canopy borne by four patriarchs.

And kings killed other kings so that they could be king. No one exactly said so, but it was clearly what happened.

But it did seem that whenever anything was actually getting done, it was the patriarchs who were doing it.

Right. Well, now the patriarchs were surely going to come to the school. And the girls would be sold, and the school would be closed.

"We have to have something we can offer them," said Chantel.

"Other than to come along quietly?" said Anna.

"We could give them the rhyme," said Bowser.

"We already offered them that, and you saw what happened," said Chantel.

"But don't you actually have the Buttoning spell now?" said Anna. "I mean, you opened that passage—"

"What *are* you children talking about?" said Miss Flivvers.

Anna briefly explained.

Miss Flivvers paled. "You went out into the Roughlands? Without asking permission? That was a terribly wrong thing to do."

"Miss Flivvers, there was a fiend chasing us," said Anna, sounding slightly impatient.

"If you must contradict someone, say 'I beg your pardon,'" Miss Flivvers instructed.

"I beg your pardon, there was a fiend chasing us."

Anna turned to Chantel. "Anyway, you opened Dimswitch; can't you seal it, now that you know where it is? You're good at wards."

"The spell is more complicated than that," said Chantel. "It's not a simple ward. It's intricate. Even though Dimswitch looked like just one spot, it's connected to the other switches and they're all part of the wall."

"How do you know all that?" said Bowser. "You didn't know it before, did you?"

"The wall sort of told me," said Chantel. "I had this idea of, kind of, a circle."

"You mean the wall?" said Bowser.

"Maybe it was the wall." She didn't think the wall was what she meant. The idea that a circle had spoken to her had only just come to her and, infuriatingly, it was wriggling away already.

"Then—" Miss Flivvers looked like someone desperately trying to keep up. "Can't you ask the circle how to do the spell? Not that it isn't rather forward on your part to ask—"

"I can't ask it," said Chantel. "It was telling me stuff, but once we were through and the button closed, it stopped telling me."

"Chantel, you interrupted me. I am becoming very concerned about your deportment."

Chantel ignored this. "Anyway, the main problem is

what we do when the patriarchs get here."

"What if we told them we were still looking for the spell?" said Anna. "What if you gave them the rhyme, and —there's that bit about lost lore, right?"

"What *are* you girls talking about?" said Miss Flivvers.

"'This remains from long lost lore. The rest is gone. We know no more,'" Holly recited.

"When we did prognostication with Miss Ellicott, and you saw into the Ago—" said Anna.

"I just saw a bleeding crown," said Chantel. "That's no help."

"But you really *can* see the Ago," said Anna. "Not like the rest of us. If you could convince the patriarchs that you were looking in the Ago for the right way to do the Buttoning, then maybe they'd leave us alone while you looked. And that would give us time to find the sorceresses."

"How can we find them?" said Chantel. "Lord Rudolph says the Marauders without the gates took them."

Miss Flivvers gasped in dismay. "Marauders! Poor Euphonia!"

"Who's Euphonia?" said Bowser.

"Miss Ellicott to you," said Miss Flivvers. "Oh, poor dear Miss Ellicott, alone with all those hairy, unwashed Marauders!"

"She's not alone. They took all of them," said Chantel.

"And we do bathe," said Franklin.

Miss Flivvers turned on him. "Well, young man? Where have you taken them?"

"Nowhere," said Franklin.

"There are different kinds of Marauders, Miss Flivvers," said Chantel.

Miss Flivvers shuddered at the thought. "How do you intend to find out which ones have taken poor Miss Ellicott, then?"

"I don't know," said Chantel. "But if we tell Lord Rudolph I'm searching the past for the spell, that will at least give us time to look."

"Seems like that would work for a while," said Franklin. "But eventually you'd have to come up with a spell."

"Well, so we *would* come up with it," said Anna. "If Chantel looks through the Ago, maybe she can find the long lost lore—"

"This is only going to work," said Bowser, "if Chantel can stop acting like she has a snake in her head."

"True," said Anna. "Chantel, you need to use your deportment."

"That was precisely my point," said Miss Flivvers sniffily.

"I mean *use* it," said Anna, frowning at Miss Flivvers.

"But," said Chantel. "If they get hold of the whole spell and figure out how to do it, then they'll strengthen Seven Buttons, which is the exact opposite of what the

Marauders told them to do, and the Marauders will kill Miss Ellicott and all the other sorceresses."

"What?" cried Miss Flivvers. "Chantel, you can't possibly know this."

"I do, because I asked Lord Rudolph. He told us that the sorceresses had been kidnapped by the Marauders," said Chantel. "And that the Marauders want the wall taken down, or they won't return them alive."

"You *questioned* Lord Rudolph?" Miss Flivvers looked shocked. "Chantel, I want you to recite for me, right now, the 42 Rules of Hierarchy and the 19 Signs of Modesty."

Chantel ignored this. "Miss Flivvers, don't be so—so helpless. Please. We need you to act like a grown-up when the patriarchs come. Let us do the talking but . . . but act like a grown-up. Because if you don't—" She thought of a threat that might work. "Mrs. Warthall will come back."

Miss Flivvers looked horrified. She began to sob softly.

Chantel remembered that Miss Flivvers had once said something quite spirited to Miss Ellicott about pedestals. There had to be more to Miss Flivvers than met the eye.

Chantel hoped it would show up soon.

From down below, there came a knock at the street door.

11

The Battle of Miss Ellicott's School

It was not so much a knock as a banging, a pounding, a yanking, a thoroughgoing effort to rip the door from its hinges.

The crowd of girls parted to let Chantel through. She opened the door.

Four city guards stood on the steps, resplendent in the purple uniform of the Order of Watchful Sentinels of Lightning Pass. They wore swords and daggers and carried spears tipped with shiny-sharp blades.

"Yes?" said Chantel.

"You're under arrest," said the captain of the sentinels.

He made a grab at Chantel. They all watched as his arm hit an invisible rubbery wall and bounced back.

Of course, he was the sort of person who doesn't feel he has to believe something just because it's happened. He shot his arm out again, and it came boinging back and punched him in the nose. The smaller girls laughed, and Chantel heard Anna behind her hushing them.

"Please tell Lord Rudolph," said Chantel, "that I have an offer to make."

Instead of answering, the captain surged through the doorway—for about two feet. Then the shield bounced him back, throwing him down the steps to land on his rear in the street.

Again Anna hushed the little girls' laughter.

"Please tell the patriarchs—" said Chantel firmly.

The captain was back on the top step. "You there, boy! What's your name?"

"Me? Bowser."

"Can you make these girls see sense?"

"No sir," said Bowser.

The man cursed, and turned to Franklin. "What's your name?"

"He can't talk," said Bowser hurriedly. "He's my cousin. His name's Rob."

"Well, I have no orders to arrest him," said the captain. "He can be in charge of the females until we send another manageress to look after them."

"You're not arresting anybody," said Chantel, struggling

for deportment. The snake inside her head was wriggling furiously. "You can't come in here, so you can't arrest us. We'll only talk to Lord Rudolph. Please send him up here."

And she closed the door gently, although the snake was urging her to slam it.

She looked around her. Miss Flivvers had stayed upstairs.

It became a very long day.

More guards arrived—dozens of guards. They tried all the windows and doors, including the roof door, which they reached by dropping down from the roof of the house above. They tried to knock bricks out of the wall, which really worried Chantel, and she had to run around putting wards on the walls themselves.

Meanwhile the younger girls were doing adhesion spells to stick the guards' boots to the street, and gelid spells that turned puddles to ice on which they slipped and fell.

It was dusk by the time the men finally went away. It had been a long, cranky, hungry day in which nobody had had time to cook anything, and anyway there was very little food in the house.

Finally Lord Rudolph climbed the many stairs of Fate's Turning and knocked on the door of Miss Ellicott's School. He came accompanied by six sentinels and his clerk, Mr. Less.

"Only Lord Rudolph comes in," said Bowser. He had suggested that he do the talking, because of Chantel's snake problem.

Miss Flivvers stood behind him. Chantel and Anna had insisted on this. Miss Flivvers's job was to look like a grown-up.

And Franklin was there simply because Miss Flivvers didn't want him wandering around the school, being a boy all over the place.

Lord Rudolph opened his mouth to protest, but Mr. Less spoke first. "That seems fair. After all, sir, we're not afraid of children, are we?"

"Of course not," said Lord Rudolph. "But we don't allow children to set the terms of discussion, either. Leila, take down the ward."

And to Chantel's utter fury, Leila stepped from behind the guards.

The snake in Chantel's head reared. Patriarchs upset the snake, Miss Flivvers and Mrs. Warthall and Franklin upset the snake, but nothing made it angrier than the treachery of Leila.

Leila began a spell. Using magic against her own school and classmates! Chantel was furious. She wanted to scream. She wanted to break things.

But she had to stop Leila instead. Quickly she made the eighth sign with both hands. Out of the corner of her eye she saw Anna doing the same.

The patriarch turned to Leila. "What's the matter? Can't you do a simple spell?" He reached out and pushed at the ward.

Leila abruptly stopped. "It's two against one!" she said.

Miss Flivvers pushed Bowser aside. "Really, Leila. I'm shocked to hear you address a patriarch in those tones. Where's your curtsey?"

"I already curtseyed, you old—"

"Leila, I think you should copy down for me the 140 Lesser and Greater Reasons for Good Deportment," said Miss Flivvers.

Chantel and Anna took advantage of this distraction to extra-stengthen the ward.

"You seem like a reasonable woman," said the patriarch approvingly. "Will you let us in?"

"Only him, Miss Flivvers," said Anna. "Not the guards. And not Leila."

"Anna, I will not be instructed by you." Miss Flivvers curtseyed to Lord Rudolph. "We would be honored to welcome you and your clerk into our humble school, Lord Rudolph. I'm afraid we lack sufficient accommodations for those other gentlemen."

Lord Rudolph nodded to the sentinels. They retired.

"Very well," said Miss Flivvers. "Chantel, Anna, let the nice gentlemen in. And Leila."

Chantel did not want to let Leila in. The snake inside

her head was so furious at the thought that he was positively banging on the inside of her skull. Grudgingly, she took down the ward long enough for Lord Rudolph, Mr. Less, and Leila to slip in. Then she and Anna redid the ward, strengthened it, and restrengthened it.

By the time they finished this, Miss Flivvers, Lord Rudolph, and his clerk were seated in wing chairs in the parlor. Leila was on a stool at Lord Rudolph's feet. Chantel wanted to kick the traitor right off her stool. The snake had grown so much Chantel felt as if her head would explode.

Nonetheless she and Anna stood beside the door and waited respectfully for Miss Flivvers to tell them what to do.

Miss Flivvers flicked a glance at them. "How terrible, Lord Rudolph," she was saying. "I'm absolutely horrified to hear that my students have behaved in such an unladylike manner. I'm afraid it reflects very poorly on the school. I can assure you they will face the most dire consequences."

Mr. Less turned an amused gaze on the girls. The snake in Chantel's head thrashed; she suddenly felt she hated the clerk.

"Although of course the school was *not* in my control at the time that it happened," said Miss Flivvers. "I'm afraid that dear Mrs. Warthall isn't much of a manager of girls. Had I been in charge—" she turned to the girls.

"Chantel, Anna, go and help the boys. They're fetching refreshments."

Furious, Chantel went.

"What refreshments?" she asked Anna as they went down the hall. "There's nothing to eat or drink in the house."

"I think that's probably the point," said Anna.

The boys seemed to think so too. Bowser and Franklin and several of the smaller girls had arranged a tray with a steaming teapot and the best china cups. They were laughing.

"What about to eat?" said Bowser. "What's in the bread box?"

"Mouse droppings!" said Daisy gleefully.

Bowser shook his head regretfully. "She wouldn't be able to cope. The Fliv, I mean. She'd weep, and it would ruin everything."

Holly banged open a cupboard. "Candle stubs!"

Bowser whipped out his pocketknife. "Give 'em here."

He cut a candle up into discs, and Daisy and Franklin arranged them carefully on a plate.

Franklin eyed the result. "Can't we just sprinkle them with mouse—"

"No," said Anna firmly.

"It would look like—"

"No," said Bowser.

Chantel went ahead to open the doors as Bowser

138

proudly bore the tray into the parlor.

He set the tray on the tea table. Miss Flivvers, with a sweet smile, poured out cups of brown liquid, and Chantel handed them around. Anna passed the candle-wafers.

Leila refused the wafers. She set her cup down on the floor beside her stool. The clerk, Mr. Less, had a plate of wafers balanced on his knee and a steaming cup in his hand. He looked down at the latter in amusement.

"I hope you gentlemen will forgive—" Miss Flivvers began.

Lord Rudolph lifted the cup to his lips and took a deep drink. "Waugh!" He spat it out on the floor and jumped up. Cup, saucer, and candle-wafers fell to the floor. The handle broke off the cup. The wafers bounced.

"It tastes like mud!" said Lord Rudolph.

"I believe it is mud," said Mr. Less. "And the cookies appear to be wax."

"Oh dear." Miss Flivvers turned to Bowser. "Did you bring the nice gentlemen mud to drink?"

"There wasn't any tea," said Bowser.

"And wax to eat?"

"There weren't any cookies."

"Well, couldn't you have made sandwiches?" said Miss Flivvers, sweetly exasperated.

"There wasn't any bread," said Bowser. "Or anything to put in the sandwiches."

"What a shame," said Miss Flivvers. "Still, you know you shouldn't serve people mud, young man. Go to your skullery at once."

Bowser went, cheerfully enough.

"I'm terribly sorry, Lord Rudolph," said Miss Flivvers. "I'm afraid Mrs. Warthall doesn't seem to have laid in any provisions at all, although I'm sure you must have provided her with ample means to do so."

"Of course we did! Didn't we?" Lord Rudolph turned angrily to his clerk.

"Not really," said the clerk. "Enough to feed a hutchful of rabbits, possibly. Or a rather abstemious reindeer. But not a school. No."

"See to it, then," said Lord Rudolph. "Now then, Miss Flivvers. Obviously the school needs a manageress, so I—"

"I shall do the best I can, Lord Rudolph." Miss Flivvers bowed her head modestly. "Thank you for your confidence in me."

"I meant—"

"Wonderful," said the clerk. "That's that settled, isn't it, sir?"

Lord Rudolph glowered at his clerk. "I had intended to close the school, and disperse the students."

Sell the students, you mean. The effort Chantel had to expend in not saying this made Japheth even more restless. She thought she ought to be given a medal for deportment.

"Oh, we may not want to do that just yet, sir," said Miss Flivvers. "The children were telling me that you were interested in perhaps finding a spell . . . ?"

"The Buttoning. It is vital to the defense of the nation," said Lord Rudolph.

Miss Flivvers nodded and smiled and blinked. "If I may humbly venture an idea—"

And Miss Flivvers told him about Chantel's ability to see the Ago.

Lord Rudolph directed his piercing gaze at Chantel. "Do you think you can find the Buttoning in the past?"

Snake or no, Chantel had to reply. She used all the magic of her deportment and managed to force the snake down into her stomach, where he slithered around nauseatingly.

"I can but try, sir." She was surprised at how even and grown-up her voice sounded.

"Hm. 'Try,'" said Lord Rudolph. "'Try' isn't good enough. It needs to be done by Midsummer's Eve. That's when the Marauders threaten to kill Miss Ellicott."

Chantel used her deportment to put all the confidence into her voice that she could. "I can do it."

◦◦◦

Miss Flivvers showed Lord Rudolph and Mr. Less out. Leila went with them.

"I just hope he remembers to send the money," said

Anna, as soon as they were gone.

"Anna, how can you think that a gentleman like Lord Rudolph would go back on his word?" said Miss Flivvers.

Anna shot her a disbelieving look.

"The clerk will remember," said Chantel. "If he doesn't, we'll go and remind him."

"Chantel!" Miss Flivvers looked shocked. "I am—"

"Concerned about my deportment. Yes. I beg your pardon, Miss Flivvers." Chantel curtseyed, the snake swirling angrily.

"You have interrupted me," said Miss Flivvers. "It is absolutely necessary that you comport yourself in the manner of a decent young lady, Chantel. We are all counting on you to find the Buttoning. And on Anna, of course," she added as an afterthought.

"Miss Flivvers, I beg your pardon," said Chantel. "But did you not understand what I told you before? The Marauders have Miss Ellicott and they won't give her back unless we bring *down* the walls."

"Are you actually suggesting bringing down the walls?" said Miss Flivvers.

"No, of course not," said Chantel. "But—"

"Things may not be as they seem," Miss Flivvers interrupted. "We are counting on you. You must not fail us."

The snake churning in her stomach gave Chantel the resolve and bad manners to say what she said next. "Miss

Flivvers, *we* were counting on *you*. And you *did* fail us. You let Mrs. Warthall take control of the school. You can't let anything like that happen again. If I'm going to be busy searching the Ago, you'd better be busy protecting the little girls."

Miss Flivvers reddened. "Is it your place to correct your elders?"

"No, Miss Flivvers, it's not. I beg your pardon," said Chantel. "Do we have a deal?"

Miss Flivvers looked furious. She looked as if she was about to demand that Chantel recite the 172 Rules and 38 Corollaries for Knowing One's Place. Then she, too, called on her deportment.

"You will search the Ago," said Miss Flivvers. "And you will find the . . . the lost lore, if that's what it is. And while you search, we shall all do our duty."

The snake in Chantel's belly sighed. That was probably as close to a promise as Chantel was likely to get. "Yes, Miss Flivvers."

12

Chantel decided to do the Ago spell at Dimswitch itself.
After practicing for a few days, she set off early one
morning. Anna and Bowser had gone ahead to set up the
brazier and basin. Franklin walked with Chantel, to help
her carry supplies.

They took a short cut through the Green Terraces.
They followed a stone walkway that led under arbors of
vines that held clusters of tiny green grapes. They climbed
down several staircases, past a terrace of peach and apple
orchards, and one of dark green potato plants. Chantel
wished the potatoes were ready to eat. The crops weren't
coming along quite as well as they should. There were no
sorceresses' cultivation spells to help them.

She pointed out the orchards to Franklin.

"I had a peach once," she said. "I won it as a prize for memorization and deportment."

"Once?" said Franklin.

"Well, they're very expensive, of course."

Franklin looked at her like she was crazy. "They grow all over the plains. In the summer you can buy them for a penny a peck at the markets."

Chantel figured he was making this up. Obviously he was still overwhelmed by the magnificence of Lightning Pass, and it was natural he would want to talk up the Roughlands a bit.

They passed through a tunnel formed by melon vines just beginning to work their way up wrought-iron frames.

"When the vines have finished growing," Chantel told him, "they'll form a tableau of the treachery of Queen Haywith. You can see if you look—"

"Is there anything that we can eat right now?" said Franklin.

"Of course not!" said Chantel. "It isn't ours. And anyway, you can see it's guarded."

She pointed out the guard towers to him.

"Oh, of course," said Franklin. "You people would guard gardens, wouldn't you."

The snake in Chantel's head twitched with fury. On the one hand she quite liked Franklin. She appreciated that he had many good qualities . . . none of which were his annoying twangy accent, his arrogance, or his air of Marauder superiority.

"What have the Marauders done with the sorceresses?" she demanded. "You must know *something*."

"I don't," said Franklin.

"Well, it could have been your people. Charles the Bloody?"

"*Karl* the Bloody," Franklin snapped.

The snake squirmed happily at having annoyed him.

"*We* wouldn't take them," said Franklin. "*We* don't—"

"We who?" said Chantel.

"We, the tribe of Karl," said Franklin. "The Sunbiters."

"But you ran away."

"I'm still a Sunbiter," said Franklin. "We don't take hostages. We just kill people. Properly, you know. We give them a chance to die a noble and honorable death, so that they'll go to their ancestors in glory."

Chantel's stomach gave an unpleasant lurch. "You mean you killed the sorceresses?"

"I doubt it," said Franklin. "I'm sure we never had them in the first place." He started to step over a stone wall. Chantel caught him just in time.

"You can't walk there. That's a Monday lawn."

Franklin raised an eyebrow and looked amused.

"Meaning it can only be walked across on Mondays, I suppose."

Chantel was relieved not to have to explain this, as he was looking more and more sardonic. "We do have Thursday lawns, if you want to walk on one," she said, leading the way across an arched stone bridge.

From the highest point of the bridge, they could see out over Seven Buttons to the Roughlands. The distant smudges of sea and land looked different to Chantel now that she actually knew their smells and sounds.

"There's a lot of Karl the Bloody's men out there," said Franklin.

"How can you tell?" Chantel couldn't see anyone.

"They've placed their camps to be invisible from most of the city. But you can see tracks. They're watching Dimswitch, probably, because those scouts saw it open."

"Won't we drop something on them?"

"Nah. Things are probably still at the negotiating stage," said Franklin. "We—Karl the Bloody is probably making demands."

"There's nothing to negotiate," she said. "The Marauders can't get through Seven Buttons."

"Would you stop calling us that?" said Franklin. "We're not *Marauders*. We're Sunbiters."

Chantel didn't answer. She led the way down the bridge to the Daisy Pond.

It was a nice, orderly pond, the sort that Lightning Pass approved of. It was round, contained in a stone wall, with algae-covered stone sides that went down as far as the eye could see. It was said that the Daisy Pond had no bottom.

They followed a flagstone path that skirted it.

"If your tribe didn't take the sorceresses, who did?" she asked.

Franklin frowned. "I don't know. It couldn't have been the Walatoni. They think women are sacred, so they would never bother sorceresses."

"Think women are *what*?" said Chantel.

But Franklin wasn't listening. "The Haramats wouldn't have done it, because they're like us—they let prisoners die honorable deaths. That is, the Haramats might have taken them, but if so, they're not hostages. The Elestorians will take hostages sometimes, and exchange them for Elestorian prisoners—do you have any?"

"I don't know," said Chantel.

"It doesn't matter," said Franklin. "The Elestorians are famous for not keeping their word, and only delivering their prisoners in pieces."

"Oh," said Chantel. "So isn't there any kind of Marauder who takes hostages and doesn't kill them?"

"Not that I ever heard of," said Franklin with a shrug. "And none of us call ourselves Marauders."

Chantel did like Franklin, but she was feeling a certain

urge to push him into the Daisy Pond.

Still, she thought . . . if what Franklin said was true, then the Marauders weren't holding the sorceresses. Either Franklin was lying, or the patriarchs were.

They had reached the steep stone dropoff that marked the edge of the Green Terraces. Chantel led the way down a stone staircase to the lanes and alleys below.

⟨≋⟩

Lord Rudolph had ordered the cobbled square beside Dimswitch cleared while Chantel did the Ago spell. Barriers were up, and city guards were stationed around them to keep people out.

Chantel had never actually done the spell herself, only watched Miss Ellicott do it.

Anna and Bowser had kindled a charcoal fire. Anna had set a small pot of water to boil; magical brews and potions were her thing. She dropped ingredients into the pot.

She filled a bowl with ice magically made from the Daisy Pond. She set the bowl down on the cobbles, right in front of those few green threads from Chantel's robe that marked Dimswitch.

Chantel stood before the bowl, facing Seven Buttons. She concentrated on clearing her mind of all other thoughts—like the fact that the Marauders—Sunbiters, rather—were now camped outside the wall, and that, according to Franklin, they did not really have the sorceresses. To

149

do magic you had to free your mind of distractions. This was difficult with a snake wriggling around in your head. She told the snake to be still, and it slithered down and settled somewhere in her left leg, clearing her mind.

She thought about the question she wanted answered. The one about the long lost lore for the Buttoning spell.

What do we need to do to protect the city? she asked.

And then she asked another question. *Can you show me how to find the sorceresses?*

And just in case the answer wasn't hidden in the past, she added *Or can you at least show me something that will help?*

Carefully Anna lifted the pot from the flames and poured it into the ice.

There was a hissing sound, and a billowing column of white steam rose. It smelled of tea and hay fever and late October. The others backed away. Chantel held her braids away from her face and leaned into it. For a moment, she saw nothing but steam, which was almost too hot to breathe. She closed her eyes against the heat. She didn't remember the spell being this hot when Miss Ellicott had done it.

Consider the girl now.

The girl? She has a snake in her innards.

A girl who will let a snake into her head is neither shamefast nor biddable.

Shamefast or biddable? Does that matter?

Matter!

It matters more than anything.

It has been a long time since a girl has let a snake into her head.

But will anything come of it?

She works great magic.

She works a summoning.

No, it is not a summoning. It is simply a spell for seeing the past.

The past?

Perhaps.

When _she_ does it, it is a summoning.

Chantel gazed through the steam at Seven Buttons. Then the wall faded slightly, becoming transparent, and she saw the swamp beyond. There were no Marauders there. There was just swamp.

And someone was walking toward her, from a great distance, along a path that was suddenly there. As he came closer she saw that he was wearing brown trousers, a loose green tunic, and a cap with a feather in it. A tree popped up beside the path. The man climbed onto a low branch, and beckoned to Chantel.

Hm.

Before, when Chantel had looked into the Ago, the Ago hadn't seen *her*.

The man beckoned again.

Chantel hesitated. He must have something to tell her. But would she be able to pass through Seven Buttons?

She stepped over the bowl of mist, and onto the path which she now saw ended at her spell. She felt a faint rippling as she passed through Dimswitch. The air smelled of early spring. She walked until she reached the tree.

By this time the man in the tree was eating an apple. He had short brown hair and a narrow, brown, rather graceful face. He wore useful-looking leather boots, which he swung nonchalantly as he watched Chantel approach.

Around the base of the tree was curled a large golden

lizard, about the size of a donkey. It was asleep, and snoring, wings folded across its back.

"Is that a dragon?" Chantel blurted, when she reached the tree.

The man raised an eyebrow. "Yes. He's called Lightning."

Chantel moved closer, surprised to find she wasn't frightened at all. The dragon fascinated her. She'd never seen a dragon, not a real one. She wished it would wake up so she could see its eyes.

"Not many people aren't afraid of Lightning," said the man.

His voice was rather high-pitched. He looked like he didn't need to shave, although he was certainly old enough. Was he some sort of elf, or something?

He also had a strange accent.

"I'm . . . this is the Ago, isn't it?" Chantel asked.

"I beg your pardon?"

"I did a spell," Chantel explained. "To see into the past. So, um, I guess you're in the past."

"That explains it. You look a bit wavery. So you're from the future, then?"

"From the Will-Be," said Chantel. "Er, how far back are we?"

"For you it is the Will-Be. For me it's only a May-Be. How would I know how far back you are?"

Chantel felt the conversation wasn't going well. "I don't know. Um, I beg your pardon, but I probably only have until the steam stops rising to ask some questions. Um, and I probably have to be back inside the wall by then."

"What wall?"

Chantel turned back and looked. There was the city, climbing on top of itself to the castle at the peak. Above the castle flew the familiar dragon flag of Lightning Pass. But there was no wall.

"I—came through it," said Chantel. "It's definitely there in our time."

"If you say so," said the man. "Sooner or later, the wall is in your mind. Then the stone one is just a formality."

"Er, what's your name, please?" said Chantel, then bit her tongue at this shocking lapse in deportment. "I beg your pardon. Mine is Chantel."

"Haywith," said the man.

Chantel stared open-mouthed, all deportment forgotten, but then managed to drop into a low curtsey beside the dragon (who was still asleep). She looked up at what she now saw quite clearly was not a man, nor an elf, but a woman.

"*Queen* Haywith?" she asked from the ground.

"Yes, but there's no need for such formalities here," said the queen, flapping a hand at Chantel in a get-up gesture.

Chantel got to her feet, confused. Haywith wasn't just

a queen, but the quintessential traitor. Why had the spell taken her to speak to Haywith?

The queen dug in the pocket of her tunic, fished out another apple, and proffered it.

"No thank you, your majesty," said Chantel. "I'm probably not supposed to eat anything in the Ago, or I might end up stuck here."

"Suit yourself." Queen Haywith tossed the core of her finished apple aside. Instantly a seedling sprouted from it, and began to grow into a sapling.

"Is that real?" Chantel asked.

"Probably not," said the queen, looking at the rapidly growing apple tree. "I expect I'm asleep in the palace and having a dream. How can I help you?"

It was a question often asked rudely, but Queen Haywith clearly really meant it. The traitor queen was kind, Chantel thought, even if she was a little abrupt and dressed very oddly. Suddenly Chantel was pouring out all her difficulties—the missing sorceresses, and the Marauders without the gates. And to her shame, Chantel also started crying.

"Well, crying always helps," said the queen. "So they built the wall, did they? Over my dead body, I presume. I told them that Marauders without the gates would be the least of their problems."

Chantel sniffed angrily. The queen was *not* kind. "Well,

sorry, but you'd probably cry too!"

"Probably," said the queen. "I wasn't being sarcastic. Crying *does* help. Are you finished?"

"Yes," said Chantel with as much dignity as she could muster while surreptitiously wiping her nose.

"It's a little hard for me to advise you given that I've been dead for—?"

"About five hundred years," said Chantel.

"Really, that long? How did I—no, never mind. Don't answer that. So you're doing a type of past-scrying spell, then. Do you have questions for me?"

Chantel did, and she'd forgotten all about them in the confusion of discovering who she was talking to. "Yes. Um, the missing sorceresses—"

"Unfortunately, I won't be able to help you find them," said the queen. "Remember, I'm in the past."

Owl's bowels. And she couldn't ask how to do the Buttoning. Queen Haywith seemed not to know there even *was* a wall.

What to ask, then? Chantel thought of the couplet that Miss Ellicott had given her to memorize.

"What were the words that you spoke and what was the vow that you broke?" she blurted.

"I *beg* your pardon?" said the queen frostily.

Chantel hadn't realized the question would sound so rude. "I'm sorry. It was in a rhyme we were given. 'Speak the words that Haywith spoke, and keep the vow that Haywith broke.'"

"The vow I took at my coronation was to protect the kingdom, of course," said Haywith. "And I shall *always* keep it."

"Right, of course," said Chantel hastily.

"I would not *dream* of breaking it," the queen said.

"Yes, sorry," said Chantel.

"To suggest that I *would* is terribly offensive."

Chantel curtseyed again and apologized again. She was wasting time. She felt sure the spell to see into the Ago wouldn't last much longer. "Er, what about the words you spoke?"

"I am thirty-eight years old," said the queen. "How many words do you suppose I have spoken?"

"Er, a lot," said Chantel. "But was there anything in particular that . . . Er, can you do magic?"

The queen looked at the sleeping dragon, and arched an eyebrow in a gesture that reminded Chantel of Franklin. She smiled. "Perhaps. But I know nothing of this spell you speak of.

"Those patriarchs . . . we don't have them in my time. I expect they turn up later. Hm." She was still gazing at the sleeping dragon. "Is Lightning still in the city?"

"I don't think so," said Chantel. "I've never seen a dragon." She remembered something Miss Ellicott had said. "I've got a snake, though. He's my familiar."

"What?" The queen jumped down from the branch and walked around Chantel, as if wanting to inspect her from all angles. "You managed to summon a *snake*? How old are you, child?"

"Thirteen," said Chantel, turning as the queen walked, and getting a little dizzy. "I was six when I summoned him, though."

"And where is he now?"

Chantel wouldn't have admitted this to most people, but within the spell, it seemed wisest to tell the truth. "He went into my head."

The queen looked startled. "That's where he is now?"

The question took Chantel by surprise. "No. He's—" He wasn't in her leg anymore. Chantel took a careful inventory. "He doesn't seem to be there at all anymore, actually." She felt a sharp pang of loss.

"How can that be?"

"I don't know," said Chantel. "Maybe it's something to do with this spell."

"Hm." The queen stopped with her hands in her pockets and stared at Lightning, still snoozing under the tree. Then she turned and looked at Chantel eye to eye. "There is something I can tell you. You are more powerful than any of those who seek to act against you. But they can still overcome you if you make the wrong choices. Do not, under any circumstances, make the wrong choices."

"How—"

The queen held up a hand to stop her. "Whom do you wish to help?"

Chantel thought. "The girls at school. And Bowser. And I suppose Franklin, although he's a Mar— a Sunbiter, and kind of annoying."

The queen shook her head. "Too small."

"And the sorceresses, of course, if they need it," said Chantel.

"Still too small."

Chantel wracked her brain. "The city?"

"Are you asking me?" said the queen.

"The city. The people."

The queen looked at the dragon, and then back at Chantel. "A good answer. And a natural one, given your affinity for . . . for snakes. But I'm afraid it's still too small."

"Then what—"

"You wish to find these sorceresses. It may be that they were kidnapped for their power. So you must ask yourself, who wants power?"

"I don't—"

The queen cocked her head. "I hear something. It's probably Rose coming in with my morning ale. I think you'd better go before I wake up."

"But can't you tell me—"

"No time! Quickly!" The queen made a shooing-chickens gesture. "If there's a wall in your time, you might be trapped."

The queen was right. Trapped, and in the midst of hostile Sunbiters. Chantel turned and fled up the path.

She ran as fast as she could, and even so she felt some resistance as she crossed Seven Buttons. A moment later, she was blinking away the last of the steam.

And the Order of Watchful Sentinels was dragging Franklin away.

13

A Journey to the Top

Anna was struggling to hang on to one of Franklin's arms; Bowser had the other. The guards were raining down blows on both of them, but Bowser and Anna held fast.

"Stop!" Chantel said, firmly. After all, she had just been talking to a queen. Guards didn't frighten her. Much.

The guards did stop, slightly.

"The boy is under arrest," said a Watchful Sentinel to Chantel. "Anyone who interferes will also be arrested."

"Why?" Chantel demanded

The man looked like he wanted to tell Chantel to mind her own business, but somehow he didn't. "He is suspected of being a Marauder spy."

"Well, he's not a spy," said Chantel. "I can tell you he's not. We brought him—"

"Chantel!" said Franklin loudly.

"What?" said Chantel. "They can't—"

"Chantel, leave it. Please." Franklin looked straight at her and lied. "I—they're—They're not going to harm me."

"Not as long as your friends don't interfere, and you come along quietly," said the guard. "Otherwise we might have to run you through and feed your guts to the ravens."

"Please, Chantel," said Franklin.

Chantel clenched her fists in frantic fury. Anna and Bowser clearly didn't know what to do either. And while they were standing there being indecisive, the guards marched Franklin away.

⟨✦⟩

Chantel and her friends looked after him in dejection. Chantel felt a wriggle in her stomach—Japheth the snake was back. Well, he was no help.

"I can't believe they took Franklin!" Anna fumed. "If I ran this city—"

She trailed off.

They began gathering up the detritus from the spell.

"Did you find out anything useful?" said Bowser.

"I don't think so." Chantel looked down the street where the guards had just disappeared with Franklin. Why hadn't she *done* something?

"What did you see?" asked Anna.

"I talked to Queen Haywith."

"Really? The traitor?" Bowser looked disgusted and alarmed.

"I hope you didn't believe anything she said," said Anna. "I guess we'll have to do the spell again."

"No!" Chantel was surprised by her own vehemence. "I mean, maybe later. Not right now."

The others stared at her.

"I need to think about things," she explained.

⋘⋙

"They just *took* Franklin," said Anna, stomping at the stone street as they climbed. "Why did he say he would be all right?"

"He doesn't know the patriarchs like we do," said Bowser. "Do you think they'll torture him?"

"Probably," said Anna glumly. "If I—"

"Will you shut *up!*" said Chantel.

The other two looked at her in astonishment.

"I know you have a snake in your head—" said Anna.

The snake was actually wriggling along Chantel's shin-bone at the moment. She shook her foot angrily, trying to settle him, and stomped extra hard as they climbed the next set of stone steps.

Anna looked hurt. Chantel felt bad. She didn't want to feel bad, but she did. She should apologize. If Anna had been a grown-up, it would have been easy. Chantel would have just had to curtsey and beg her pardon. But you couldn't deport with your friends.

"Sorry," Chantel muttered.

Anna looked somewhat less hurt. "Do you think we can rescue him?"

"If we tried, we'd be rebelling against the patriarchs," said Bowser. "We'd all be put to death. They'd sacrifice us on the wall."

Chantel knew this was true. People did get sacrificed on the wall sometimes.

She trailed behind Anna and Bowser as they climbed the winding streets back to Miss Ellicott's School. She thought about her odd encounter with Queen Haywith, the traitor. And the dragon. The sleeping dragon. The queen had called it Lightning. Chantel felt oddly homesick for the dragon. She wished it had opened its eyes.

They found Miss Flivvers and the others making soup from vegetables and the neck of a chicken. Mr. Less the clerk had brought money, and had escorted Miss Flivvers to a market on the north slope—the Miss Flivverses of the world do not venture forth alone. There were still no potatoes, alas.

Miss Flivvers sent Chantel, Anna, and Bowser out into the parlor, and came in shortly with a pot of tea for them.

This was not the sort of treatment to which any of

them were accustomed. The parlor was usually reserved for the sort of visitors who expect rose-covered carpets and red satin wing chairs as a matter of course.

Miss Flivvers shut the parlor door, and poured out tea and handed it around.

Chantel took a sip. The tea was warm and comforting. The snake seemed to grow calm and somnolent in its presence. He fell asleep somewhere behind her lungs.

"Well? Did you find out how to do the Buttoning?" asked Miss Flivvers, sipping her tea very correctly with her pinky sticking out.

"No," said Chantel.

"And did you learn anything of poor Euphonia's fate?"

"No."

"Well," said Miss Flivvers. "You must just keep searching while the rest of us try to find—"

"Miss Flivvers, the guards arrested Franklin!" said Anna.

"The Marauder boy?" Miss Flivvers sniffed. "I always suspected he was guilty of something."

"Just because he's been arrested doesn't mean he's guilty!" said Bowser hotly.

Miss Flivvers gave him a look that said she'd given up expecting deportment from him. He was, after all, a boy. "For what did they arrest him, pray tell?"

"They said he was a spy!"

"I suspected as much."

"I don't think he's a spy," said Anna. "He's *nice*. What will they do to him, Miss Flivvers?"

"It is not our place to ask that," said Miss Flivvers.

"But—"

"If you wish to have any influence in deciding the Marauder boy's fate," said Miss Flivvers, turning to Chantel, "you must continue to do as the patriarchs say."

Chantel had been only half-listening to this. She was frantically worried about Franklin. She was also thinking about Queen Haywith, and the things she had said. "Miss Flivvers, what's Miss Ellicott's familiar?"

"If she had wanted you to know that, she would have told you."

"Please, Miss Flivvers. It might be important."

Miss Flivvers sniffed austerely. "If you must know, a snake."

"Oh! Like mine!" Chantel thought about this. "How come I've never seen it?"

"She outgrew it," said Miss Flivvers.

Chantel had never heard of people outgrowing their familiars. She felt Japheth awaken suddenly and start slithering around her spine, and though it was extremely uncomfortable and disconcerting, the thought of him leaving her forever was even worse. "Did it, er, ever go into her head or anything like that?"

"I think it's very disrespectful, Chantel, to suggest that your headmistress might have carried a reptile about in her head. Miss Ellicott was—*is* a lady of very correct deport-ment."

"I just wondered—"

"She simply outgrew it. She became mature and under-stood her place in society, and put aside snakes and other such unwomanly interests. This is certainly not a conversa-tion we ought to be having about Miss Ellicott at *all*."

Chantel saw she was going to have to abandon this line of inquiry. "Miss Flivvers, how did Queen Haywith die?"

"Legend has it that she was locked away in the cas-tle's highest tower, where she wept for her sins until she drowned."

"That doesn't sound very likely," said Chantel, thinking of the matter-of-fact woman eating an apple in a tree. She had said crying *helped*.

"It is presumably a metaphorical way of stating that she pined away as she reflected upon her sins . . . stopped eating, perhaps."

"Like everyone in Lightning Pass is about to." Chan-tel thought of Franklin's description of what the different kinds of Marauders would do to the sorceresses. "Miss Flivvers, do you think the Marauders without the gates even *have* the sorceresses?"

"The patriarchs have said so," said Miss Flivvers. "And

that ought to be enough for you."

What an odd way to answer the question. "Is it enough for you? Do you believe it?"

Miss Flivvers looked at the closed door as if it might be spying on them. "No," she murmured.

"Then what do you think happened?" said Chantel.

"I think—" Miss Flivvers's haughty manner vanished in a moment, and she looked as young and confused as Chantel herself felt. "I think it was the patriarchs themselves who took the sorceresses."

"Oh." Chantel remembered Queen Haywith's words: Whoever had taken the sorceresses wanted power. She suddenly felt certain Miss Flivvers was right. "We've got to—"

"This changes nothing," said Miss Flivvers, becoming herself again. "You must find the Buttoning."

"But the patriarchs—"

"May be misleading us, yes. Still, if we wish to keep Miss Ellicott and the other sorceresses safe, we must pretend that we do not suspect their prevarication."

"Just do as they say?"

"Yes, indeed. And graciously."

"I don't trust them," said Chantel.

"Nor do I," said Miss Flivvers. "But we must dance to the tune that is played for us."

"I don't th—I beg your pardon, I don't think so," said

Chantel. "I'm going to talk to the king."

"The king!" Miss Flivvers couldn't have looked more surprised if Chantel had said she was going to stand on her head atop Seven Buttons. "What earthly good will that do?"

"I don't know," said Chantel. "But he ought to be able to stop the patriarchs if anyone can. And he really ought to do something about those Marauders without the gates."

Anna and Bowser had been watching Chantel in silence, as if she were some kind of strange phenomenon, Chantel thought irritatedly. The Girl with a Snake in Her Head.

"We're coming with you," said Anna, and Bowser nodded vigorously.

"You can't," said Chantel. Down, snake. "I mean, don't, please. You need to stay here and—"

She looked at Miss Flivvers, and decided not to add *and make sure the girls are safe*. It wouldn't be kind. But she was relieved to see that Anna and Bowser understood.

◦◦◦

If Chantel hadn't already spoken to Queen Haywith, she would never have had the nerve to go up to the castle.

Still, the higher she climbed, the more nervous she became.

The castle perched on the top of the mighty block of stone that formed the peak of Lightning Pass. It was accessible only by a narrow stairway, so ancient that it was impossible to tell whether it had been carved from the peak, or built on.

She started up, careful where she put her feet. Here and there a step had crumbled away completely. There was an iron railing, rusted and bent. Chantel took care not to lean on it.

She stopped to rest, and looked down on the whole city . . . its neighborhoods and factories, its houses sitting almost on top of each other, its bridges and courtyards. All filled with her people, the people of Lightning Pass.

Beyond that, you could see the Roughlands in every direction, except south where the sea flashed in the sunlight. Everything close to the walls, though, was cut off from sight. She couldn't see the Marauder army.

It was funny, she thought. If you didn't know better you might think that all the power in the city rested here, at the top.

The girl is nearly
                    at the top
                              of the stairs.
Did we expect her to do this?
Yes.
But we did not expect her to do it so
                                        soon.

Well, she has chosen.
This is the greatest danger she has yet faced.
            After all
                    the snake is in her <u>head.</u>

            The snake is in all of her.
                    It is a very serious situation.
But if she does <u>not</u> face this danger, all is lost.
            Yes.

                    All is lost.

                    And if she faces it and dies?

                    What then?

14

Somehow Chantel had expected things to be royal at the top of the stairs. She'd expected sentries, like at the gate in Seven Buttons.

Instead there was a woman sitting on a stool, knitting.

Chantel curtseyed. "Excuse me, ma'am, I—"

"Just a minute." The woman counted stitches to the end of the row. "There. Yes?"

"I . . . I'm here to see the king." It suddenly seemed like a ridiculous claim.

The woman set her knitting down carefully in a basket at her feet. "What's your name?"

"Chantel."

"Shon·tell," the woman repeated. "Hm. I think you're

the one they've been waiting for." She got to her feet and peered at Chantel closely. "You are tall and black. You are neither shamefast nor biddable. Yes, Chantel. But you have no snake."

"No," said Chantel, rather taken aback. She was not about to say the snake was inside her. This woman was sharp and brusque and did not invite such confidences.

Besides, the fact that she'd been expected was somehow not at all comforting.

"I'll go see what's wanted." The woman left through a wicket embedded in the huge oaken door of the castle.

Chantel waited impatiently.

After a while the great door was flung open. A man appeared, dressed in a white uniform so clean and crisp that Chantel felt sorry for his laundress. He had a high, fluffy white hat with a long feathered plume, and a sword at his side. He marched out, stopped in front of Chantel, clicked his heels together, and saluted.

Chantel curtseyed.

"You are Chantel?" He looked down his nose, which was nearly rectangular and sat over a trim little mustache.

"Yes," said Chantel.

"The king desires that you be brought into his presence."

"Thank you," said Chantel. "That's what I'm here for. I want to tell him—"

"You are far too quick to speak," said the man. "You

must be meek and biddable. You will tell him nothing until spoken to. Do you know how to make a court curtsey?"

"No," said Chantel. "But I need to tell him—"

The man turned and snapped his fingers. The knitting woman came up.

"Teach her to do a court curtsey, Lady Moonlorn," said the man.

And so Chantel, who was burning to just go in and talk to the king, had to practice doing a court curtsey under the watchful eye of the knitting woman and the man in white. It involved crossing her ankles, bending her knees outward, and going right down to the ground and staying there, neck bent, until bidden to rise. The really hard part was the rising.

Finally, with very sore ankles, Chantel was deemed good enough. She followed the man in white into the castle, into a high room with an arched ceiling painted with scenes of battle. Chantel craned her neck to look at them.

But the man in white hurried on.

"You ought to have done a court curtsey to me," he said, "as I myself am a prince. I am My Royal Highness, Prince George. But as you didn't know, I shall be lenient."

"Thank you," said Chantel, annoyed at having to thank him for nothing.

They passed through a hallway in which the paintings

reached down to the floor. Chantel stopped to look at a picture of a woman being chased from the city by what looked like wild dogs—only they were the size of horses. The woman, terrified and bloodied, was fleeing through the city gate, pursued by the beasts.

"What's this?" Chantel asked.

"*The Exile of Queen Haywith*," said the prince. "A very famous painting by a noted artist of the last century."

"Are you sure? That it's Queen Haywith, I mean?"

"Of course I am sure, girl," said the prince.

Chantel kept staring at the painting. The woman was wearing what was left of a flowing white gown. She had clouds of red-gold hair, and her eyes, wide with terror, were green.

"Was there more than one queen named Haywith?" Chantel asked.

"Of course not. Who would name a girl after a traitor? Now come along. You are keeping the king waiting."

They walked on, although Chantel kept looking back at the painting, which looked nothing at all like the Queen Haywith she had met in the Ago. And Miss Flivvers had said she'd died in the castle.

The prince held up a hand to stop Chantel, walked through an archway, and shouted ringingly, "My lord King! The girl Chantel!"

He stepped aside and nodded, and Chantel went in.

The enormous, octagonal room was painted red all the way up to its high, groined ceiling, with details picked out in gold. In the center of the room, pacing around a small table, was a tall man in green velvet.

He stopped pacing when he saw Chantel.

"Curtsey!" the prince reminded Chantel in a loud whisper.

Oops. Chantel crossed her sore ankles and sank to the floor, her robes spread around her. She bent her neck until her nose almost touched the tiles. They had little dragons painted on them.

"The king is signaling for you to rise," said the prince. "Approach him, but do not sit."

Chantel got to her feet. Her legs were trembling, as they hadn't been when she'd met Queen Haywith. Fortunately her robes hid this. She stopped halfway to him, as the knitting woman had instructed her, and waited.

"So. The girl Chantel comes to us."

King Rathfest's voice was fruity and rich, and Chantel found it oddly comforting. But his eyes and mouth narrowed into a smile that struck her as smug.

"We expected you to come bearing a snake."

Chantel felt the snake inside her twitch uncomfortably.

"You are surprised to find we were expecting you, no doubt," the king continued. "And that we set our own mother to watch. She has been waiting out there for a

176

week, in fair weather and foul, during which time she's knitted seven scarves and a mitten. You took your time, girl. We almost grew impatient."

"Oh," said Chantel, nonplussed. "Er. Do you know why I'm here then, er, Your Majesty?"

"We do," said the king. "But it would amuse us to know why you *think* you're here. Please sit down. We shall sit first, as is proper."

The king sat, and looked at Chantel expectantly.

Chantel cast a nervous glance at Prince George, in case he disapproved, and then sat on the velvet-cushioned chair the king indicated.

King Rathfest turned to the prince. "Do bring us some refreshments, George, Your Highness, won't you? The sort of thing girls like."

The prince sniffed, nodded haughtily, and left.

"Now then." The king smiled encouragingly at her. "Tell us your story."

So Chantel did. She talked about the disappearance of the sorceresses, and about her visit to the patriarchs. But when it came to her flight through the catacombs, she decided not to say that she had ended up outside the wall. She felt it would merely complicate matters.

She did not mention Franklin.

She wondered what terrible dangers he was facing, while she sat on a velvet cushion and talked to a king.

The prince came back, wheeling a little cart that rattled across the tiles.

"Excellent, Your Highness," said the king. "You may leave us now, as we discussed. Will you be so good as to serve, Chantel?"

The prince bowed and withdrew.

Chantel got up and took the things off the cart, managing to do it quite gracefully thanks to her deportment. There was a pot of tea, and two extremely breakable-looking cups of breath-thin china, and a plate of little cakes with pink icing, and another of raspberry and blueberry tarts. Chantel tried not to stare in disbelief at these delicacies.

You would hardly know that, down in the city, eggs were selling for five dollars each.

When the tea was poured, the king urged her to take at least two of everything. Chantel did, and tried to eat slowly. The cakes were rich and buttery, and the tarts oozed sweet jam that she had to catch with her tongue to keep it from glopping on her robe.

The king merely nibbled at a single bit of cake. Chantel wondered if there would be leftovers, and whether she might be allowed to take some to the girls at the school. She could not possibly ask such a thing, so she said, "Thank you, your Majesty. We never have anything like this at the school."

"No?" said the king. "And why is that? We thought

girls liked cakes and so forth."

Chantel told him about the shops and markets, and how little there was to buy and how much it all cost, and how the patriarchs bought things in the harbor and then sold them for much more inside the city walls.

"Oh yes, they control the markets," said the king. "We ourself suffer from it. We have been reduced to living without servants, as you see, and being waited on by our mother and our siblings."

Too small, Chantel thought. Who had said that to her? She couldn't remember. Anyway, the king's concerns were too small.

She expected to feel the snake inside her writhe with impatience. But Japheth was oddly still. Waiting.

"The patriarchs want to strengthen the wall," Chantel told the king. "Even though, according to them, the Marauders have demanded the walls come down or they'll kill the sorceresses."

"Kill the sorceresses? How will the Marauders do that?" said the king.

"I don't think they can." Chantel took a deep breath. "I think the patriarchs kidnapped the sorceresses themselves."

"Dear, dear," said the king, shaking his head. "Well, you do right to bring this to our attention, Chantel. We have been concerned about these overreaching patriarchs for some time."

This isn't about you and the patriarchs, Chantel thought. *Too small!*

"'So why didn't Your Majesty do something,' you are thinking," said the king. "Well, we had to wait until the time was right. Now, we believe, the time may be right. For, you see, we have you. And that is not all."

He snapped his fingers in the air, and Prince George was instantly by his side. "Yes, my lord King?"

"Send them in," said the king.

The prince in white marched away, straight and tall. He flung open a pair of doors that formed an arch. And through the doors, in a moment, for they had clearly been waiting just outside, came the sorceresses.

15

In Which Chantel Has a Headache

Chantel sprang to her feet. She watched as the miss-ing sorceresses walked forward in a line, gracefully encircled the table where the king sat, and dropped into deep court curtseys. Their robes spread out around them, like the petals of a many-colored flower, with Chantel and the king at the center.

Miss Ellicott, in her green robe, was right in front of her.

"You may rise," said the king.

The sorceresses rose elegantly, each one a perfect model of deportment.

"The girl, Chantel, has come." The king nodded at Miss Ellicott. "As you told us she would."

"Of course, Your Majesty," said Miss Ellicott.

"But she has no snake," said the king.

The snake, Japheth, was in fact squirming madly, as if sensing Chantel's confusion.

"Nonetheless, she is unusually powerful, Your Majesty," said Miss Ellicott. "As I told you, that is why I chose her."

"Ptishptush," said the king. "You told me you'd chosen any number of them."

If being ptishptushed annoyed Miss Ellicott (and Chantel was quite sure it did), the sorceress managed to conceal it. "Any of them might have been chosen," said Miss Ellicott. "But I always thought Chantle the most likely."

"And none of them might have," said the king. "The important thing is, this one was chosen, and now we have her in our castle. And we have you. The patriarchs never let us have any soldiers, but this should be almost as good, eh?"

"I should think it was a great deal better, Your Majesty," said Miss Ellicott with a touch of asperity.

Chantel hadn't been spoken to, but she couldn't hold back any longer. "Miss Ellicott! What is this all about? We thought you were kidnapped! The patriarchs said the Marauders had you."

"The patriarchs lie," said Miss Ellicott.

"But . . . you mean you just left us?" Chantel began to feel really angry as the realization came to her. The snake slithered up into her head and battered at the inside of her skull. "You left us alone, and we had nothing to eat and we had to chase out a horrible manageress woman—"

"Nonsense," said Miss Ellicott. "I left you in Adelika's care. I knew I could trust her to look after the school."

Adelika was Miss Flivvers's given name. "She didn't! She went all to pieces and we've only just gotten her back together again."

"That's unfortunate," said Miss Ellicott. "But it was a necessary temporary measure. Things have taken slightly longer to develop than I expected. We had hoped you would arrive sooner."

"Why didn't you send for me, then?" Chantel demanded. The inside of her head began to feel hot.

"We did not wish to draw attention to you," said the king. "We had far too much to lose. How you ladies do chatter on. The important thing is, we have you now."

"Why?" said Chantel. "Why did you need me? You had all these sorceresses. I'm not a sorceress! I'm still learning. Why me?"

"Now, Chantel," the king chided. "Were you brought up to ask why?"

"Chantle," said Miss Ellicott, "where is the snake?"

"He . . ." Chantel looked at Miss Ellicott. She looked at the sorceresses all around her. She didn't understand what was going on. Miss Ellicott, who ought to have been at the school, protecting her students, had instead gone off to the castle, without telling anyone. This was not a Miss Ellicott you could trust. This was not a Miss Ellicott to whom you confided that a snake had crawled into your ear.

"He's away," she said.

"How long has he been away?"

"Not long at all," said Chantel, as the snake twisted angrily in her brain. "I've heard from him *quite* recently."

She wanted to lose her temper, but she had a feeling her deportment had never been more important. "Miss Ellicott," she said. "What happened to *your* familiar?"

"It is not your place to ask me questions," said Miss Ellicott.

The other sorceresses shook their heads and tsk'ed.

"Really," said the king. "We expected your student to be more shamefast and biddable, Miss Ellicott."

"My apologies, Your Majesty," said the sorceress, with a brief and rather angry curtsey.

"I know your familiar was a snake, the same as mine," said Chantel, fighting for calm. The sorceresses still encircled her. She felt more angry than frightened—but really, she felt plenty of both. Japheth seemed to be burning mad; the inside of her skull felt as if it were on fire.

She just managed not to clutch her head in pain. "What happened to your snake, Miss Ellicott?"

"I outgrew him," said Miss Ellicott coldly. "I became an adult, and I put away childish things. And you? What about you, Chantle? Have you put your familiar away?"

"No," gasped Chantel, squeezing her eyes shut.

"Good," said Miss Ellicott. "For the moment, there is power in that. And we need power."

"Why?" said Chantel.

Miss Ellicott turned to the king. "I beg your pardon, Your Majesty. It seems she is going to keep asking why."

"In order to help her king," said the king. "What could be more fitting?"

"Chantle," said Miss Ellicott. "Far too many people have worked far too hard to bring events to this point, to have you spoil it now."

"You should *want* to help," said one of the other sorceresses.

"What could be more proper for a girl than to serve her king and country?" said another.

"I don't understand what you want from me*!*" Chantel said, much more angrily than she'd intended. Japheth thrashed and burned in her head. She struggled for deportment. The sorceresses were using lots of it. Chantel drew on it as hard as she could—she *summoned* deportment—and managed to still the snake's antics.

"I beg your pardon, Miss Ellicott," she said. "But could you please explain why you wanted me here, and what it is you want me to do?"

"We ourself shall explain," said the king.

Chantel turned to face him. "Thank you, Your Majesty."

"Do sit down," he said.

She sat, and folded her hands in her lap, and kept her eyes on his face, as she had always been taught. Which turned out later to be a serious mistake.

"It has long seemed to us," said the king, "that the patriarchs do not govern the city in the best possible manner. They control everything: the soldiers, the sorceresses, the markets, the money, and, most of all, Seven Buttons.

"Therefore we have long sought a means of displacing the patriarchs, and returning the city to the king's own rule, as it was in the time of our grandfather's grandfather, before our dissolute cousins lost the reins of kingship. We have summoned the sorceresses here to help us with this, and now we have summoned you."

He looked much larger than he had before, and kinder, and his voice seemed very wise. A Gleam spell, Chantel thought. One of the sorceresses is doing it. She ignored the Gleam. "What is it that you want the sorceresses to do, Your Majesty?"

"Why, use magic, of course, to overthrow the patriarchs, and to turn the soldiers to our side. And you, of course, will use your familiar. You can use him, can't you?"

"I'm not sure," Chantel admitted. "But, Your Majesty. If you use magic to fight the patriarchs, people could get hurt."

The king smiled. "A wise man once said, Chantel, that

one cannot make an omelet without breaking eggs."

"I see. And once all the, er, eggs are broken, Your Majesty, what will happen?"

"Why, we shall be a true king, of course!" said the king. "And we shall command the soldiers to make quick work of the Marauders without the gates, and we shall order the sorceresses to seal Seven Buttons, and we shall cause the dr—the sorceresses to patrol the city and make certain that nothing threatens our reign, from within or without the walls."

"And . . . and that will make things better for the people?" said Chantel.

"Of course!" said the king. "We shall control the markets, and gold shall fill the royal coffers again, and the castle will be full of servants, and thus the people will all be better off."

He's not stupid, Chantel thought. I can see that in his eyes, no matter what stupid things he says with his mouth.

"But the people . . . Will food still be expensive?"

"If it is," said the king, "at least the money will go to a worthy cause."

Meaning himself. "Thank you for explaining everything, Your Majesty," she said. "You've certainly given me a lot to think about, once I get home. I—"

"You're not going home, Chantel," said the king, with an annoying little smile.

He stood up. Chantel hastily scrambled to her feet too;

it would not do to sit while royalty stood.

And then she saw what the sorceresses had done.

She and the king were surrounded by a cage of glowing red bars of light.

The king smiled at Chantel, nodded, and stepped through the bars.

When Chantel tried to follow him, the bars were searingly hot. They crackled and spat sparks.

"You'll stay right where you are, Chantle," said Miss Ellicott. "Until you see reason and agree to work with us."

The sorceresses walked in a circle all around the cage, making so many signs with their hands and feet that Chantel couldn't keep track, and then they stood outside the cage, with the king beside them, and smirked.

Chantel was angry. She was furious. The fire inside her head burned white-hot.

She grabbed again at the bars, but it was like trying to grab fire. Fire that writhed and spat, fire that grabbed back.

She put her burned hands to her mouth. She *had* to get out. Everyone at the school was depending on her, and there were the Sunbiters outside the gates, and Franklin in prison.

She needed mighty magic. And she tried to summon it. It had worked with Dimswitch, but it wasn't working now. Maybe because she was so furious.

She was in a flaming rage. She wanted to do something

horrible to the vile king and the traitorous Miss Ellicott. But she couldn't find any magic strong enough. She could only tell them what she thought of them.

"You're terrible!" she said. "You don't care about the city at all, you only care about yourselves!"

Inside her head, the snake had grown bigger, and hotter, and she felt as if her skull would explode. She hardly noticed the pain in her hands now.

"There are Marauders without the walls!" she yelled. "You ought to be thinking about how you can drive them away. How you can *help!* Instead, you're thinking about what you can *get* out of the situation!"

"Really," said the king, "not at all shamefast and biddable."

"Not at all," echoed a sorceress.

"It will be worth it, Your Majesty," said Miss Ellicott. "You'll see."

"You're—" The pain in Chantel's head was stifling. "Absolutely—" She struggled with her brain, trying to make it summon magic. "You're—" Pain filled her throat, and her mouth. Something horrible was happening. She couldn't breathe. She fell to her knees. The world flashed red and green.

Something slithered out of her mouth.

Scaly and golden, fiery and strong.

The sorceresses and the king stumbled back in surprise.

The thing kept coming out. Everything began to go black around the edges of her vision.

Then, with a furious, writhing wriggle, the thing leapt out into the air and flew at the king and the sorceresses.

It was a dragon. It breathed fire. It swiped at the sorceresses with gleaming scimitar claws. They fell back, barely escaping the jet of red-orange fire it sent at their heads.

"I told you, Your Majesty!" cried Miss Ellicott, as she and the king and the others fled.

The dragon crashed around the room. He smashed into the walls, splintering beams and sending chips of red and golden paint flying. Then he landed. He paced over to Chantel's cage, claws clacking on the tile floor. He sat on his haunches, rather like a cat, his ridged tail curled around his feet.

He was golden and alive and beautiful, and his eyes flickered like deep orange flames.

Chantel was afraid, but not in a bad way. Not the kind of fear you feel when you face something terrible, but the kind you feel when it's time to leave your old life behind, take an enormous leap, and hope you land on something.

"J-Japheth?" she whispered.

There were certain things that were the same. A way of tilting the head and flicking the tongue. The shape of the head around the eyes. Those told her that this enormous, fire-breathing dragon had been her little green snake Japheth.

He extended a claw and beckoned.

"I'm stuck in here," said Chantel.

The dragon opened his mouth several times, his forked tongue struggling. It seemed he was trying to talk. But his throat and his mouth weren't built for it.

"Come out," he managed at last, rasping. If metal—gold, perhaps—could talk, its voice might sound like that.

Chantel examined the spell that had made the cage. It was complicated. It used the power and magic of each of the sorceresses. There was no way a lone magician could undo it.

"I can't come out," said Chantel, casting an anxious look at the closed doors through which the king and the sorceresses had vanished. "These bars burn."

The dragon snaked his tail around and held it over one of the bars. Like a jet of water when you stick your hand in it, the bar of light stopped shooting upward, and sputtered every which way.

"Just a minute," said Chantel.

There was no point in leaving the cakes and tarts behind. She bundled them in her handkerchief.

The dragon laid his tail across several bars. Droplets of fire splattered. Chantel winced as one hit her in the hand. She seized her robes and her bundle tightly and half-leapt, half-stumbled through the gap. She tripped over the dragon's tail and fell sprawling. Her left leg had a stinging burn. Her hair smelled singed.

Footsteps rang behind the double doors. "I heard something," said a voice.

Chantel scrambled to her feet and ran toward the hallway where she'd come in. She felt a jerk at her robes. The dragon had caught her with his teeth.

"'is way!" he said, around a mouthful of cloth.

"The way out is this way!" said Chantel, struggling.

The dragon made a growling sound in his throat and tugged. Chantel tried to pull free. The dragon held fast.

The door opened, and several men entirely dressed in iron clanked into the room, their faces obscured by iron helms.

"She got out!" cried one of them, in Prince George's voice.

The iron men rushed at her. Chantel frantically started doing signs for an adhesion spell to stick their feet to the floor.

The dragon seized Chantel in his claws and took flight.

They flew around and around the room, dizzyingly. Chantel's feet dangled just a few feet from the floor. She was still trying to do the adhesion spell. The dragon's claws on her shoulders *hurt*. The prince grabbed at Chantel's leg, and she kicked, struggling. Then someone grabbed the hem of her robe.

The dragon faltered in his flight, tottered, and brushed against the wall. Furiously Chantel tore at her robe and kicked, trying to get rid of the man holding her.

The dragon surged upward. There was a jarring crash that made Chantel's teeth rattle. The stupid dragon had flown right into the ceiling!

And through it. There was a fury of plaster dust and tumbling bricks. The man who'd been clinging to Chantel's robes was suddenly shaken loose, and Chantel heard him scream as he fell.

Then Chantel and the dragon were out in the bright blue world, sailing free. They soared high over the city, and out over the Roughlands, where the Sunbiter army was an anthill beneath them.

Then Chantel and the dragon sailed over the wide gray sea.

Have we misunderstood?

Is she not the girl we think she is?

That dragon was <u>real.</u>
That was no illusion. It breathed fire. It
carried her, and it flew.
Of course it was real.
But the girl has fled.
She is not ours. She has broken free.
She

is

a

storm.

Nonsense. No human ever really breaks free.
Certainly no girl. What are we without the rules
and walls that contain us?

No one would want to live like that.

Yes, yes, that is all very well. But she, the
girl Chantel Goldenrod, has broken free.
With the dragon, mind you. I think she
will probably die.

And if she dies, that is no help to us at all.

16

The dragon flapped down just low enough to set Chantel on a rock in the sea. For a moment she stood and gasped, catching her breath.

Then she looked at where she was. A brown ripple of stone, rising just a few feet out of the sea.

Waves crashed against the rock, sending up spouts of white water that splatted down almost at her feet, then slid away.

The dragon was high above her, flying around in joyful spirals and loop-de-loops. Then he dropped into a wide, wide circle, swept once around the sky, and glided toward the horizon.

Chantel watched in dismay as he became a smaller and smaller dot in the distance. She looked down at the bundle of cakes still clutched in her hand. She looked toward Lightning Pass, a barely visible toy city on a thin arc of land. Even the mountains climbing behind it looked small.

She jumped up and down and waved her arms. "Help! I'm stuck on this rock out here!"

No one heard her, of course. She hardly heard herself above the smashing waves.

There were small pools of water in hollows on the rock. Chantel dipped her finger in one and tasted the water. Yech. Salt. There was no fresh water here. There was no *anything*.

Maybe the dragon had thought she could swim.

Or hadn't really thought about her at all.

A fog rolled in.

It hung low on the ocean, obscuring the land and then even the sea. Soon Chantel was completely enveloped in pearl-gray mist. She could hear the waves around her, and feel droplets of seawater splashing her skin, but she couldn't see anything.

What if she jumped into the water? Maybe she would discover that she really could swim. But then a particularly strong wave smashed against the rock and splatted into her face, and she decided not to try just yet.

Maybe later. When she started to get thirsty.

Immediately, she started to get thirsty.

The important thing was not to panic, she told

herself. You couldn't make a rational plan when you were panicking.

Especially not when you were standing on a rock, invisible, surrounded by ocean, and nobody even knew where you were.

And who would help, if they knew? Who could you count on?

Nobody, that's who. Not Miss Ellicott, nor any of the other sorceresses. They had betrayed Chantel, betrayed the school. And not Miss Flivvers—if she knew Chantel was stuck on a rock in the ocean, she'd probably flap her hands helplessly and tell Chantel to recite the 423 situations in which a magical maiden must never find herself.

Not the patriarchs—they only cared about themselves. And the king was no better. And the other girls, even Anna, well, they really relied on Chantel to know what was best. Bowser wouldn't know what to do.

An image of Franklin came into Chantel's head. The one person who might actually know what to do, but he'd been captured by the—

A wave washed over Chantel's feet.

She took a step backward and almost fell. She scrambled to regain her footing. The entire rock was underwater now except the little bit she was standing on, and the waves were lapping over that.

The tide was coming in. She'd read about that in

books. The dragon had left her on a rock that disappeared at high tide!

She was going to have to swim for it. Or drown for it, more likely . . . she couldn't even remember which way the land was. She—

There was an almighty crash, and a wall of water knocked Chantel off her feet. She was in the ocean, fighting the waves and her entangling robes.

Then a dragon head loomed out of the mist. "Sorry," it said. "Forgot."

"You—!" Chantel swallowed salt water and sank.

The sea roiled around her, and then she was rising, the dragon beneath her. The dragon gave a grunt and a small shrug, and Chantel slid into a space between his back and his neck.

The rock was completely submerged now, but he rose up, standing on it.

Chantel was just feeling around desperately, realizing there was nothing at all to hold on to on a dragon, when the dragon's muscles bunched. He sprang forward and glided out over the open sea.

Chantel threw herself flat and wrapped her arms around as much of his neck as she could reach. The dragon sailed upward, rising through the fog. They broke out into sunlight. Chantel saw the fog like a sea below her, and then it slowly broke apart and she saw the ocean, deep blue and spreading to the horizon. Here and there it was dotted with ships like toys. She saw a cluster of fish at the surface—no, not fish, she thought. Whales! I'm seeing whales!

She felt a rush of joy. Whatever happened now, even if she fell off the dragon and died—she had flown. And she had seen whales.

The dragon flew higher still, over the harbor and over the city and over the marshes where the Sunbiters were camped, and up to the mountains.

And there he landed, on a shelf of rock, his claws grating and sending up sparks.

Chantel slid from his neck. She was shivering with cold.

"Sorry," said the dragon again, in his odd voice. "Forgot the tide." He gave an apologetic shrug. "Snake a long time."

"What's your name?" Chantel asked. She had named the snake Japheth herself. It seemed to her now to have been a terribly forward thing to do.

"Lightning."

Chantel remembered the dragon asleep under the apple tree in the Ago. Queen Haywith had called him Lightning. But no—it wasn't possible. That dragon had been much smaller. And after five hundred years? Besides, Miss Ellicott had said a snake was an immature form of dragon.

Miss Ellicott. She wasn't ready to think about Miss Ellicott just yet.

"Shoulders?" Lightning inquired. He lifted a claw and pointed.

"Oh," said Chantel. "Um, they're fine—"

Actually, they hurt. She pulled her robe off one shoulder and looked. There would be claw-shaped bruises later.

"It's fine," she said. "Thank you."

She gazed down at the marshes. She got her first good look at the Sunbiter camp.

There were thousands of Sunbiters.

Thousands upon thousands. Their camp went on for miles. She saw men cooking and men eating. There were men polishing shields and sharpening weapons. There were enormous catapults, poised to fling huge rocks into the city, and there were siege engines, tall wooden towers on wheels for reaching the top of Seven Buttons.

The camp stretched nearly to the harbor walls—which, Chantel saw, were bristling with Lightning Pass soldiers.

Chantel saw more camps, further out in the marshes—the Sunbiters' families, she guessed. Laundry flapped in the breeze. There were tiny people tending tiny herds of cattle and flocks of geese.

A procession was coming from the harborside, headed for the Sunbiters' camp. From the bright colors of their velvet capes and hats, Chantel recognized the patriarchs.

"Can we go down closer?" Chantel looked around for a path. There was nothing but a sheer cliff down to the road below—which must be the toll road, Chantel realized.

"Can fly," said Lightning with a shrug.

"Wouldn't they see us?"

The dragon cocked a sardonic eyebrow at her. This was the first time Chantel had noticed he even had eyebrows.

"Well, they *would*," she said. "And then what?"

"Then they see us," said the dragon laconically.

That was probably an easier attitude to take if you were an enormous firebreathing dragon than if you were a Chantel. Still—

"Maybe you could set me down on Seven Buttons?" Chantel suggested. "So that I can see what happens. And then you could come back for me, so that I don't get captured by the king or—or the sorceresses. That is, if it wouldn't be too much trouble."

She considered curtseying, but her robe was too wet and she was too tired.

The dragon nodded. "Can do that."

She mounted by using the dragon's front leg as a step, just above the elbow. It was like stepping on slightly slippery metal tiles.

"I beg your pardon," she said. "I hope I'm not hurting you."

There was a fiery rumble deep inside the dragon which Chantel thought might be laughter.

Right. Next step. Chantel reached up and put her

hands flat on the dragon's back. She heaved herself up. She bunched her soggy robe underneath her.

"Hold on," said Lightning.

And with no more warning than that, he plunged from the crag.

Chantel fell forward and held on as tightly as she could. They swooped and circled over the Sunbiter camp. Chantel heard shouts of alarm down below, and a thunder of feet running in all directions. She half-hoped (and half-feared) that the dragon was going to blast the Marauder camps with fire.

Then suddenly she found herself sliding off Lightning's neck onto the wall-walk atop Seven Buttons, and Lightning was flapping away.

And nobody even noticed she was there. Of course they didn't. They were too busy staring, running, and yelling. When a girl rides in on a dragon, nobody notices the girl.

She did a self-abnegation spell anyway.

Keeping close to the parapet, she hurried along the wall-walk. She reached a spot near the patriarchs and stopped, peering through a crenel.

The patriarchs were marching out in a body, all nine of them, resplendent in blue velvet capes and hats with white ostrich plumes. Behind them came a phalanx of guards, and in the midst of the guards, walked Franklin.

The Sunbiters sent out a procession too. It was led

by a man wearing a shaggy fur robe, and a sword on one side and a dagger at the other, and a heavily dented helmet adorned with two blood-red horns. Behind him came a mob of armed men.

The patriarchs are going to be hacked to pieces, Chantel thought.

Of course, they had a hostage. They had Franklin. But he wasn't worth much, surely. Chantel quite liked him, herself, even if he did have an annoying voice and an annoyingly superior attitude. But to the Sunbiters, he was just a deserter. Or that's what he'd *said*, anyway.

Franklin walked with his chin up, as if he wasn't afraid at all.

Chantel bet he was terrified.

The patriarchs weren't carrying the dragon flag of Lightning Pass. They were marching under a white flag of truce.

The two processions stopped twenty paces apart.

A man stepped forward from the fur-clad ranks. He threw back his head, and yelled, "Who comes to speak to Karl the Bloody?"

So that man with the horns is Karl the Bloody, Chantel thought. Franklin had said that when he captured people, he let them choose the stake he was going to impale them on.

"The Nine Patriarchs of the Kingdom of Lightning

Pass," replied Lord Rudolph, his voice calm but carrying.

"The Nine Patriarchs of the Kingdom of Lightning Pass!" yelled the Marauders' herald.

"I heard, thank you," said Karl the Bloody. He took off his horned helmet and tossed it over his shoulder. One of his men caught it and held it reverently. Karl's red hair glinted in the sun. "Greetings, Nine Patriarchs. Do you bring me word from your king?"

"Indeed," said Lord Rudolph. "King Rathfest the Restless demands that you cease to surround his kingdom with belligerent troops, and go away peacefully."

"We hold the toll road through the mountains," said Karl the Bloody. "And we surround the harbor. We await the king's response to our demands. Open the harbor!"

"It is His Majesty's pleasure to point out," said Lord Rudolph, "that the harbor is already open to such shipmasters as pay the fees."

"Which are ruinous," said Karl the Bloody.

Chantel was surprised to hear that all this trouble was about the harbor. Weren't there other harbors?

But no . . . Franklin had said there weren't any for three hundred miles.

"The king is put to great expense to maintain the harbor," said Lord Rudolph. "Nonetheless, he will graciously consider your request, if you go away."

Karl the Bloody sneered. "A worthy try, Mr. Nine

Patriarchs. But we find ourselves comfortably situated here. We have plenty to eat—unlike you, I daresay. And it would be most inconvenient to move our catapults, with which we can hurl deadly missiles into your city, and our siege engines, which we've been at some trouble to build high enough to top your city walls. No, we'll stay."

"Do you not see the mighty dragon of Lightning Pass that circles in the sky, ready to wreak havoc on your camp, your women, and your children?" demanded Lord Rudolph.

Chantel looked up. Lightning was flying overhead, in plain view of everyone. People in the streets of Lightning Pass were crying out in excitement and alarm.

"I see an illusion, no doubt cooked up by your wise women," said Karl the Bloody. "It is cleverly done. I congratulate them on their artistry. It doesn't frighten us."

"The dragon is not all we have," said Lord Rudolph. "We have a hostage."

He turned, and made a signal.

The patriarchs stepped aside, and the phalanx opened up enough for Karl the Bloody to see Franklin, who held his head high and glowered.

Karl the Bloody came a few steps closer to gaze at the hostage.

Chantel gulped in surprise. Franklin's hair was exactly the same shade of red as Karl the Bloody's. Their eyes were the same dark brown, and their teeth were crooked in the same way. Their noses had been broken differently, however.

"Oh, a hostage. I see," said Karl the Bloody. "Well, boy? Do you find you have improved your lot by deserting your liege-lord?"

Franklin looked up at Karl. "I haven't made it any worse."

Karl smiled. "Bravely said, at any rate." He turned to Lord Rudolph. "And I suppose the offer is that, if we leave, you won't kill him."

"That is correct," said Lord Rudolph. "However, if you refuse to depart—"

"Understood," said Karl. He shrugged with one shoulder. "Kill him."

Chantel gasped aloud.

Lord Rudolph pursed his lips. "Do not make the mistake, sir, of thinking that ours is an idle threat."

"Of course not," said Karl. "Having threatened to kill him, you must do so. Otherwise, you lose face and, worse, cause me to doubt that you are a man of your word. And if we are not men of our word, what are we? I quite understand." He nodded to Franklin. "Die bravely, son. At least do that right." He turned back to Lord Rudolph. "Are we finished here?"

"So it would seem," said Lord Rudolph.

And, still bearing the white flag of truce, the patriarchs and their attendants turned and marched back toward the harbor district. Franklin was almost hidden among the guards, who were clutching him more tightly than ever as they hustled him along. From where Chantel stood, he was just a tiny patch of red hair bobbing amid the uniforms.

Chantel was still staring after them in horror when Lightning swooped down on Seven Buttons. A hail of arrows bounced off his scales as Chantel scrambled hurriedly onto his back.

They took off, fast. They sailed higher and higher, and Chantel began to feel quite ill. At last they landed on the high mountain crag.

Chantel slid hastily off the dragon's back. "I don't believe it! They're not really going to kill him, are they?"

"Who?" said Lightning.

"Franklin! The boy with the red hair!"

"Probably," said Lightning.

"Why didn't the Sunbiters stop them! There's thousands of them, they way outnumber the patriarchs and the guards! They could—"

"Honor," said the dragon.

Chantel grabbed Lighting by the shoulder urgently. "Do something!"

The dragon blinked a golden eye. "Such as?"

"Rescue him! Dive in there with flames and kill all the patriarchs!"

"And people?" said the dragon.

In the distance, far, far below, the patriarchs were making their way through the gate into the harbor district.

Crowds pressed out of their way on the street.

"Well, no, of course not, not the people, but—" Chantel struggled to calm herself. "When are they going to kill him? And where?"

The dragon cocked his head thoughtfully. "On the wall?"

"On top of the wall," said Chantel. "Where sacrifices are made. And where his people can see. Why? Oh, right, so the patriarchs can be men of their word. When?"

"Now?" the dragon suggested.

"I'm sure you're right," said Chantel. "Okay. We're going to stop them."

Chantel climbed back onto the dragon's back—she was getting quite good at this now.

Lightning dropped from the mountain ledge, spread his wings, and flew. He circled high over Lightning Pass.

They didn't have long to wait. The guards and patriarchs marched Franklin to the wall. There was a staircase, almost ladder-steep, up to the wall-walk. Franklin was forced to climb up, a difficult job with his hands tied behind him. Patriarchs and guards climbed beside and behind him. Last of all came a hooded executioner bearing an enormous two-handed sword.

17

The Dragon's Lair

Honor was a thing Chantel had trouble understanding. Honor meant that the patriarchs, having said they'd kill Franklin, now had to kill him.

And honor meant that Franklin had to act as if he didn't much mind.

He was doing that now, as he stood on the wall, elevated on a shooting-step and visible to the Sunbiters who had gathered below. Guards held him by the arms. The official executioner made his way along the wall, bearing the sword with which to strike off Franklin's head.

Chantel clung to the dragon's neck as they dove.

"There's a very nice view from up here," said Franklin, his voice trembling slightly.

"Put your head down on the parapet," said a guard. "It's easier that way for everybody."

Then everyone looked up at the plunging dragon. The guards squawked in terror. The executioner screamed, dropped his sword, and fell off the wall. Lightning seized Franklin in his claws.

The dragon swooped up in the air again, high over the city. Chantel just had time to see a volley of Marauder arrows rising. One struck a patriarch, and Chantel saw him tumble from the wall. Then Lightning soared away, over the sea, and Chantel couldn't see what happened next.

Lightning dropped Franklin in the ocean.

The dragon skimmed to a landing in deep water beside a cliff, sending up silver fans of water. Chantel cried out in dismay as Franklin sank straight down.

"Do something!" she yelled at the dragon. "If you please, I mean!"

"He'll be back," said Lightning.

And a moment later Franklin bobbed to the surface. He wasn't choking at all. He could *swim*, Chantel saw with a twinge of envy. He was kicking furiously, though, and his face kept getting smacked by waves that crashed against the cliff and then rolled back.

Chantel managed to catch hold of his collar and drag him halfway onto the dragon's back.

"Climb up," she said.

"I can't! My hands are tied!"

Chantel tried to undo the leather thongs binding his wrists, but it was impossible. The seawater had swollen and tightened the knots.

"Lightning!" said Chantel. "Can you cut him free?"

In answer the dragon directed a sharp, sudden flame at Franklin's hands. Chantel was so surprised she almost fell into the water.

Franklin's hands were free. He hauled himself up on the dragon's shoulders.

"You have no eyebrows," he told Chantel.

"Neither do you," said Chantel shortly.

"Hold your breath," said Lightning. "Hold on."

Chantel just had time to take a deep gulp of air as the dragon plunged straight under the water. It was icy cold.

Chantel tried to hold on, but she felt herself floating away as the dragon dove. She felt Franklin grab her arm. She struggled furiously. She was being dragged deeper. Water pushed at her, trying to make her take another breath.

Then suddenly she was thrust upward. She gasped for breath too soon, and got saltwater instead.

Franklin was hauling her through shallow water, and she struggled again, coughing—she could *walk*. She wasn't drowning! She couldn't talk, however, and so she ended up being dragged, and deposited on what felt like stone. The darkness here was total.

She went into a furious fit of coughing that sent white stars of light flashing around her eyes.

"Okay?" said the dragon.

Franklin, apparently not sure what to do, hit her on the back a few times.

"Turn her over," the dragon suggested.

Chantel hastily turned herself over, and coughed some more. Franklin knelt beside her. "You okay?"

"Argh," Chantel managed to say.

She staggered to her feet and did the light spell. She held the light-globe cupped in her hand, and looked around.

They were in an underground cavern.

"Where are we?" she asked.

Lightning tilted his head, and gestured with one wing as if to say *look and see*.

Chantel walked around the rocky ledge, shining her light. There was an opening in the wall, a tunnel into darkness.

She glanced back at the water. "They might try to follow us."

The dragon shook his head emphatically *no*.

Franklin had gone to the passage mouth. "Hey, I hear something. Bring your light."

Chantel heard it too—a sound of water dripping.

She and Franklin followed the sound, into the close, clammy passage. They had to duck under outcroppings here and there, and step over unexpected crevices in the floor. The dragon crept along behind them, his tail dragging and scraping against the stone.

The tunnel widened into a cavern.

"Hey, c'mere," said Franklin. "Look at this."

Chantel held up her light, and it reflected like the moon on a clear pool of water, with white sand at the bottom. Water fell into it from the stalactites that hung above, and the drips echoed loudly in the silence.

Beside the pool, on a sloping wall of the cave, were human handprints, outlined in red. And there were drawings. Chantel could make out something that looked like it might be a horse, except that it had horns; a man with antlers; and—a dragon.

"Is . . . is there a dragon down here?" she asked.

"Me," Lightning croaked.

Chantel looked from the drawing to Lightning and back again, doubtfully.

"How did you know this place was down here?" said Franklin. "Oh, and, I mean. Thanks for rescuing me." He looked from Chantel to the dragon. "Both of you I mean."

"You're very welcome," said Chantel politely. "It was no trouble."

The dragon indicated the cave—the passage, which led

back to the ocean pool and ahead into darkness—with a nod. "Mine."

"The cave is yours? But—" she looked at the drawings on the walls. They looked very, very old. She peered at the sketch of a dragon. "But—"

But he'd been a snake just a little while ago. And Miss Ellicott had said—

She winced. The thought of Miss Ellicott's betrayal still hurt.

"Always mine," said the dragon.

"Wow," said Franklin.

Miss Ellicott had said a snake was an immature form of dragon. If Lightning had been immature until just recently, then that couldn't be him on the wall. Unless—

Unless, Chantel thought with some embarrassment, it had been *her* that had been immature.

"How old are you, Lightning?" said Chantel. "If you don't mind my asking."

"Old as the city," said the dragon, his tongue darting back and forth as he flicked the words out of a mouth shaped all wrong for speaking. "Older. Old as first humans. Called."

"You mean they summoned you? Like I did when I was six?"

Lightning looked slightly offended. "Was *here*."

"Oh, of course," said Chantel, not quite understanding this.

The dragon preened his golden wings. "Genius loci," he said modestly.

"Okay," said Chantel. "Um, good."

This seemed to satisfy the dragon. He turned away from the pictures, squeezed past Franklin and Chantel, and slithered up the dark passage.

Chantel followed his long gold-scaled tail as he swished, snake-like, through caverns and galleries. Marvelous ripples of flowstone hung like glistening curtains. Crystals sprouted up from the floor in places, and there were curious rubbles of rounded rocks that were really, Chantel found when she touched them, all one stone.

Yet it seemed to Chantel that someone had been at work here, sometime, forming the stone, smoothing out places to walk and even places to sit.

Once they passed a drawing of stick-figure people standing in a circle.

Chantel's heavy wet robes clung to her legs and tired her.

At last they reached a huge chamber, bigger than the room where Chantel had met the king. This was very clearly a dragon's room. It had an arc-shaped dragon bed along one wall, and several chests which, in the nature of things, must contain treasure. A waterfall tumbled from halfway up the wall, filling a shallow pool that fed a stream that babbled away into the darkness of a side passage. Beside the pool were a human-sized table and chairs.

We're not the first people to come here, Chantel thought with a stab of jealousy. And then—of course we're not. If he's really as old as he says, maybe he's been other people's familiar over the centuries.

The dragon settled himself along the couch with a contented sigh. His tail snaked around and tapped one of the chests. "Things."

"You want me to open it?" said Chantel.

The dragon nodded.

There was a key in the chest. She turned it and lifted the creaking lid. Inside were mostly ordinary things: blankets, sheets, a winter cloak, some old-fashioned-looking robes, all slightly musty. Some dishes and silverware, and a couple of pots. Housekeeping, in fact. The only unusual thing was a cup made of gold, with an elegant enameled painting on it, showing the sea and a high green hill beside it. On the hill were tiny people, standing in a circle. They reminded Chantel of the stick figure people she'd seen on the tunnel wall.

She turned the cup over in her hands. She thought it must be very, very old.

"Clothes," said the dragon. "Wet."

He was right. Chantel put the cup back. She dug around in the chest and found some robes. She handed one to Franklin.

He made a face at it, but they both changed their

clothes anyway, turning away from each other.

She quite liked the robe she'd found that fit her, which was warm and purple and had many interesting pockets, inside and out. It had an enormous dragon embroidered in green and gold, wrapping all the way around the robe with its head on one shoulder and its tail at the hem.

She looked at her reflection in the pool. Mistake. Her eyebrows weren't completely gone from the dragon's flame, but her eyelashes were. Her sea-wet, flight-swept hair was a mess. And there was something else. Maybe it was just the ripples in the pool, but she didn't look the least bit shamefast or biddable.

She looked like a girl who rode dragons.

She was surprised to discover the bundle of cakes had stayed in her sodden robe. She hung up the wet clothes on rock outcroppings in the wall, while Franklin stood around looking annoyed, and also rather old-fashioned in a red silk robe with gold lions embroidered on it.

"Think now," said the dragon. "Plan. Sit."

What Chantel was thinking was that she wanted to get out of here. But you couldn't very well argue with Lightning.

She sat. Franklin sat across from her. She undid her handkerchief full of cakes and looked inside. Everything was smooshed. She reviewed in her head in what order she properly ought to offer the cakes. She and Franklin were the guests, but the dragon was certainly the oldest. "Would you care for a cake?" she asked the dragon.

He shook his head.

Franklin grabbed a tart without waiting to be asked. He looked at it dubiously, and then wolfed it down and reached for another.

Chantel took a battered pink-frosted cake. But she wasn't really that hungry. She set it down on the table, where it oozed pink seawater.

"Now," said the dragon. "You choose."

She knew he wasn't talking about the cakes. "Which side I'm on, you mean."

He nodded.

"And which side you're on?" Chantel asked, because after all he was her familiar. But she immediately felt stupid for saying it. It was quite clear that while he might be her familiar as a small side job, he was something very much more than that in the main.

"No," said the dragon. "That I know."

He was watching her closely. She had a feeling she was being tested. She spread her hands on the table and looked at them. There was a dab of pink frosting stuck to one thumb. "Well. The patriarchs want to rule the city. I mean they want to go *on* ruling the city. If I'm on their side, that means I help them with what they're doing. Controlling everything, and keeping everyone . . . locked in."

She looked up at the dragon to see if he agreed with her. He blinked his great golden eyes.

"But it also means I can help the patriarchs repel the Marauders. Sorry. The Sunbiters," she added, looking at Franklin. "After all, the patriarchs are the ones who command the soldiers."

The dragon merely waited.

"If I help the king—" she licked the salty frosting off her thumb. "Then I'll be doing what Miss Ellicott wants me to do, and I ought to do that because I'm grateful for my education and for having a home and not being a servant or a factory girl."

This gratitude had been urged upon her from the time she was small, of course, and she felt she really *ought* to be grateful for these things. The problem was that her education, and so forth, were so much a part of her that she found it impossible to be grateful for them. It was like trying to be grateful you were born.

The dragon was still waiting.

"If I help the king, then I'll be doing my duty," said Chantel uncertainly.

The dragon nestled his enormous head on a scaly forearm and stared at Chantel and waited.

"I don't know who I ought to help," said Chantel. "The truth is I don't actually *like* the king *or* the patriarchs."

And as for the sorceresses—Chantel felt suddenly as if she might cry. She pressed her lips together hard. Franklin was watching her intently, and so was the dragon.

"I . . . can't I just be on the *city's* side?" she asked.

Lightning smiled, and flames deep inside reflected off his long white fangs. "Yes."

He yawned hugely, ending in a ROWRR that shook the cups on the table. "Sleep now."

"But—" Chantel said, dismayed. She wanted to go home. She wanted to make sure the girls and Bowser were all right.

The dragon was already asleep.

"Come on," said Franklin, finishing off his fourth saltwater-soaked tart. "Let's find a way out of here."

"I don't think we should," said Chantel, doubtful. "He's expecting us to wait for him."

Franklin made an exasperated noise. "Well, let's at least look around."

Chantel lifted the light-globe high. There was that tunnel by the waterfall, through which the stream ran away into the darkness. But there was also a dragon-sized doorway at the far end of the chamber.

Beyond it was another passage, and it split immediately.

"We could get lost," said Chantel.

"Not as long as we can hear the dragon," said Franklin.

In fact, the dragon's rumbling snore filled the passage.

On the left, the passage opened into another cavern. This room was full of . . . well, not treasure exactly. It was more of a junk room. There was furniture, much of it broken. There were weapons, and an entire suit of armor. There were flowerpots, for some reason. And tools of various sorts. A large brass cauldron. An old cart. It was all a jumble and a terrible mess.

"Let's go the other way," Franklin suggested.

They reached another chamber. And stopped and stared.

"Owl's bowels!" said Chantel.

"It's some kind of library, isn't it?" said Franklin. "We, er, burned one once."

It was like no library Chantel had ever seen. Darkwood shelves lined the walls of the chamber, twenty feet high. They had been carefully crafted to curve and slope where the cave did.

Besides that, there were other shelves that twisted their way into smaller caves, high in the wall, and within these caves Chantel could see more shelves and more books.

Spindly spiral staircases climbed the shelves in the main chamber, and insubstantial-looking green copper walkways stretched before every seventh shelf. These were for the humans to access the highest books, Chantel supposed. Lightning could simply reach for any book he wanted, and probably stretch his long neck into the high caves, too.

Chantel had never seen so many books in her life. She

hadn't known there *were* so many books.

She took a book from a shelf. It smelled of leather and old, old paper. She paged through it. It was about plants. Plants did not interest her particularly. But this did: there was no purple stamp on the book anywhere. Every book she'd ever read had had APPROVED stamped inside it, sometimes covering the words.

Was this the long-lost lore?

She put it back, and took another book. And another. None of these books were approved! They were unapproved books.

"Chantel," said Franklin.

There was an odd diffidence in his voice. Chantel turned to look at him. His red hair was still wet, and plastered flat on his head. He rubbed his crooked nose nervously.

"I was wondering," he said. "Um, how did you find a dragon?"

"He came out of my head," said Chantel.

Franklin looked hurt. "Well, if you don't want to tell me, that's fine."

Chantel managed to avoid sighing in exasperation. Her deportment was that good. "Remember how I had a snake in my head?"

"I thought that was just an expression."

"No, it wasn't an expression, it was a snake," said Chantel. "And I went to see the king, and he took me prisoner, and the snake came out as a dragon, and broke through the roof of the castle and we escaped. Then we saw you about to be executed, so we flew down to rescue you."

Franklin gave her a pained look. "That didn't really happen. About your head, I mean."

"All right, suit yourself," said Chantel. She turned back to the books.

There were books about architecture, and books about geography. There was a long book about a country Chantel had never heard of. There was a book about beetles. None of these books were approved. Not one of them. Not even the most boring one she'd seen yet, which picked sentences apart and laid them out on stick drawings.

"Well, say that was really what happened—" said Franklin.

"I beg your pardon. I believe I *did* say that," said Chantel.

"What's the dragon going to do with us now?"

"I don't know," said Chantel, putting the book about sentences back on the shelf. "I've never met a dragon before today, and I'm not familiar with their habits. I think he'll probably show us the way out of here, if we ask nicely."

"You don't think he'll eat us?"

"He might," said Chantel, and then felt mean for saying it. "No, I don't think he will. This is his house. Do you see any signs of eaten people around here?"

"Just that empty suit of armor," said Franklin. "And these clothes." He pulled at his crimson robe in disgust.

Chantel felt an uncomfortable twinge. But she really didn't think Lightning was going to eat them, and she did her best to convince Franklin of it. It was odd he needed reassuring, she thought, when he'd been so brave about being executed on the wall.

The fact was, now that the snake was out of her head, she didn't find Franklin nearly as annoying. Even his twangy accent didn't bother her as much.

"Is Karl the Bloody your father?" she asked.

Franklin looked down at the floor. He walked over to a table and sat on it. He swung his feet so that they thumped against the table's stone leg.

"Yeah," he said. "But we don't get along."

Chantel didn't know what to say. She remembered how Karl the Bloody had jerked his head at Franklin and said *kill him*. It seemed to her that that went a little beyond not getting along.

"Well, so you ran away from home," she said.

"Yeah. And I thought if I could just get into the walled city, I'd never have to see him again."

"Karl's not attacking the city *because* of you, is he?"

"Nah. He's always hated all that stuff about the pass and the harbor and everything. Even before my mother died. Everybody hates you guys for the toll road and the harbor fees."

"Oh," said Chantel.

"Plus we hate the wall. And maybe we hate the whole idea of having a city on a hill looking down at us."

It was hard to continue a conversation after being told that everyone hated you, so she turned back to the books.

"If I promise to believe you, will you tell me what happened?" said Franklin.

"Why, if you hate me?"

"I don't! I didn't say that!" Franklin looked distraught. "I didn't mean it. Girls, sheesh."

"You did say it," said Chantel. "And don't blame girls."

"Okay. I'm sorry," said Franklin. "Everyone hates the toll and the harbor fees. Is that okay?"

"I suppose so," said Chantel. "I didn't even know there were harbor fees until you told me. Maybe because I'm a *girl*."

"I said I was sorry," said Franklin.

Chantel knew she was being difficult. She'd had a hard day. But then, she reminded herself, so had Franklin.

So she left the books, and sat down on a bench, and told him everything that had happened.

"Huh," said Franklin, when she finished. "So you found your Miss Ellicott, and she turned out to be just as bad as my dad."

"She did not," said Chantel.

"What does she want from you?"

"I'm not sure. I—do you think she could have known about the dragon?—"

"Stands to reason," said Franklin with a shrug. "You said her familiar was a snake, right? Did the dragon ever come out of *her* head?"

Chantel could not imagine a dragon emerging from Miss Ellicott's very proper mouth, or a snake ever daring to crawl into her ear.

"We could ask him, I suppose," she said doubtfully.

"I bet it didn't," said Franklin. "Otherwise what would she need you for? It's obvious she wants you because you've got the dragon."

"I didn't, then." Chantel thought. "And she told me she outgrew the snake."

Franklin looked skeptical. "I wonder if she even had the snake."

Chantel wasn't used to hearing Miss Ellicott's veracity doubted.

"I wonder if Karl the Bloody will think I'm dead now," said Franklin.

"But he must've seen us rescue you—"

"Nah," said Franklin. "He saw me captured by a big dragon. That's what it must've looked like, if you think about it."

He sounded hopeful.

"Why—" Chantel had been taught not to bring up difficult subjects. "Why would he—" she faltered.

"Want me dead? Because I don't want to be a chieftain."

Franklin swung his feet, kicking the stone bench. "My older brother was supposed to be heir, but he died."

"I'm sorry." Chantel wondered if this was also her city's fault. "Was it spotted swamp fever?"

"Nah. Crossbow bolt. In a battle with the warrior tribe of Shone. He died covered with honor. But you couldn't see it for the blood."

"Oh," said Chantel. "Er. That's too bad. But why do you have to be the heir? Couldn't they just give the, er, job"—she wasn't sure how these things worked—"to the person who's best at, er, crossbow-bolting or whatever?"

"I suppose. But that would be me," said Franklin, with a touch of pride. "I can shoot the head off a chicken at three hundred paces." He frowned. "But I don't like to. I mean, I like it better when it's a stick. And in battle, you know, it's not sticks *or* chickens."

"I see," said Chantel. "So you ran away. Well, you're free of that now, anyway."

Franklin looked doubtful. "I don't . . . well, maybe I am."

They talked of other things. They speculated about Lightning, and how old he was, and how many times he had been a snake and a dragon over the centuries.

It wasn't until they were both too tired to talk anymore that Chantel remembered Franklin had wanted to look for a way out. But she didn't remind him. They went back to the dragon's lair.

There was no place to sleep except the dragon's couch. It was squashily soft and covered with rich purple velvet. Franklin and Chantel got blankets from the chest and found places at the tail end of the dragon. Franklin fell asleep immediately.

Chantel did not.

First, for a long time she couldn't stop staring at Lightning. He had gotten so very much bigger, and he was clearly an old and powerful dragon and not just a little creature she wore around her neck.

And he was snoring so loudly. Also, the waterfall was loud. And the tunnel beside it, down which the stream flowed, seemed like a place fiends might lurk. Things kept rolling over and over in her head. The sorceresses. The king. The patriarchs. Queen Haywith. She felt she had asked the queen the wrong questions. Queen Haywith had had Lightning beside her, under the apple tree. Had he once been her familiar? Had he crawled into her ear?

18

A Position of Strength

She must have fallen asleep eventually. Because later, she awoke to find the room bathed in a deep red glow.

She sat up. Gradually she took in the cave, the water-fall, and the sleeping dragon, and the woman perched comfortably atop his belly.

"Oh, good, you're awake," said Queen Haywith.

Chantel blinked and stretched. She gave things plenty of time to resolve themselves into one of those dreams where you only think you're waking up. But when she climbed out of bed, the stone was warm and solid beneath her feet.

She looked over at Franklin. He was sound asleep.

Finally she said, "Good morning?"

"Good morning," said the queen. "Is this the second time we've met?"

"Yes," said Chantel, miffed that the queen didn't remember.

"It is for me as well," said the queen. "So much better when these things happen in order."

"Will we—did we—will we meet a third time?" said Chantel.

"If we do, there will be a price to pay," said the queen. "Magic is like that. Summonings particularly."

"I don't think I summoned you," said Chantel.

"You must have."

"I didn't do any magic!"

"Let us surmise that you are a person with unusually strong summoning skills." The queen looked down at the sleeping dragon. "But as this is only our second meeting, we are safe. On what may I advise you?"

"I don't know," said Chantel. "Er, can I trust Lightning?"

"It depends," said the queen. "He is a dragon, and so he will always see things differently."

"Will he hurt us?" Chantel blurted.

"These questions are too small, Chantel, girl from the May-Be."

Chantel remembered the things she'd been wondering about. "Was . . . Is Lightning your familiar?"

"Something of that sort," said the queen. She slid down from the dragon and came over and sat on a rock beside the pool.

"You're a sorceress?"

"A Mage of the Dragon. Why don't you tell me what's going on?"

Chantel described her visit to the castle. "Miss Ellicott used to have a snake for a familiar," she added.

The queen looked startled. "Are you quite certain?"

"Miss Flivvers told me so. And Miss Ellicott said she outgrew him."

"You don't grow out of having a familiar. You grow *into* it," said the queen. "If Lightning appeared to Miss Ellicott first—"

"Couldn't it have been some other snake?" Chantel interrupted. She curtseyed. "I beg your pardon, Your Majesty."

"No," said the queen. "Another dragon would not have tried to manifest in Lightning Pass. That would have led to a dragon battle, which would have destroyed the city."

"Oh." It seemed to Chantel that the queen's answers only raised more questions. "Are all snakes dragons?"

"If they appear as familiars, yes. That is, they have the potential to be dragons, just as the people to whom they appear have the potential to be more than they are. From what you describe, though, every step has been taken to prevent that from happening. And if Miss Ellicott never let the snake into her head, then—"

"I didn't let Lightning into my head!" Chantel curt-seyed again to cover the interruption.

"Do stop bobbing up and down," said the queen. "You must have. At least, you had a head into which he could crawl."

"Because I wasn't shamefast and biddable enough?"

"You?" The queen smiled. "I'm sure you weren't."

Chantel knew she ought to have felt horrible; she had failed at deportment so badly that she had welcomed a snake and caused a dragon. Miss Ellicott had done no such thing. Miss Ellicott had dismissed the snake, and gone from being shamefast and biddable to being proper and correct.

Chantel failed to feel horrible.

"He grew in your head," said the queen. "And this means that until his next incarnation, he is under certain constraints."

"Constraints?"

"He won't do anything you wouldn't do," said the queen.

"But I wouldn't fly or breathe fire!"

The queen made a dismissive gesture. "Of course you would, if you could. And you, of course, have been changed by the dragon. I can see that quite clearly from here."

Chantel pressed her lips together to keep from making

an angry retort. The queen was talking in riddles when Chantel needed plain answers.

"You are becoming a Mage of the Dragon," said Queen Haywith. "But it is a difficult journey, and it is easy to fail along the way, as—"

As you did, Chantel didn't say.

"—as your Miss Ellicott appears to have done."

At this point Chantel actually did forget herself so far as to sigh in exasperation.

The queen smiled. "You are more concerned with your immediate situation."

Chantel was immediately embarrassed. Belatedly, she offered the queen a cake.

"No, thank you," said the queen. "I am not quite here, you know. Besides, you may need them. Lightning is not a poor host, except that he himself eats only every year or two, and he forgets that humans are different.

"In fact," said the queen, "he tends to take a long view, which is often rather useless to us humans."

"Like leaving me on a rock and forgetting the tide would come in," said Chantel.

"Precisely. So, you will return to the city, and there you feel you must choose between two equally distasteful powers?"

"Yeah." Chantel sat down at the table, put an elbow on it, and leaned on her hand, then remembered herself hastily and folded her hands in her lap. "Yes. The patriarchs are power-hungry and deceitful, and the king is just the same. I'm sorry," she added hastily. "I didn't mean to speak ill of your family."

"My family? The king? It's possible." The queen shrugged. "After five hundred years, it's equally possible that you are my family. You must realize I have no idea who this king is."

"King Rathfest the Restless," said Chantel.

"Indeed?" said the queen, without much interest. "And is he?"

"Is he . . . oh, restless, you mean? I'm not sure. Maybe. He seems to actually want to be king," said Chantel. "And I guess he might have killed his cousins who were kings before him. No one really dies of lettuce, do they?"

"Only in the most unusual circumstances."

"Hm."

"Well, I can't advise you about the king, except in a general way. I can advise you to set little store by what men say, and much by what they do. Women too. What do *you* think you should do, Chantel?"

"What's best for the city," said Chantel. "I said that to the dragon, and it seemed like he thought that was the right answer. But you said that was too small."

"The city cannot survive alone. And even if it could, mere survival is not enough to offer to the world."

"Oh," said Chantel.

"Now, what are you fighting against?"

"The Sunbiters," said Chantel promptly.

The queen dabbled a hand in the water. "I would have expected you to say, 'Anything that can hurt my people.'"

Chantel looked down at her hands, as she always did when she got a question wrong. "Yeah. I mean yes. I mean that is what I meant."

The queen looked at her impassively, not answering. The dragon let out a loud snore, and two orange-pink puffs rose from his nostrils.

"Which I guess . . ." Chantel stopped, and thought.

Still the queen said nothing.

"The patriarchs are hurting the people," Chantel explained. "Just to make money and have power. And the king doesn't really intend to help. He just wants money and power himself."

"That is so often the case," said Queen Haywith unhelpfully.

"That question that I asked you before . . ." Chantel trailed off uncertainly.

"What question was that?"

"Um, well, the one you didn't like very much."

"You'll have to remind me." The queen was clearly not going to make this any easier.

"Um, about breaking a vow."

The queen's dark eyes sparked. "I have taken only one vow in my life."

"Would—would you mind telling me what the exact words were?"

"'By the power of the dragon, I swear to protect the city of Lightning Pass and its people from any force, within or without, that may harm it,'" said the queen.

Obviously the queen had broken the vow, but it wouldn't do to rub it in. "So. I . . . I think I should go and check on the girls and Bowser. And Miss Flivvers," said Chantel.

"You may be arrested."

"Well, what would you do?" said Chantel.

"I would establish a position of strength. And then I would try to gather as much information as possible," said the queen. "Does that help?"

Chantel thought about it. She was in a position of strength. And the books in the library were information. It was possible that— "Yes," she said. "Thank you."

"Not a problem," said the queen graciously. "And now I really think I'd better be going."

She skirted the edge of the pool and stepped into the stream. Then she sloshed away down the dark tunnel.

"Oh, and Chantel." The queen's voice echoed weirdly from the tunnel. "Don't forget—at the third summoning a price will be exacted. Good luck."

Then she was gone.

Chantel did not go back to sleep. She paced around the library and thought. She took books down from the shelves and piled them on a table. She paced some more.

There was no escaping it: if Queen Haywith was telling the truth, then having had a snake in her head made Chantel more like Queen Haywith than like Miss Ellicott.

Well, Chantel could still make choices. And she could be more like Chantel than either of them.

She went back to the dragon's chamber and found that Franklin was just waking up and the dragon had opened one orange eye.

"Good morning," she said. "I'm going to go back to the school and check on the girls, and Bowser."

"King," said the dragon drowsily.

"I'll try not to get caught by him," said Chantel. "Franklin, there's something I'd like you to do, please."

She took him into the library and showed him her stacks of books. "Can you read through these, please, and see if there's anything about Queen Haywith? I especially want to know how she opened a breach in the walls, and what happened to her afterward. How she"—Chantel hesitated, because it seemed a strange thing to say about someone she'd just been talking to—"died."

"I—" Franklin began, then stopped.

"Thank you," said Chantel. "And the other thing I need to find is anything at all about how the spell that strengthens Seven Buttons is done."

"Why do you need spells to strengthen a wall like that?" said Franklin.

"Don't you think your father could knock a hole in it if he tried?" said Chantel.

"I don't know," said Franklin. "I know that if he decided to try, he wouldn't give up till the wall was down, or he was dead."

"So look for the spell, please," said Chantel. "And if there were some famous words that Queen Haywith spoke . . . well, if you run across anything she said at *all*, actually, write it down. I found paper and pencils here." She opened a drawer at the bottom of a bookshelf.

Franklin didn't respond. He was sulking, Chantel thought, because he had to stay behind. Well, at least she was showing him how to do something useful. "Over here," she said. "On the wall, there's a list of all the books. Do you see how it works?"

It was almost like a book itself, composed of hinged wooden panels. But she couldn't get Franklin interested in it. He just leaned against the bookshelves and sulked.

"Well, you'll figure it out," she said, trying not to sound exasperated. "And I'll be back as soon as I can. And we'll figure out what to do with you."

"I don't want you to figure out what to do with me," said Franklin, scowling.

"I meant you and me would figure it out," said Chantel. "I'm trying to help you."

"Yeah. Okay." Franklin looked disagreeable.

"So if you could help me by—"

"Enough already!" said Franklin. "I'm coming with you. There's going to be people looking for you, and I know a lot more about evading the enemy than you do." He cast a hostile look at the books. "Even if I can't read."

"Oh," said Chantel.

19

Miss Flivvers Misses the Point

Lightning led them to a passage that went to the surface. Chantel had changed back into her school robe, although it was torn and pocketless and stiff with salt. The purple dragon robe seemed altogether too grand for Miss Ellicott's School.

The passage decanted into a narrow cleft between two buildings in Bannister Square. There was an abnegation spell concealing it—Chantel had noticed the spell a few days before, when she'd been searching for the sorceresses.

"Now, you need to stay here," said Chantel.

Franklin smiled in a very annoying and supercilious way. "Don't give me orders."

"I'm not giving you orders," said Chantel firmly. "But

if you come out into the city you'll be in grave danger."

"I'm not afraid."

"You'll be in grave danger from me," said Chantel. "Because I'll cast a horrible spell on you. And if you're not afraid of that, you're st—" Chantel's deportment caught up with her. "Unwise."

Franklin stayed, grumbling.

The wind chased curtains of rain across Bannister Square, turning the buildings gray and indistinct. Chantel made her way upward, fighting the water that gushed down the hill.

It was always like this in Lightning Pass when the rain came. The streets became rivers, the bridges became aqueducts, the alleys became rushing torrents. When it rained it seemed the only direction in Lightning Pass was down.

Chantel lost her bearings. She felt her way along until she came to an arched doorway, where she stood until the rain cleared enough for her to recognize *something*. Then she started on again, up streets and across bridges, with some brief rainfree interludes in which she squelched along arched alleyways, until at last she was splashing up the stairs of Fate's Turning.

When she arrived, dripping, in the hallway of Miss Ellicott's School for Magical Maidens, everyone came running, cascading down the stairs.

"It's Chantel!" said Holly.

"Chantel!" Anna came out of the kitchen, then stopped and stared. "We thought—are you all right?"

Miss Flivvers folded her hands and stared at Chantel in dismay. "Goodness, you look a fright. We were dreadfully worried."

"Chantel, there was a dragon!" said Daisy, jumping up and down.

Holly grabbed Chantel's soggy sleeve. "A big green dragon in the sky!"

"Now, girls." Miss Flivvers frowned. "The patriarchs have decreed that there was *not* a dragon. Daisy, go find Chantel a dry robe."

But Anna was already bringing one.

"But we saw—" Holly quailed under Miss Flivvers's frown. "I mean, I beg your pardon, we saw a dragon."

"What you saw," said Miss Flivvers, "was a symbolic expression of the city's power and destiny. The image of a dragon was a sign that the city will triumph over her enemies."

"Why is the city a her?" asked Holly. "When all the patriarchs and the king are hims?"

"Do not ask silly questions," said Miss Flivvers. "Go and fetch a mop."

Soon Chantel had changed into the dry robe, and the other was dripping on the kitchen hearth, making a puddle that ran down the hearthstone and hissed in the fireplace.

Miss Flivvers poured Chantel a cup of hot oniony broth. Chantel wrapped her hands around it to warm them. Holly and Daisy set about fixing Chantel's hair, and Chantel tried hard not to wince at each tug. They meant well.

Anna sat and looked at Chantel with a concern that was equally uncomfortable. The other girls crowded around. There was definitely something missing from the kitchen—

"Where's Bowser?" Chantel asked.

"He was called up," said Miss Flivvers.

"Called up?" Chantel said, bewildered.

"To serve in the army," Anna said, looking down at the brick floor. "To defend the city."

"What does Bowser know about defending cities?" Chantel demanded.

"All of the boys over the age of nine have been called up," said Miss Flivvers. "The situation is—is desperate. No, I shouldn't say that. We should not despair, because the patriarchs have told us we have the dragon on our side. Even if he is metaphorical."

"How—" How desperate could it have gotten, in the time that Chantel had been underground? "What happened?"

"There was a terrible attack on the patriarchs when they were up on the city wall. A treacherous volley of Marauder arrows, under a flag of truce. Lord Rudolph was killed, along with several other patriarchs. Sir Wolfgang is now in charge," said Miss Flivvers.

Chantel stared at her in dismay. "Lord Rudolph? Killed? But—"

"It is most unfortunate," said Miss Flivvers. "He had a certain leadership quality that it would be disloyal to suggest the other patriarchs lack."

"He could hear us when we talked to him," said Chantel. "But—"

"Do not be impertinent," said Miss Flivvers. "About an hour after the first attack, the Marauders launched three missiles into the city. The upper stories of two houses were destroyed, and two people were killed."

"Oh." Chantel suddenly felt terrible. By rescuing Franklin, it seemed, she and Lightning had caused several deaths. "Lord Rudolph was up on the wall to execute Franklin, you know."

Anna gasped, and the little girls let out cries of dismay.

"He's not dead," Chantel added hastily.

"I suspected that boy was a spy," said Miss Flivvers.

"I beg your pardon, he is not!" said Anna hotly.

"I don't think he is," said Chantel. "He's the son of Karl the Bloody, you know."

"Who's Karl the Bloody?" said Holly.

"The leader of the Marau—the Sunbiters," said Chantel.

"Then the boy clearly was a spy," said Miss Flivvers.

"Though I am still sorry that he was killed, as I know you girls had a sentimental fondness for him."

"He wasn't killed! I beg your pardon. I just said. I— The dragon and I rescued him."

"I knew there was really a dragon," said Holly, giving an extra-hard tug with the comb.

"Did you ride on it?" said Daisy.

"Yes," said Chantel.

"Do not fill the children's heads with foolishness," said Miss Flivvers, warily.

"Where did the dragon come from?" said Anna.

"Inside my head," said Chantel.

"Not just inside *your* head. We *all* imagined we saw a dragon," said Miss Flivvers.

Chantel explained.

"Chantel, really—" Miss Flivvers looked stunned. "I have always known you to be an essentially honest girl—"

"The dragon came out of your *mouth*?" said Daisy.

"You went through the *roof*?" said Holly.

"Yes. And . . ." Chantel took a deep breath. This next part was going to be difficult. "And I've found the sorceresses."

A gasp from all around the kitchen.

"Oh, marvelous! Why didn't you say so at once!" Miss Flivvers jumped to her feet. "Is Euphonia—are Miss Ellicott and the others safe? Are they well? Where are they?"

Chantel told her.

"But this is excellent!" said Miss Flivvers. "If they are helping the king, then all is saved!"

"I'm not sure it is." Chantel hurried on before Miss Flivvers could tell her to beg her pardon. "Really it's the king fighting against the patriarchs, and meanwhile we've got those Marau—Sunbiters without the walls. The king tried to get me to help him—"

"Then it was your duty to do so," said Miss Flivvers firmly.

Do your duty, Miss Ellicott had said.

"No, it was my duty to protect the city and the people," said Chantel. "And it's the king's and the sorceresses' duty too, but instead they'd rather fight for power. And they want me because I've got the dragon."

Chantel expected Miss Flivvers to argue some more, but Miss Flivvers was silent.

"Then if they want you," said Anna, "that explains why there was a man here looking for you yesterday."

"What man?" said Chantel.

"He looked like death," said Anna.

"Oh," said Chantel.

It was very like Bowser's description of the man who'd come for Miss Ellicott.

Just then there was a knock on the street door.

Everyone in the kitchen drew closer together.

"Oh dear, I suppose someone ought to answer it," said Miss Flivvers.

"I will," said Chantel, freeing herself from Holly's and Daisy's ministrations.

"I'll come with you," said Anna.

They started down the hall. Chantel heard Miss Flivvers following behind.

Anna opened the door. It was still pouring down rain outside. A skeletally thin man in a soggy black cowl stood on the doorstep, rivulets cascading off his cape.

Chantel saw what Anna had meant. The man did look like death.

"The king has sent for the girl, Chantel," he said, in a cold, sepulchral voice.

"She's not here," said Anna, before Chantel could speak.

"Then the king wishes the girls in the school to come to him." The man who looked like death shivered.

"Why?" said Anna.

"For safekeeping. The situation in the city may become difficult, especially should the Marauders without the walls gain entrance."

Chantel, meanwhile, was making signs with her thumbs, strengthening the ward spell on the door.

"Thank you," said Miss Flivvers, stepping forward. Chantel could tell Miss Flivvers was having a lot of trouble not inviting the soggy man in to dry off. "I am touched by

His Majesty's concern for my humble charges. Truly, he is a good king. If there should be any signs of danger, it is a comfort to know—"

"You fail to understand me," said the man, his voice like an echo from a tomb. "His Majesty demands that the girls be sent to the castle *now*."

"Unfortunately, I can't do that without the approval of the headmistress," said Miss Flivvers. "If she were to return and—"

"Miss Ellicott requires it," said the man.

"Then she must come and tell me so herself," said Miss Flivvers firmly. "Good evening."

She closed the door on the rain and the man who looked like death.

"What if she does?" said Chantel quickly. "What will you do then, Miss Flivvers?"

"If Miss Ellicott comes here—" said Anna.

"She'll be sent by the king," said Chantel. "And she'll be taking the girls hostage."

"What a way to speak of Miss Ellicott!" said Miss Flivvers.

"Hostage for what?" said Anna.

"To make me cooperate," said Chantel. "And no, Miss Flivvers, it is not my duty, and I won't let the king use the dragon to fight the patriarchs when they *all* ought to be defending the city."

"Can we make the wards strong enough to keep Miss Ellicott out?" said Anna.

"What a thing to say!" said Miss Flivvers.

"I kind of really doubt it," said Chantel. "I think she'll walk right through our wards."

Chantel and Anna looked at each other hopelessly.

"I hardly think Miss Ellicott would—" Miss Flivvers began.

"We have to get the younger girls out of here," said Chantel. "We'll take them to the dragon's lair."

"Oh, they'll love that!" said Anna.

"What a shocking idea," said Miss Flivvers. "And I, for one, have no desire to—"

"We'll leave you here, Miss Flivvers," said Chantel. "That is, if you don't mind. We'll need you to talk to . . . anybody who comes knocking."

20

IN SEARCH OF BOWSER

The rain had let up. Water still chuckled down the streets and gurgled in the gutters, on its way to the culverts and the sea.

Franklin was waiting for them at the entrance to the lair, inside the abnegation spell, in Bannister Square. He was still in a rotten mood, but the small girls were so delighted to see him that he had to cheer up, and was soon happily recounting how he'd nearly been executed.

One or two tiresome girls squealed in fright at the darkness of the underground passage. Most of them, though, were sensibly fascinated. Those who knew how did light-globe spells, and they began the long descent into the caves. The girls stopped to shine their lights on tall wedding-cake columns of glistening stalactites, and to press their hands into the soft moonmilk that coated the walls.

They arrived at last in the library, where the girls ran to climb the spiral staircases.

"Careful!" Anna commanded. "Don't fall."

Just then Holly let out a squawk and froze, staring.

Lightning's golden dragon head came through the doorway, followed by a long sinuous stretch of dragon neck, and then the rest of the dragon.

One of the smaller girls buried her face in Anna's robe. But the rest gazed, awestruck.

"It's beautiful," said Daisy.

"Not an it," said the dragon.

"His name is Lightning," said Chantel. "Lightning, I, er, brought you some guests."

"Not lunch?" said the dragon.

Several girls backed up against the bookshelves, trying to get out of sight.

"He's joking," said Chantel. "Er, you are, right?"

The dragon nodded solemnly. The girls looked only slightly reassured. But they went back to exploring the side caverns, and the walkways that crisscrossed the bookshelves.

Chantel turned to Anna. "These books—"

"The long-lost lore?" said Anna.

"Maybe," said Chantel. "But so far all I've found is boring stuff."

"The lore could be boring," said Anna. "I mean, it could *look* boring. We need to know—"

"I know!" Holly interrupted, hanging down from the railing of a spiral staircase by one hand. "What the words are that Queen Haywith spoke."

"Right," said Chantel. "And I also want to know . . . what happened to her. What she did, and what happened afterward."

"*I* know *that*," said Daisy, who was crouched beside Lightning's left front foot, examining his sword-sharp claws. "She breached the wall, and then they locked her up in a tower and she drowned to death in her own tears."

"Nobody could drown in their own tears," said Holly thoughtfully. She was hanging by her knees now. "Especially not if they were in a tower."

Overhead, the walkways (which did not have railings) rattled as girls ran along them, shrieking. Franklin was watching them with a slightly worried expression.

"I want to know what happened to Queen Haywith in books that don't have a purple patriarch stamp on them," said Chantel.

Anna picked up a book from the table and flipped through it. "You're right. They don't."

She kept paging through the book, fascinated.

Then she set it down. "What we really need to know, though, is what the rest of the Buttoning spell is."

"Right," said Chantel. "And I'll bring more food as soon as I can find some, and . . . and there are blankets and things here, you'll find them, and there's water in Lightning's room, he won't eat you—" she looked at the dragon. "Right?"

The dragon nodded, looking, Chantel thought, amused. It was hard to tell facial expressions on a dragon. You mostly had to go by the eyes.

"Wait, you're leaving?" said Anna.

Overhead, a small girl named Ivy tripped on the hem of her long school robe and fell.

Everyone watched in horror for a fraction of a second, and then Lightning spread a wing. Ivy hit it and rolled, with a metallic rustle of scales, to land safely on the dragon's back.

The girls up on the walkways applauded.

"All of you come down from there!" said Anna.

Chantel suddenly felt the little girls were going to drive her insane if she had to be in the same cave with them for one more minute. "I have to go find Bowser," she said.

"I'm coming with you," said Franklin.

"You can't leave me alone with them," said Anna. "I won't be able to find anything in the books. I'll be too busy mopping up blood!"

Chantel looked up and all around. "Come down!" she said. "And do as Anna says. Or, or the dragon will eat you!"

"No he won't," said a girl on the top walkway.

Chantel turned to Lightning in despair. "Can you—"

In answer the dragon breathed flame. The flame formed into an orange ball. The ball grew larger and larger, a roaring, burning sun. It began to grow uncomfortably warm in the library.

"Um, thank you, Lightning," said Chantel. "That's—"

The ball of flame grew larger still. Now it was really hot. Chantel felt her face burning. Some of the smaller girls looked quite overheated. And very frightened.

"Really, Lightning—" said Chantel.

"You'll set the *books* on fire!" said Anna.

The flame ball popped out of existence.

"Right," said Chantel, casting a nervous look at Lightning in case he was going to do it again. "Everybody please listen to Anna and do what she says, and help her search the long-lost lore so that we can do the spell to seal Seven Buttons."

She gave them all the Look. That quieted them. Most of the girls came clattering down the stairs and went off to explore the storeroom.

Chantel turned to Anna. "Miss Ellicott told me the sorceresses do a Contentedness spell, to make people happy with the way things are—"

"So that's why you people haven't killed your patriarchs and your king," said Franklin.

"Probably," said Chantel, exasperated with him. She
turned back to Anna. "We might be able to—"

"Do a spell on the girls? No." This came from the
rock-hard part of Anna that had never been shamefast or
biddable. "No. I can manage them."

"They seem pretty happy with the way things are
already," said Franklin.

Screams came from the storeroom. Chantel shrugged.
She slid past the dragon and went into his chamber. Her
green robe had gotten wet again in the rain, so she put on
the purple one.

She had just finished buttoning the embroidered dragon
together when the real dragon oozed into the chamber,
gave an expressive sigh, and flopped down on his couch.

From out in the storeroom came the mostly gleeful
yells of little girls.

"I'm sorry," Chantel told the dragon. "They're not usually like this. Or at least, they never have been before."

The dragon grunted.

"I think it's getting away from the school," she added.
"They—um, I'm sure they'll calm down."

More shrieks from without. The dragon snorted.

Chantel sat down by his head. "Were you Miss Ellicott's familiar? When she was a girl?"

"Snake," said Lightning,

"Well, yes, I know, as a snake, but—"

"I change," said the dragon.

"Oh." Chantel didn't really feel this had answered the question, but from a dragon point of view it apparently did. "All right. Um, I was wondering. About the Mar—the Sunbiters. Can't we, um, do something?"

The dragon peered at her orangely. This had the effect of making her feel stupid for asking. But it was important, so she went on. "I mean, if you burned those catapults of theirs first, what could they do? And then you could just fly in and flame them—"

"Would you?" said the dragon.

"Well, no. But I'm not a dragon."

"You wouldn't." Lightning said this with finality, and closed his eyes.

"But, well, don't you eat people?" said Chantel.

"Sometimes."

"So what's the difference?"

"You."

Chantel's toes curled with frustration.

"Grew with you," said the dragon.

"Right," said Chantel. "Queen Haywith said something about that."

And the dragon had changed her too, the queen had said. Chantel wondered if that had really happened. She hadn't noticed anything.

There was a distant thud and a smash, followed by sobs. Chantel jumped up and ran out. She found Franklin and Anna picking up several small girls from the library floor.

"Chantel, we found a cart!" said Holly, emerging from the wreckage. "In the storeroom. And I was giving them rides, and—"

"Is everyone still alive?" said Chantel.

"Seems to be," said Franklin.

"I think so," said Anna.

"The cart's wrecked," said Holly. "But look, we found this!"

She waved a small gold crown, just a circlet, really.

"That looks very valuable," said Anna. "Perhaps Lightning ought to put it in a treasure chest."

Chantel hooked the circlet on her finger, and took it to the dragon.

He blinked an orange-gold eye at it. "Not mine," he croaked.

"But shouldn't you put it somewhere for safekeeping? It might get damaged or lost or—" Chantel didn't want to say stolen. She couldn't imagine any of the girls would try to steal it. Then again, she didn't know. You couldn't count the way they'd behaved at Miss Ellicott's School as real deportment, perhaps.

The dragon's eyes glowed dangerously. "Not. Mine."

"Okay," said Chantel hastily. "Well, I'll, um, find somewhere to put it."

But she didn't, not right away. She stuck it in one of the many inside pockets of her dragon robe.

✿

Franklin and Chantel climbed the tunnel to Bannister Square.

The rain had stopped. The last of it was sluicing down the steep gutters, winding its way around the twisting streets. People were everywhere. And they were doing one of two things: standing in line or marching.

If they were boys or men, they were marching. Chantel and Franklin passed columns of unlikely-looking soldiers everywhere, bearing swords, spears and crossbows, trying to stay in formation as they rounded quirky bends in streets not made for marching.

The girls and women were standing in line, at shops and market stalls.

"Shortages and rationing," said Franklin. "And people panic, too. They want to get their share before it's gone."

"How are we going to find Bowser?" said Chantel.

"It won't do any good to find him," said Franklin.

"I just need to talk to him," said Chantel. "Make sure he's okay."

Franklin shrugged. "They'll have him drilling with new recruits the same height as him."

"The same height?" Chantel looked at him to see if he was joking.

"Yes," said Franklin patiently. "And he comes up to here on me." He touched the bridge of his nose.

They found a troop of boys the height of Franklin's nose down near Dimswitch, in a market square called Traitor's Neck. There were at least a hundred boys, standing ramrod straight, in ranks and columns. They moved their arms and stamped their feet in response to the things a guard captain standing on a box yelled, which sounded to Chantel like "Hut! Hop! Yop! Yup!"

The boys weren't wearing uniforms—there probably weren't enough to go around—but they were all wearing floppy gray hats. That and the fact that they were all exactly the same height made it very hard to tell them apart. Chantel hurried along, peering at their faces, trying to find Bowser.

"Don't," Franklin had said, once, and then he faded into the background.

None of the boys looked at Chantel as she scanned their faces. They all stared straight ahead and hopped and yopped on command.

Then suddenly she saw Bowser, near the middle of the formation. His floppy cap was at exactly the same angle as everyone else's floppy cap, the loose empty space creating the impression that there wasn't very much room for a brain. This made Chantel sad, because it was what people tended to think about Bowser anyway, but she was awfully relieved to see him. She turned sideways and worked her way quickly down the row.

She stopped in front of him. "Are you all right?" she whispered.

Bowser ignored her.

"What are they going to make you do?" Chantel whispered.

Bowser's eyes flicked once in her direction, then he stared straight ahead. He hopped. He yopped.

"Listen, you can't fight the Sunbiters. I've seen them. There're too many. And we—"

"They're in the harbor," Bowser whispered urgently, still staring straight ahead.

"Halt!" yelled the commander.

All hopping and yopping stopped. Absolute silence filled Traitor's Neck, except for the sound of the commander's boots snipping the cobbles. He had a stick under one arm.

"We are all stopping our important military drill, essential to the defense of our nation," said the commander, in the same loud voice, "because number 8-217 has to talk to a girl."

Chantel realized she should leave now, but her feet somehow wouldn't move.

Bowser continued to stare straight ahead, his face red.

"Maybe," the man yelled, his mouth now three inches from Bowser's ear, "number 8-217 wants to *be* a girl.

"Is that what you want, number 8-217?" The commander's eyes squeezed shut and his face became all mouth when he yelled.

"No, sir!" said Bowser, very loudly, still staring straight ahead.

Chantel at that moment was feeling extremely grateful that she *was* a girl.

"Maybe," yelled the man, "you already are a girl!"

"No, sir!" yelled Bowser.

This whole time nobody had looked at Chantel or even seemed to notice she existed. Nonetheless, she was the problem, and finally her feet listened to her brain's commands and marched her away. She didn't turn around as she heard the sound of the commander's stick whacking repeatedly.

She felt the angry prickle of tears starting in her eyes. She did not let them fall. She had deportment.

"I told you," said Franklin, who was suddenly by her side.

"Where were you?" she demanded.

"Not making a fool of myself like you," said Franklin, without rancor. "You can't interrupt a military drill, for the Swamp Lady's sake."

"That man is just nasty!" said Chantel. "I'm sorry, but he is. What's the point of all that yelling and hitting?"

"To make them obey perfectly," said Franklin, looking

at the ground. "And to make them mad enough to kill someone." He kicked a cobble.

"Does your father do all that?" said Chantel.

"There's no way those kids can stand up to my father," said Franklin. "It's going to be a slaughter, once he gets over the wall. The streets will run with blood."

"Bowser said the M—Sunbiters are in the harbor."

"Well, yeah. That would be the sensible thing for them to do," said Franklin. "Take the harbor."

"But that woman and her daughter, the ones who gave us the stew—"

Franklin looked uncomfortable and didn't say anything.

"Will they be all right?" said Chantel.

"Maybe," said Franklin.

"Maybe's not good enough!"

"Now you see why I hate the whole thing," said Franklin.

Chantel thought, frantically. If she could get Lightning to come out, if she could fly over the harbor and flame everybody—

Everybody would include the kind woman and her daughter.

"I'm going to the Hall of Patriarchs," said Chantel. "And I'm going to tell them they need to give in to your father's demands."

"You're wasting your time," said Franklin, hurrying

along beside her. "Men don't do what girls tell them to."

"I have to *try*," said Chantel. "But I guess you'd better go hide again."

She immediately realized she shouldn't have said it. She was afraid now that he would refuse to hide, and the patriarchs would find a new executioner and lop off his head. But Franklin said nothing, and by the time she reached the Hall of Patriarchs he was no longer beside her.

21

MISS ELLICOTT DOES A SPELL

Chantel made her way through the chilly gloom of the kings' tombs and into the clerk's well-lit office. After everything that had happened, she was rather surprised to see Mr. Less, once again sitting at his sharply slanted desk.

"Miss Chantel," he said. "What a surprise."

No one had ever called Chantel "miss" before. She took it in stride. "Good afternoon, Mr. Less," she said. "I've come to see the patriarchs. Are they in?"

"Those who remain," said the clerk. "Lord Rudolph we lost to the Marauders' arrows, along with Sir Botolph, and Sir Twang."

"Not to the dragon?" said Chantel.

"You will surely have heard, Miss Chantel, that there

was no dragon," said Mr. Less. "If you know something to the contrary, you may wish to keep that to yourself." He nodded at the door. "You know the way."

The remaining patriarchs were bruised and bandaged. Sir Wolfgang had a black eye, and his arm in a sling. Chantel was dismayed to see that he sat at the head of the table. Sir Wolfgang, unlike the late Lord Rudolph, couldn't hear girls.

And so he went on talking when she came into the room, until one of the other patriarchs—Sir Faraday, Chantel thought his name was—held up a hand to interrupt the flow of eloquence, and nodded at her.

The patriarchs all turned to look at her. She did not curtsey. She was neither shamefast nor biddable. She was not afraid of them. She had ridden a dragon.

"Good afternoon," she said. "I've come to ask—"

"Who's that?" said Sir Wolfgang.

"It's that girl," said Sir Faraday. "The one we were told was supposed to be something out of the ordinary."

"Looks ordinary enough to me," said Sir Wolfgang. "Doesn't she curtsey?"

"I've seen the boys marching in the city," said Chantel. "And I've seen the Marauders without the gates—Sunbiters, they're called. And they're in the harbor now, and who knows what's happening to the people there? You've *got* to give the Sunbiters what they're asking for. It's the only way to save the harbor and the city."

"Why's she alone?" said Sir Wolfgang. "Weren't there more children before? A yellow-haired girl, wasn't there? And some kind of boy?"

"Maybe the dragon got them," said Sir Faraday.

"There was no dragon," said Sir Wolfgang.

Several of the patriarchs chuckled, but wearily. They had not been having a nice time lately.

"There was a dragon," said Chantel. "I was riding it."

"Run along," said Sir Wolfgang. "We have no time for the pretty chirruping of little girls. This is men's business."

Chantel felt anger building up in her like magical strength. There were empty chairs at the table. Gathering the hem of her purple dragon-robe in one hand, she climbed onto the chair of a dead patriarch. Then she stepped up onto the table. The patriarchs exclaimed in surprise and dismay. She marched down the table and stopped in front of Sir Wolfgang.

"Listen to me," she said. "I'm speaking! Don't pretend you can't hear me!"

Sir Wolfgang looked up at her. "No decent young lady," he said, "stands on a table."

"The dragon is real," said Chantel. "I rode it. I flew out over the Sunbiters' camps. Karl the Bloody has thousands of men. If he gets into the city, the streets will run with blood."

"This is like something out of an old tale," muttered one of the patriarchs. "Girl in a dragon robe up on the table saying portentous stuff."

"I never heard that tale," said another patriarch.

Chantel turned her Look on them. "There are only two things to do," she said. "The first is to tell the Sunbiters that you'll give them what they want. Lower the port fees and the tolls."

"You know nothing of such things," said Sir Wolfgang. He'd finally heard her.

"The second," said Chantel, "is to have the sorceresses strengthen the walls. And I know where the sorceresses are."

"So do we," said Sir Wolfgang irritably.

"Lord Rudolph told us the Marauders have them," said Chantel. "But that was a lie, to control us. If you'll agree to lower the port fees and the tolls, I'll tell you where the sorceresses really are."

A silence greeted this. Chantel had no idea if it was a thoughtful silence or an angry silence.

There was no telling how the patriarchs might have responded to her demand if they'd had a chance to answer it.

Instead, a man's voice in the hall outside cried out "Way! Way! Make way for the king!"

And then the king and all the sorceresses burst into the room.

The patriarchs jumped to their feet. There was a lot of shouting and shoving, and the sorceresses were busy making signs. Chantel leapt down from the table; she had no desire to be caught in a cage again.

Amid the hubbub the king cried, "There she is! The girl! Seize her!"

Chantel fled.

She ran down the hall. Footsteps came pounding behind her. Whoever was chasing her was much faster than the patriarchs had been. She burst into the hall of tombs and dodged, careening from one tomb to another. She saw a flash of white as her pursuer jumped over a tomb—it was Prince George, the king's brother, in his spotless white uniform. She ducked and made for the door. He tackled her.

Chantel hit the floor hard, the breath knocked out of her. She rolled, kicking and punching furiously. Then she felt cold steel touch her neck.

"You'll serve your king," said the prince, "or die."

Chantel froze. The blade bit into her skin. Behind her, she could hear the sounds of battle in the patriarchs' council room. If only Franklin had come with her! He at least knew how to fight. If only she'd run down the steps to the catacombs . . . but no, the fiend was down there . . .

"The dragon," said Prince George. "What have you done with it? Where is it?"

The fiend . . . Chantel was supposed to be good at summoning, wasn't she? Queen Haywith had said so. . . .

A ringing smack on the side of her head made her see bright flashes of light. "Answer me, girl!"

"He's in his lair," Chantel gasped. "The dragon's in his lair." The fiend . . . Not Franklin, she probably couldn't summon a Sunbiter boy . . . but the fiend . . .

"Summon him!" the prince demanded.

"I can't summon a dragon!"

He hit her again. "The Ellicott woman said you could! Summon him now!"

The prince had his hands around her throat. He shook her. Her head banged against the stone floor. Summon . . . summon . . .

She clawed desperately at the prince's hands, and she struggled to remember the fiend—the catacombs—the smell like a flooded grave—

And then there was a sound like cloth brushing against stone. And then something breathing impossibly evenly, like a bellows with pneumonia.

When Prince George turned to face the fiend, Chantel rolled quickly away, scrambled to her feet, and charged for the door.

Franklin was running up the front steps.

"Why—" Chantel gasped as they fled. Her throat still hurt and her head ached. "Why did you come here?"

"I saw the king and the wise women headed this way and I thought I'd better check up on you," said Franklin, not out of breath at all as they ran through the streets.

"You didn't . . . feel summoned?"

"Summoned?" said Franklin. "No."

As they climbed the city, Chantel hurriedly told Franklin what had happened.

"Who was winning?" said Franklin.

"I don't know. The patriarchs will probably win; they've got the guards."

"Were there any guards *there*?"

"No," said Chantel. "But—"

"People side with kings," said Franklin. "The guards will go over to him once they see he's got the wise women."

Chantel didn't see that this made a whole lot of difference. "Either way, your father's going to—"

"But if the wise women win, they can do the Buttoning," said Franklin.

"What there is of it," said Chantel.

⁂

It took the girls from Miss Ellicott's School a long time to fall asleep. Chantel had to roar at them, almost like a dragon, to get them to settle down, and she wouldn't have minded being able to breathe fire as well. The dragon merely watched in amusement.

Chantel went to sleep on the dragon's purple couch,

near his tail, and woke with a start to find Lightning staring down at her.

She remembered everything that had happened the day
before. The city. The patriarchs. The king—and Miss Ellicott. Was the king in control of the city now?

"Is it dawn yet?" she asked.

"Soon," said the dragon.

There was still time.

She conjured a light-globe, got dressed, and made her
way alone through the dark cavern, up through the tunnels, and then down through the still-slumbering city of
Lightning Pass to Dimswitch.

It was a windy night—morning, rather. Chantel could
feel another storm brewing.

The steep straight stair that had been used for Franklin's execution was unguarded. Chantel did a self-abnegation
spell, climbed over a low iron gate, and scaled the stairs.
She stood on the wall-walk and looked out over the parapet.

The Sunbiters' catapults stood assembled and loaded
with heavy boulders. The siege engines, tall rolling towers
of wood that protected ladders for scaling the wall, had
been moved closer to Seven Buttons.

Black storm clouds loomed on the horizon.

If the king had won, then the sorceresses should be
arriving soon to do the Buttoning. Chantel turned and

looked down into the city. She heard footsteps crossing the cobbles.

Chantel felt some trepidation—she needed to talk to Miss Ellicott, to find out what had happened. But she did not want to be captured and handed over to the king.

"Good morning, Miss Ellicott," she said.

Miss Ellicott glanced at Chantel and nodded absently. The sorceress had probably not had time to go to the school yet, and discover her pupils were gone, Chantel thought.

A new sound began—a distant, rhythmic thumping. "What's that?" Chantel asked.

"A battering ram, most likely. The Marauders are at the gates," said Miss Ellicott.

Her eyes were on the lightening sky overhead.

Chantel followed her gaze and saw something circling in the sky. Lightning, the dragon, almost too far away to see.

Chantel sat down, and waited to see what Miss Ellicott would do.

"Chantle, don't dangle your feet like that," said Miss Ellicott. "It's not ladylike."

"I beg your pardon, Miss Ellicott," said Chantel, tucking her robe around her legs. "Could you please pronounce it shahn-TELL?"

"Have I pronounced it incorrectly?" said Miss Ellicott. "I beg your pardon."

"Thank you," said Chantel. "Um, did the king's brother . . . die?"

"I have not seen Prince George since the glorious battle of King's Hall," said Miss Ellicott.

And you probably won't, thought Chantel. I . . . I killed him. Or as good as. Oh dear. "King's Hall is the Hall of Patriarchs?"

"It is now," said Miss Ellicott. "You must learn, Chantel, to be on the winning side. A girl must obey. It behooves her to obey those who are winning."

The battering ram thumped steadily on. Chantel looked toward the city gate. In the growing light, she could make out the rocks and arrows raining down from the towers, onto the attackers below.

"Miss Ellicott, are you going to do the Buttoning now? It's dawn. And—"

"Just a moment, Chantel. I am telling you important things. Do not take advice from poor advisors. They will lead you astray. And do not fail to obey your king, or you will find yourself in a place that you do not like. You will find yourself there very soon indeed."

Chantel watched the dragon circling the city. Flickers of lightning rippled across the horizon. Along the wall, she saw guards pointing to the dragon and exclaiming.

Miss Ellicott's advice, Chantel thought, was much too small.

"Are there sorceresses at all of the buttons?" she asked.

"Of course," said Miss Ellicott. "The Six are positioned to do the spell."

"It's—It's not the real spell, is it, Miss Ellicott? The rhyme you hid in our heads said the real spell was gone."

Miss Ellicott looked all around to make sure no one was within earshot. "It is part of the real spell," she said, her voice so low Chantel had to strain to hear. "It brings comfort."

"If we found the long lost lore—"

"It is lost," said Miss Ellicott.

Chantel thought of the vast library far beneath their feet. "What if we made a new spell—"

"Making new spells is far too dangerous. You never know what they'll do. Now we must begin. And we would like your help."

"What kind of help?" said Chantel warily. She had no intention of winding up inside a cage again.

"If you come down here, I will show you," said Miss Ellicott.

"I think I would rather help from up here, thank you," said Chantel.

Miss Ellicott gave her a cold stone look. "I expected you to be more dutiful, Chantel."

"I—" Chantel began.

I think I am dutiful. I'm not sure what my duty is, but

I know it's not to the king. That would be too small. I think it's to the people, but that might be too small, too. She wanted to say these things, she wanted to *talk* about these things. But Miss Ellicott did not like questions. Only answers.

Questions are more important.

"If you're doing the spell now," said Chantel, "does that mean the patriarchs are . . ." She searched for the acceptable word. "Deceased?"

"Those who remain alive have sworn loyalty to the king," said Miss Ellicott. "Real loyalty this time, for which they will be properly rewarded. They have seen the advantages of being his men, not his masters."

"What about you?" said Chantel, curious.

"I'm afraid I don't understand the question."

"Is the king rewarding you? Or is he just rewarding the patriarchs?"

There was a rumble of thunder in the distance.

"Chantel, I find your questions impertinent. I did not raise you to ask questions."

"No, you didn't," said Chantel. "And I wish you had. But, um—" This was hard to say. "You took me in, and fed me, and had me taught to read and do spells, and . . . and I want you to know that—" she looked down at her feet, and then further down at Miss Ellicott. "That I'm, um, grateful for that, whatever happens now."

Miss Ellicott nodded. "That sentiment becomes you very well, Chantel. Now, your dragon can best be used in service to the king, so if you will summon him—"

"I beg your pardon." Chantel pulled in her legs and got to her feet. "He's not mine, and he's not to use."

A loud crack of thunder made her start. It was accompanied simultaneously by a jagged pink streak of lightning.

"Chantel!" Miss Ellicott sounded worried. "Come down from there before you're struck by lightning."

The dragon was circling lower now. In the distance, the battering ram had stopped.

"I . . . I think I'd better not," said Chantel. "But, if you don't mind, I'll watch you do the spell."

A sudden gust of cold wind blew deep black storm clouds toward the city from the west. In the east, dawn was just beginning to break. Bells rang; trumpets sounded, announcing the day. Thunder rumbled overhead, and lightning flashed and flickered in all parts of the city.

Miss Ellicott began doing the spell.

Chantel watched carefully. She recognized the sign that Miss Ellicott did as the one from the rhyme.

And Chantel tried, without really thinking about it, to summon what was missing from the spell. But she couldn't figure out what that was. Something—she had a sense of something to do with a circle—was that the wall itself? Whatever it was, she couldn't reach it.

She saw Miss Ellicott scatter dust; it must be from seven tombs. She listened carefully for the words that Miss Ellicott spoke, the words of Queen Haywith.

"Derval sabad ijee. Dwilmay kadapee pasmines choose maul," Miss Ellicott intoned.

And Miss Ellicott reached out and touched the wall.

That ought to have strengthened it.

That was not what happened.

22

Octopus Stew

Two lines near the end of the rhyme, Chantel remembered, were:

> Bring the peace that Haywith stole
> And touch the wall, and make it whole.

Miss Ellicott had just made the third sign with her bare feet. She placed her hand on Dimswitch.

Thunder, lightning, and the earth shook . . . no, the *wall* shook. There was a sound of rending and breaking, of rocks shifting. Chantel fell to her knees.

At last the shaking stopped.

And Seven Buttons was cracked, a crack that went right through the wall.

The battering ram? Chantel peered over the parapet.

No . . . There was no battering ram at Dimswitch. But some of the Sunbiters had heard the noise, and they were running toward the breach. It was only a couple inches wide, but they dug their fingers into it, and then their swords, and then men came with more tools, long iron bars that looked exactly right for prying a wall apart.

The Lightning Pass guards fired arrows down at the attackers. A hail of Sunbiter arrows came back, zinging over Seven Buttons.

Hunched behind the parapet, Chantel ran. "Lightning," she said aloud. "I need you *now*."

The storm overhead broke, and rain poured down, emptying the sky. The dragon came bursting through the downpour and landed, his claws screeching on the stone wall-walk. Chantel clambered onto his back. They took off into the storm.

Arrows rattled against the dragon's scales. Chantel felt one hiss past her leg. Flashes of lightning rippled all around them. Thunder rolled across the sky. The city below was invisible, just a grayed-out map of vague shapes, the wall an indistinct gray line.

"Lightning," Chantel called over the singing wind. "*Now* they are attacking the city and now I would breathe fire on them!"

And then she couldn't help adding, "Wouldn't I?"

Lightning dove sickeningly through the storm, leaving

Chantel's stomach behind. He breathed fire at the masses of Marauders working at the crack in the wall. The flames hissed in the driving rain, but the men cried out and fell away. Chantel couldn't see how badly hurt they were—or whether they were alive—but she couldn't afford to think much about that. She remembered what Franklin had said. *The streets will run with blood.*

Lightning spiraled away, came back, and breathed fire again. More Sunbiters came, but the rain had soaked their crossbow strings and they couldn't fire.

Chantel leaned against Lightning's neck and called, "The crack! Close the crack!"

"How?" croaked the dragon.

"Melt the stone!" said Chantel. "Please, I mean!"

The dragon breathed flame after flame onto the crack in Seven Buttons. Hissing and steaming in the rain, the stones glowed red hot and then white hot. Finally the stone fused, closing the crack.

"Now we have to look at the rest of the wall!" said Chantel. "There might be more cracks!"

There were. There were five more places where there were great cracks in the wall, and Chantel supposed that these, and Dimswitch, made up six of the seven buttons. Where was the seventh? she wondered, as Lightning heated and fused each of the cracks in turn.

Then the dragon wheeled out over the sea, and deposited

Chantel on the same rock island.

And left her. Chantel watched in dismay as he flew off, circling, plunging, diving—for fish, she guessed. Maybe all that fire-breathing had made him hungry. Meanwhile the storm raged, and everything Chantel had read about thunderstorms suggested that a rock in the middle of the ocean was a very, very bad place to be during one.

The rock was slippery. Chantel found cracks and crags to cling to, and she hung on. The wind whipped across the rock and tried to sweep her into the sea. Her sopping-wet robe clung to her skin. She chattered with cold.

At last the rain let up, and the sun flashed out from behind dark clouds. In the distance Chantel saw the dragon happily diving after a fish, and she momentarily hated him.

"Lightning, come back *now!*" she said.

She wished she'd thought of that before. The dragon, far away, halted in mid-gambol and came flapping back.

"Was hungry," he said by way of apology.

"Well, now I am too," said Chantel irritably. "And cold, and—yuck."

The dragon looked hurt as Chantel recoiled from the large dead octopus he dropped at her feet.

"I beg your pardon," said Chantel hurriedly. "Thank you. We'll take it home and, er, cook it or something, and I'm sure the girls will love it."

As they soared over the city, octopus and all, Chantel

saw that something strange was happening. People were climbing the streets—mobs of people, thousands of people—carrying their possessions on their backs. Babies were strapped atop bundles, and small children clung to skirts and cloaks. Everyone looked grim, terrified, and wet.

The sun reflected off a plane of water covering the lower city.

"What about the drains and culverts?" Chantel wondered aloud. It always rained hard in Lightning Pass—sometimes as hard as it had rained today—but the drainage system sent everything out to sea.

The dragon glided down into Bannister Square. People scrambled to get out of his way, yelling and stumbling, their bundles tumbling.

Chantel dismounted to pick up a fallen child. A woman came running to claim it.

"What's happened in the lower city?" Chantel asked.

The woman chuddered with fear. "Flood, Dragon Girl."

"Why don't they open the city gates and let the water out?" Chantel asked. "That would force back the attackers with the battering ram too."

"The city gates don't open," said a bearded man carrying what looked like part of a sawmill on his back.

"Of course they open," said Chantel. "I mean, I know they're usually closed, but if they didn't open, we wouldn't have—"

"Oh, I see now dragons fall from the sky and girls correct men," said the sawyer. "Excuse *me*. I should have realized the world had turned upside down."

And he stalked off with his sawmill bits. The woman with the child turned and fled.

"But why doesn't the water drain away?" Chantel asked the empty square.

Later, back in the cave, she asked the same question of Anna, as they worked together to invent octopus stew. This involved figuring out which parts of the octopus were to eat and which parts weren't, and lighting a fire with broken furniture and dried seaweed, and filling the cave with a steamy octopus-scented fug which Chantel was sure would hang around for days.

"The drains must not be working," said Anna, ladling up octopus stew for one of the smaller girls. "No really, you'll like it," she told the child. "Well, at least try it. Well, you can't be that hungry if you won't try it."

All of this was said in the same patient, calm tones. Chantel felt an urge to bop the whiny child with an octopus tentacle, but she overcame it. "All of the drains at once? And the city gates?"

"Do the city gates open inward?" said Anna.

"Only if the architects are stupid," said Franklin, wiping up octopus stew that one of the little girls had knocked over. "In a defensive wall, the gates open outward."

"So the walls cracked, the drains and culverts sealed up, and so did the gate," said Anna. "All of that happened when they did the spell."

"Maybe it was because they weren't doing the real Buttoning," said Chantel.

"It was because they did the Buttoning without you," said Anna.

"Without *me?*" Chantel was astonished. "They've always done it without me!"

"But you weren't a dragonbound sorceress before," said Anna.

"I'm not a sorceress at all!"

"But you are dragonbound," said Anna pedantically. "And according to the books, when there *is* a dragonbound sorceress, also called a Mage of the Dragon, no great working can be done unless she has a hand in it. The Buttoning must be a great working."

Chantel cautiously tasted a bit of octopus. It was just as she'd expected . . . rubbery. And salty and fishy and . . . rubbery. She disagreed with Anna. You could probably be quite hungry and not want to eat octopus.

I was helping the sorceresses, she thought. I was trying to summon that circle, whatever it is. I was probably helping wrong.

So the Buttoning had gone wrong because of Chantel. It was completely unfair. What was she supposed to do, anyway? "Can I fix it?"

"I don't know," said Anna.

"If the sorceresses did the spell again, and I helped them—"

"I'm not sure how you're supposed to help exactly," said Anna.

"Oh." Chantel imagined a blood sacrifice, with herself in the starring role.

"I kind of think dragonbound sorceresses don't 'help' so much as take control," said Anna.

The sorceresses had put Chantel in a cage. This did not suggest a willingness to let her take control.

"Well, at least we sealed the cracks in the walls," Chantel said.

"How?" said Anna.

"With fire," said Chantel. "Lightning breathed flames on the cracks in the wall, and fused the stone where the Sunbiters were trying to pry it apart, and—what?" she demanded of Franklin, who was staring at her.

"Fusing stone doesn't strengthen walls," he said. "It weakens them."

"How do you know?" said Chantel.

"Everyone knows it," said Franklin. "Parsifal the Peacemaker used magic fires to seal the walls of his fort, and the marauding Coriscanders were able to pick the wall apart in a matter of weeks using the jawbones of asses."

This was very depressing news.

"Chantel, I wanted to tell you . . . I've found a few

things." Anna led the way to a library table, with several books lying open on it. Silver hairpins and bits of velvet from the dragon's storeroom were stuck in them for bookmarks.

"This," said Anna, pointing to a page, "talks about Queen Haywith. She was one of the dragonbound sorceresses. In those days queens were usually sorceresses. All the kings and queens have always taken a vow to defend the city and its people. There are words to it here." She pointed to a book.

"So that's the vow she broke?" Chantel remembered how offended the queen had been at the mere suggestion.

"Some people might say so," said Anna. "In fact, *this* book says so." She tapped a page. "I think we have it at school. But this *other* book here says that what happened was that some of the people wanted to build a wall around the city—"

Chantel remembered her journey into the Ago. "There was no wall in her time."

"Right. And Queen Haywith refused to have one. She said a wall becomes a wall in the mind, and she wanted no walls for her people. So *this* book"—Anna reached for another one—"says she broke her vow by refusing to build the wall and then by refusing to abdicate in favor of her son."

"Then she left the city open to attack," said Franklin.

"She doesn't sound like a very good queen."

"She was an excellent queen!" said Chantel hotly, and then stood aside and looked at herself in surprise. When had she decided that?

"She said a wall wasn't necessary," said Anna. "She said there was no threat. She used to go out into the marshes—"

"Dressed like a man?" said Chantel.

"It doesn't say. But she had a house out in the marshes, just an ordinary house, and people would come and talk to her and stuff. People from anywhere."

"She had a dragon?" said Franklin.

"I saw him," said Chantel.

"The Swamp Lady," said Franklin. "I bet that's who she was. I didn't know she had a name, though."

"Everyone has a name," said Anna. "Who was the Swamp Lady?"

"A sorceress, you'd call her," said Franklin with a shrug. "Very powerful, but she never did any harm. Advised people and stuff."

"Well, she was dragonbound," said Anna, reaching for another book. "And dragonbound sorceresses are powerful. But they're bound. They can't do anything a dragon wouldn't do, and the dragon can't do anything they wouldn't do."

She and Franklin both looked at Chantel expectantly.

"I know," said Chantel.

They were still looking at her, so she added, "I'm not a sorceress."

"Not yet," said Anna. "But you got the dragon at the right time. You let him into your head, and he grew, and he learned from you, it says here, and you learned from him. And now that you're bound, that goes on happening."

"So have you found the real Buttoning spell yet?" said Chantel.

"No," said Anna.

"Well, I'm sure you'll—"

"No." Anna cast a despairing glance at the books spread out on the tables. "I've looked everywhere it could possibly be. Chantel, I don't think there *is* a Buttoning."

"But . . . but . . . the Sorceresses wouldn't . . ." Chantel trailed off.

"Sure they would. Makes them seem more important," said Franklin. "I wouldn't think you'd need a spell for a wall that thick. Well, I mean, if you hadn't—"

"I didn't know fire was going to weaken it!" Chantel turned back to Anna. "We're going to have to *make* a Buttoning."

"Yes," said Anna. "I know the sorceresses say never to try anything new but . . . do you ever get the feeling that what we were taught was maybe a little . . ."

"Too small?" said Chantel.

"Yes." Anna picked up a book and frowned at it. "I

think this one talks about how to make new spells. But it's all written in very old-fashioned flowery language."

Chantel reached for it. She wasn't afraid of old-fashioned flowery language. The book smelled ancient. Bits crumbled off the edges when she touched it.

"There are some other spells I found that look useful," said Anna. "There's one called Inversion, where you make your enemies see everything upside down."

That did sound useful.

"I wonder why I only found six cracks in the wall?" said Chantel.

"Because the gate is the seventh button," said Anna.

⬥⬥⬥

Chantel went back to the city the next day to see if there was anything she could do. She changed into her green school robe, because the purple one attracted too much attention. People were busy fixing iron bars to their doors and windows and preparing to be invaded. Panic reigned; it seemed the sorceresses had not had time to do a Contentedness spell.

The water was ten feet deep in the lower city. An unpleasant dirty-water smell drifted through the streets. It hadn't rained again yet; the floods would get deeper when it did.

Chantel could think of no spell to fix this problem.

Men in boats were hammering and prying at the sealed

289

city gates. They even tried to bore a hole in one of them, but their auger broke.

At least the Sunbiters with the battering ram had given up.

The sorceresses attempted the Buttoning several more times over the course of the next few days. Chantel could tell, because things got worse and worse. The ground trembled, and one of the towers of the castle collapsed, raining blocks of stone down on the city. Several entire houses in Donkeyfall Close sealed up, their doors and windows becoming solid stone, and men pounded vainly at the walls with sledgehammers. Finally the people inside were rescued by pulling apart the roofs.

The message was clear: the sorceresses could seal everything *but* Seven Buttons.

The attackers were at work on the walls with pickaxes and levers. The sentinels and boys of Lightning Pass rained arrows, rocks, and boiling water down on them. The Sunbiters responded with crossbow bolts and catapult missiles. There were many casualties, and Chantel couldn't find Bowser anywhere.

The sorceresses kept trying to do the spell. And more strange things happened.

Sinkholes opened at random places, dropping people suddenly twenty feet down. Then a thick hoar-frost formed over everything, and ice coated the trees and the potato plants and melon vines in the Green Terraces.

Meanwhile, Chantel and Anna had figured out that the book with the flowery language was a sort of chart for making spells. There were different signs, and magical ingredients, and times of day that worked for doing magic in certain places, and on certain objects. For example, any spell that had to do with stone required a thorn from a rose that had bloomed at the full moon. A spell related to water required hair from a mouse's tail.

"We need ingredients," said Anna.

"I'll get them from the school," said Chantel.

"I'll go with you," said Franklin.

"And see if you can find out what happened to Bowser," Anna called after them.

But they couldn't. They never could.

They knocked on the door of Miss Ellicott's School for Magical Maidens.

Miss Flivvers opened the door a crack, then threw it wide when she saw who it was. "Oh, Chantel! The most wonderful news!"

"What?" said Chantel warily, as she and Franklin came in and wiped their feet.

"Miss Ellicott was here! She's safe!"

Chantel clenched her teeth in exasperation. "Of course she's safe. She's in control of the city, Miss Flivvers."

"What a dreadful thing to suggest about a lady like Miss Ellicott!" Miss Flivvers said. "The *king* is in control."

And that, Chantel reflected, was probably more or less the truth. "What did—"

"Miss Ellicott was very concerned at finding the students missing," said Miss Flivvers.

"Because she wanted them for hostages. We talked about all this. . . ." A sudden thought struck Chantel. "Miss Flivvers, you didn't tell Miss Ellicott where they were, did you?"

Two pink spots appeared on Miss Flivvers's cheeks.

"Um, she might've figured it out for herself," said Franklin.

Miss Flivvers shot him a grateful glance.

Well, the damage was done, Chantel thought. No time to worry about it. The king might know the girls were in the dragon's lair, but the dragon was, after all, a dragon. Meanwhile Chantel and Franklin had to hurry in case Miss Ellicott came back.

"I need some things from Miss Ellicott's supply cupboard, please," said Chantel.

She had a list of ingredients in the pocket of the purple dragon robe. When she reached for it, the gold circlet from the dragon's storeroom fell out and rolled. Franklin caught it as it went wuppa-wuppa-wuppa on the floor.

He looked at it thoughtfully, then handed it to Chantel.

She stuck it back in her pocket and unfolded the list.

"Can you help me find everything please, Miss Flivvers? I'm in kind of a hurry."

"I hardly think—"

"Please, Miss Flivvers. It's an emergency. You don't need to think."

And to Chantel's relief Miss Flivvers didn't. She led the way upstairs, rattling her keys, and opened the supply cupboard. Chantel handed her the list, and together they gathered . . .

. . . dried powder made from the first red oak leaves of spring

. . . a small phial of dew gathered on May morning

. . . silver scales from a fish that had been caught by a left-handed fisherman with seven sons and seven daughters

. . . six hairs from the tail of a cat named Herman

. . . and a few other things that Anna thought could be turned into useful spells.

Chantel tucked these things into the pockets of her dragon robe. Then she and Franklin left hurriedly, in case Miss Ellicott came back.

༺✦༻

Anna and Chantel worked on inventing a new Buttoning, matching up magical elements. The new spell was going to have to be different from what the sorceresses did. For one thing, Chantel didn't think girls could be stationed at each of the six buttons to do the spell. Not in the middle of a war. It wasn't safe.

"I wish the king would just give in to the Sunbiters' demands," said Chantel.

"He can't," said Franklin. "You can't give in to force. Not if you want to rule."

He watched Chantel carefully as he said this.

"It's not giving in to force if you just offer what you should've offered in the first place," said Chantel.

Anna looked uncomfortable. "The king must know better than we do."

The streets will run with blood, Chantel thought. They didn't have much time to come up with a new spell. Maybe she should ask the sorceresses for help.

They wouldn't help, though. They wouldn't approve. They'd say making new spells was dangerous. And they'd put Chantel in a cage.

So Anna and Chantel worked into the night, matching ingredients to spell elements, trying out new signs, trying to invent spells of fortification.

They couldn't make anything stronger, though. They tried to make a spare octopus tentacle as strong as an iron cable. Instead, it merely shattered, sending tiny bits of octopus everywhere.

"I just don't think we can do it," said Chantel, as she crawled around under the table picking up the shards.

Anna seemed to be thinking the same thing. "You should at least go talk to the sorceresses. If you just explained to them . . . and didn't get close enough for them to put you in a cage . . . I mean, they have to help, it's their city too . . ."

Chantel sighed. "All right."

Lightning had been asleep all this time. Chantel supposed he was tired from having breathed so much fire.

⟨⟩

The next day, Chantel set out to talk to the sorceresses. She was on her way up to Bannister Square—in fact, she was almost at the top of the tunnel—when she saw a light floating toward her through the murk. A smell of soap and magic came with it.

The light resolved itself into a globe borne by Miss Ellicott herself.

"Miss Ellicott. I was just coming to see you." Chantel stood in such a way as to block the passage.

Miss Ellicott held up her light-globe and tried to see past Chantel. "Is this where you have secreted my kid-napped pupils?"

"I didn't kidnap them, Miss Ellicott. I brought them here to keep them safe." The sorceress tried to sidestep, and Chantel put out a hand to stop her. "Miss Ellicott, no. I beg your pardon, but no. There's a dragon down there, and he's dangerous."

"And this you call keeping them safe? The king intended to keep them safe. Do you think you know better than the king?"

From above, a grating sound echoed and rang down the tunnel.

"They're safer than anyone else in Lightning Pass right now," said Chantel.

Miss Ellicott peered over Chantel's shoulder. "To ascertain that, I require to see the dragon."

"I—I'm sorry, Miss Ellicott. You can see him if he comes out."

"I have every right to see him. He was mine once," said Miss Ellicott.

"The *snake* was your *familiar*. You had your chance, and you didn't take it." Chantel felt a twinge of sympathy. It must be awful to look back and feel you had made the wrong choice, when it was too late. "I'm the dragonbound sorceress now."

Miss Ellicott looked down her nose sharply at Chantel, and Chantel thought she was going to tell Chantel that she was not a sorceress, she was just a child. Miss Ellicott did not do this.

"You can't do the spell on Seven Buttons without me," said Chantel. "Any great working is going to require my help."

"Then you will help us," said Miss Ellicott.

"On one condition," said Chantel.

"You make conditions? The city could fall at any moment."

"That's *why* I'm making conditions," said Chantel. "What are the Sunbiters asking for, Miss Ellicott?"

"Some nonsense," said Miss Ellicott. "It's no affair of mine. Or yours, I might add."

"Are they still asking to have the tolls and port fees lowered? Because I think it would be better to give them that than to have them invade."

"You know nothing of statecraft," said Miss Ellicott.

"Of course not. I didn't learn it in school," Chantel said. "But that's still what I think. They're much stronger than us, and they can lay siege to the city and starve us. Would you please be so good as to tell the king that I'll help strengthen the wall when he agrees to give the Sunbiters what they want. And not before."

From up the tunnel came a metallic clang.

"I will ask you one last time, Chantel, to do your duty."

"I'm doing it, Miss Ellicott."

Miss Ellicott's mouth became a thin, hard line. "You will regret this, Chantel Goldenrod. You will come to wish you had done as the king asked. You will come to wish it very much indeed."

And she turned, her robes sweeping the rock floor, and marched away into the darkness.

Chantel wasn't entirely sure she'd done right.

She would talk it over with Anna. But first, having come so far, she might as well go into the city.

It was only a hundred yards or so, and a couple of turns in the passage, before Chantel reached a point where sunlight filtered in. The light threw a yellow beam onto the rough rock wall. The beam was crisscrossed into neat squares.

Her heart in her mouth, Chantel ran to the end of the passage.

A metal grid covered the mouth of the tunnel. The grid was padlocked on the outside. And it was so tightly guarded with wards that Chantel couldn't even touch the bars.

23

The Finer Points of Crystallized Rat Urine

Chantel screamed. She yelled. She hollered. She would have banged on the copper bars had the wards not been in the way. The people going about their business in Bannister Square seemed not to hear her.

Then she remembered the abnegation spell hiding the cave entrance. She undid the spell, and shouted some more.

A man stopped and looked at her.

"It's no good your yelling," he said. "You're imprisoned by order of the king. It says so right here."

He pointed to a wooden sign wired to the outside of the grate.

"I need to get out so I can save the city," said Chantel urgently. "Without me the sorceresses can't protect the city, and I've got to get the king to—"

"It says you'll say that," said the man, squinting at the sign. "It says there's treasonous magic in your voice, too, and that we're not to listen."

And he clapped his hands over his ears and hurried away.

⚜

They had run out of octopus. Finally. Lightning was still sleeping off the effects of having fused the walls and burned the siege engines. Breathing fire seemed to take a lot out of a dragon.

Once he woke up, Chantel figured he'd be able to melt the grate . . . Miss Ellicott couldn't have put an anti-dragon spell on it, could she?

If she had, they'd still be able to escape through the underwater passage.

Just in case that was necessary, Franklin taught the girls to swim.

And Holly, who had a knack for such things, put together a makeshift fishing rod and caught some peculiar-looking fish.

After they had eaten the fish, Chantel went to dispose of the guts. She carried the bundle far away from the dragon's lair because fish guts don't make very good company.

She wandered through passages, glad to be away from everyone for a bit, even if she did have her hands full of dripping fish entrails. She wasn't particularly worried about getting lost. Long ago, someone had marked out routes through the caves with colored stones at every turning. She was following a route marked by glittering green stones now.

She reached a deep shaft and dropped the guts down it, hearing them *sploosh* far below. She wiped her hands on a dripping stalactite, and then on the hem of her school robe. Then she sat down on a mushroom-shaped rock and thought.

Maybe Miss Ellicott was right, and she should do what the king said. After all, someone had to know best. That was what kings were for, wasn't it? To know best. Even if they did usually become king by killing the old king. That was just human nature, wasn't it? Didn't kings really know best? Well, granted, this particular king seemed rather foolhardy. But kings in general?

She got up and strolled further along the passage.

She came to an odd little cave, almost perfectly round and domed, with stone benches in a circle. There was a painting on the wall. Chantel held her light-globe close and studied it.

The picture showed men and women, standing in a circle. A few of them were wearing purple robes with dragons on them. Lying behind them, half-encircling them, was a dragon.

Chantel looked at it for a while, then she walked on. She'd seen several pictures of people standing in circles, and she didn't know what it meant. She wanted answers. She didn't understand a lot of things. If only someone—

She saw a person coming toward her through the gloom.

Her heart jumped. She had an awful feeling she'd just done a summoning by accident. That seemed to be a danger of being good at something. Queen Haywith had warned her that if she summoned her a third time, there would be a price to pay.

The person coming toward Chantel wore a long red robe. And a circlet of gold around his head . . . a crown, Chantel realized.

"Who are you?" he asked. "And why don't you curtsey?"

Chantel did a quick curtsey. Not a court curtsey, because there wasn't room. "I'm Chantel. Who are you?"

"People don't ask me who I am. I am the king, of course."

"Which one, please, Your Majesty?" asked Chantel politely.

The king blinked. "Oh, so it's that way, is it? Is this a summoning? Are you a sorceress? I am King Beaufort."

"King Beaufort the Basically Benign?" said Chantel.

"Is that what they call me?" The king smiled. "This must be a summoning, then. Certainly nobody would dare call me such a thing while I am still alive. How long have I been dead?"

Why did people always ask that? "About three hundred years, I think," said Chantel.

The king sighed. "Well, it comes to us all, I suppose. How did I . . . never mind. What do you want to ask me, sorceress?"

Chantel thought fast. She hadn't been aware of wanting to ask him anything. "Um, well, it's like this. We're underground—"

"Yes, I can see that. We're between the subterranean royal chambers and the draconic lair."

"I've just been trapped here by the sorceresses—"

"But you are yourself a sorceress," said the king, surprised.

"I beg your pardon, no. I'm just training to be one," said Chantel. "But the sorceresses have locked me underground—"

"How can they possibly have done that?" said the king.

"They sealed the cave in Bannister Square."

"And the dragon is party to your imprisonment?" said King Beaufort.

"He's asleep," said Chantel. "When he wakes up, I'll ask him to—"

"You speak to the dragon?" said the king. "You're a dragonbound sorceress?"

"I guess so," said Chantel.

"Hm." The king frowned. "I'm not sure whether I ought to help you or not. *Who* has imprisoned you?"

"The—" Chantel stopped herself from saying the king had done it. Kings probably stuck together. "The sorceress Miss Ellicott."

"She ought to obey you, as you're the dragonbound sorceress," said the king. "Isn't that how you girls organize things? I suppose you're rather young, though. Well, if she's used copper smelted under the full moon, the dragon's flames may rebound into the tunnel and that would be disastrous."

"Oh," said Chantel. "Then—"

"But there is still egress through the castle," said King Beaufort. "Or the underwater tunnel, if it comes to that."

"The castle?" said Chantel.

"Of course. The green stone trail goes to the castle," said the king. "As for the sorceresses, they shouldn't be messing about sealing caves. They should be guarding the seven gates."

"Seven gates of what?" said Chantel.

"Of the city," said the king, giving her an odd look. "Are we not beneath the great walled city of Lightning Pass?"

"Yes," said Chantel. "But there's only one—"

"The sorceresses," said the king, "are the keepers of

the seven gates. But they are too trusting. They allow too many people in. They lack discernment. They would do better to be guided by wise men." He looked up suddenly. "I hear something. You'd better go. It would be terribly unlucky if my courtiers were to waken me during a summoning."

Chantel curtseyed, and watched the king leave.

Then she followed the way he had gone.

She passed through marvelous caverns, great halls bedecked with glistening stalactites and columns. Human hands had been at work here, fashioning seats hidden away in alcoves, and walks beside dark streams, and a long, curved bench that Chantel was sure must be intended for a dragon to recline on.

A green stone marked the path beside an arch that led to a steep tunnel hewn from the rock. The passage was too neat and precise to be natural. Yes, and it had steps in it, here and there.

And it ended abruptly, blocked by a pile of rubble that went all the way to the ceiling.

It must have caved in at some point in the last three hundred years.

Chantel picked up a slab of fallen rock and, with considerable effort and pinched fingers, moved it. There was an ominous rumbling, and several other slabs shifted and slid toward her. She jumped back. The passage had collapsed before and could collapse again. She hurried back down the human-made passageway.

⋙⋘

Chantel loved swimming. It was almost like flying. But she didn't much care for being underwater.

Nonetheless, all the girls and Franklin practiced diving deep, and staying under as long as they could. Chantel disliked the feel of the water pressing in on her, and being so far down frightened her.

But she was desperate to find out what was happening in the city. And so she swam deeper and deeper, searching for the entrance to the underwater tunnel.

She groped in the darkness. Her ears rang and she saw deep red flashes at the corners of her eyes. And something moved toward her . . .

"Are you summoning me for a third time, sorceress?" Queen Haywith's voice rippled through the water.

"No!" said Chantel, her voice coming out in bubbles. "I mean, no, thank you. Not yet. Go away, please, and when—if I need you, come again. Thank you."

She was out of air. She fought her way to the surface.

She hadn't found the tunnel, and the thought of being trapped in it terrified her. She was going to have to wait for Lightning to wake up.

⋙⋘

Chantel had never seen Anna so excited about anything as she was about inventing the new Buttoning. The other girls caught the excitement from her, and they worked for hours on end, practicing new signs and new combinations of magical ingredients.

There would be no drawing signs on the cobbles with their feet. The cobbles were deep underwater.

Chantel told the others how she'd felt the interconnectedness of the switches, and the whole wall. If the girls worked all the spells from a rooftop near Dimswitch, and if Chantel herself touched the wall, it might be enough.

When Chantel wasn't working on the spell, she taught Franklin to read. He was quite disagreeable about it at first, which Chantel supposed she could understand. After all, even the smallest girls could read. It must be embarrassing.

And they explored the caves. Anna sent the younger girls to look for a magical ingredient she said was called amberat, which she insisted could be found sticking into crooked crannies in the upper regions of the cave.

"It's crystallized pack rat urine," Anna explained.

The girls howled in gleeful disgust and went running off in search of it.

"Does it really exist?" Chantel asked skeptically. Anna had gotten good at coming up with distractions to keep the girls from running amok.

"Oh yes," said Anna. "Could you go after them and make sure they don't fall into anything?"

Chantel went, but slowly. Most of the things to fall into—shafts and potholes and the like—were in the lower, more distant regions of the cave, the ones that hadn't been worked on by humans.

She wandered off along the green-stone path to think. Weirdly, she didn't see the round chamber with the painting of the robed men and women. It seemed to have disappeared. She went up through the royal chambers to the rubble that blocked the passage. She looked at it.

What was going on up above? Had the city fallen? Were the streets even now running with blood?

There was no way to know. There was nothing she could do.

She went to help the little girls gather amberat.

The spell still had to be done at dawn, Anna insisted. The rising sun strengthened spells of opening and closing.

⚜

At last the dragon woke. Chantel told him about the collapsed passage up to the castle.

"We were wondering if maybe you could help us dig it out," said Chantel. "If you please."

The dragon gave a huge yawn, showing a flame-lit throat which could have swallowed Chantel whole. "Help?" he asked, sounding amused.

And of course it wasn't *help*. Lightning did all the work, and the girls and Franklin kept well back as he flung rocks.

Chantel hoped it wasn't too late to save the city.

They packed up all their magical equipment and

ingredients. And they followed the end of Lightning's tail as he snaked his way up through passages that began to look more and more like a part of the city of Lightning Pass, until finally they came out in the castle cellars, deep inside Castle Rock.

The castle cellars were very ancient, and had several layers, starting with sub-sub-sub-basements. The children passed through dungeons where long-forgotten skeletons were manacled to the wall, and Chantel was uncomfortably reminded of fiends. They passed through an armory, stripped bare of everything except broken swords, leather armor that came to pieces in their hands, and a battle-ax with only half a head.

On the next level up there were storerooms . . . these were better stocked. There were barrels of wine and ale, and of flour, and even sugar. There were jugs of honey and bins of potatoes and vegetables. All the things, in fact, that you couldn't get anymore in the markets of Lightning Pass.

Following the dragon, Chantel and the others climbed the last steep stone staircase out of the basements. They emerged into a tiled hallway. Everything was quiet. Either the city was still unconquered, or . . . Chantel clenched her fists.

There was the painting of Queen Haywith, inexplicably red-haired, being driven from the city by dogs.

They moved as quietly as they could along the deserted

corridor. Nonetheless, the dragon's claws and scales rattled against the tiles, and their own feet echoed loudly in the night stillness. Chantel kept expecting someone to cry "Halt!"

Where was everyone?

They reached the front door of the castle. The great iron hinges creaked horribly. Outside, the moon was full and the night was cold. Chantel guessed it might be halfway between midnight and dawn.

Lightning stepped out onto Castle Peak. And before Chantel could say anything to stop him, he took flight. Chantel watched him soar away over the city.

Meanwhile, the king's mother sat on a small stool, knitting in the cold moonlight.

24

In Which Just One Thing Goes Very Badly Wrong

Lady Moonlorn looked up sharply. "So! It's you again! And how did you get into the castle, eh?"

"We came in by the back way," said Chantel, curtsey-ing briefly.

She looked down over the city. There were lights here and there in the higher neighborhoods. Down in the lower city, there were many more lights. Some of them were moving. She thought she could see torches reflecting off the floodwaters. A battle? No, it was too quiet for that. Men preparing for battle?

"There is no back way." Lady Moonlorn reached the end of a row, and set her knitting aside. "Did you just see a dragon? It is not real, you know. It is a symbol of the city's power, which is to say, my son's power."

Lightning was coasting over Seven Buttons. Chantel could feel a connection to him in her mind.

"There are a great many of you," said Lady Moonlorn. "The king wishes to have you under his protection. You will place yourselves in my care."

"What's going on down there?" Chantel asked.

"My son is handling matters," said Lady Moonlorn repressively.

"It looks like they're massing to defend the wall near Dimswitch," Franklin muttered, too low for the king's mother to hear. "Karl the Bloody's forces must be attacking there."

Chantel and Anna looked at each other. They'd intended to take the smallest girls, those too young to help with the spell, down into the city with them. This now struck Chantel as too dangerous. But leaving them with the king's mother, as hostages, was out of the question.

"Couldn't you stay here with them, Franklin?" Anna asked.

"No," said Franklin firmly. "I have to—" He looked down at the ground. "I have to do something."

"It'll have to be Miss Flivvers, then," said Chantel. "Can you just wait with them till I get her please? Then we'll go to the battle."

Franklin assented, grumbling.

"What do you think you're talking about?" Lady Moonlorn demanded. "Battle? You? My son is in charge of defending the city. Do you think my son is a coward?"

Chantel thought about this. "I'm not sure."

The old woman scowled. "It was a rhetorical question, girl. You'll stay here. My son will deal with you when he returns."

"Where is he?" said Chantel.

"That's not your concern. Nonetheless, I shall tell you, lest you doubt his courage. He is in the Hall of Patriarchs, renamed the Hall of Kings, and he is commanding the forces that defend the city."

Chantel looked out over the city. Torchlight broke the darkness here and there, especially in the lower city. Lights reflected off the floodwaters, which seemed to cover much more of the city than before. And outside the walls, she could see the glow from the Marauders' watchfires.

"It's strange the people haven't come to the castle," said Franklin, beside her.

"Why would they?" said Chantel.

"For safety," said Franklin. "It's the whole point of castles."

"I wonder if they've had a Contentedness spell put on them," said Anna.

Chantel watched Lightning's distant shape, like a shadow sliding across the ground.

"Come back, Lightning," she said softly.

And the dragon turned slowly and gracefully, and rode the wind back up to the Castle Peak.

〈❦〉

Lightning and Chantel delivered the girls who were going to do the spell to a flat rooftop near Dimswitch. Franklin stayed at the castle minding the little girls, with a very bad attitude and instructions to head back down to the dragon's lair at the first sign of trouble.

It was still more than an hour before dawn when Chantel banged on the roof door of Miss Ellicott's School for Magical Maidens.

She had to bang a long time before she heard footsteps on the ladder and a tremulous voice on the other side quavered "Go away!"

"Miss Flivvers, it's me."

There was a long pause. Then came the brassy rattle of bolts being shot back, and the door creaked open.

"Oh, it really *is* you," said Miss Flivvers. She peered out, saw Lightning, and nearly fell down the ladder.

"It's all right. It's only Japheth," Chantel lied.

Miss Flivvers stared at the dragon. "Where are the girls?"

"The littlest ones are up at the castle," said Chantel hurriedly. "The king's not there—"

"He's down overseeing the defense of the city, of course," said Miss Flivvers. "They say the Marauders have

314

nearly breached the crack at Dimswitch. It could fall at any moment." She seemed to recollect herself, and added, "But our king is doing everything for the best."

Yes, definitely a Contentedness spell. Chantel could feel wisps of it in the air.

Miss Flivvers was still staring at the dragon. "The littlest ones are at the castle . . . Where are the others?"

"They're safe," said Chantel. If you could call standing on a rooftop in the midst of a flood, just one damaged wall away from masses of invaders, safe. "Can you get on the dragon please, Miss Flivvers? I'm in a hurry."

Miss Flivvers, who was afraid of mice and cockroaches and almost anything with more than two legs, went on staring.

"You'll be safer up at the castle," Chantel said. "They— well, the invaders will get there last, anyway."

That seemed to convince Miss Flivvers. She allowed Chantel to help her onto the dragon's back, and they flew up to Castle Peak.

Chantel hurriedly whispered to the little girls that if things looked bad, if the Sunbiters got through Seven Buttons, they were to go to the dragon's lair at once. If Miss Flivvers wouldn't go, they should go without her.

And she climbed back on the dragon, and Franklin climbed up behind her, and they took off into the early morning twilight.

A stench rose from the flood—of dirty water, and rot, and dead things. Chantel tried to breathe through her mouth.

The scene in the lower city was chaotic.

The water had climbed to the top of Seven Buttons. Chantel was glad the girls could all swim now, although the water was so foul and dark, and so crammed with boats and rafts manned by soldiers and guardsmen, that falling in could still be disastrous.

They went to the roof where the girls, hidden by an abnegation, were getting ready to do magic. The girls were calm and serious. They used light-globes as they sorted their ingredients, practiced the new signs one last time . . .

"Chantel, it might still work if you stayed here," said Anna.

"No, I'm going to the wall. There's more chance of it working if I'm touching Dimswitch."

Anna nodded. It was true.

"If it all goes wrong," said Chantel, "head for the castle if you can. Don't wait for me. I'll . . . I'll follow."

"It won't go wrong," said Anna. She clenched her jaw. "It . . . " She swallowed, and hugged Chantel. "Just remember you're a Mage of the Dragon."

Chantel nodded. She turned to Franklin. "You should stay here and . . ."

"No," said Franklin. "If my father gets through . . . Well, anyway, I'm coming with you. There's . . . something I need to do."

Lightning was waiting patiently, treading water beside the rooftop, sending out waves.

They climbed on his back and he dragon-paddled through the lapping waters. All around them bobbed boats and rafts, full of boy-soldiers and sentinels silhouetted black against the sky. Chantel could see them pointing and muttering. They weren't sure if Lightning was a good omen or a bad one.

"Hurry, Lightning, please," Chantel urged. "We're supposed to do the spell at dawn."

A boat cut across their path. It was full of soldiers. Lightning started to swim around it.

"Halt!" called the sentinel standing in the bow.

Lightning swam on. Nobody tells dragons to halt.

"Chantel! Wait!" cried a voice from the boat.

Chantel's heart leapt. "Wait, Lightning! It's Bowser!"

The dragon stopped, with something of a shrug, and trod water.

Bowser stood up, making the boat rock. "Chantel, listen! The king wants—"

"His Majesty requires," said a sentinel, casting a nervous glance at Lightning, "that the girl Chantel and the boy Franklin put themselves at his disposal immediately."

"Bowser!" Chantel called. "I've been looking for you everywhere!"

Bowser goggled at the dragon. He blinked. Then he remembered Chantel. "The king's been keeping me close.

To get *you* to come to him." There was a note of warning in his voice.

"But he had me locked up!" said Chantel.

"He must've known you'd get out. Everyone knew. There's been talk."

"Even with the Contentedness spell?"

Bowser frowned. "Is that what it is? I knew there was something weird. Anyway, people have been asking questions, about the dragon and—"

Bowser trailed off as one of the guards gave him an angry shake.

"Well, the king shouldn't worry," said Chantel. "I'm going to do the Buttoning. That's what he wants. And I have to do it *right now*, because—"

"It's not all he wants," said Bowser.

"Oh goodness no," said another voice from the boat. "No more spells on the wall, please. You'd better talk to the king."

Chantel recognized Mr. Less, sitting among the guards. She could make out his curlicue mustache in the growing light.

He nodded a greeting. "Miss Flivvers is well, I hope?"

"About as usual," said Chantel.

"Such a brave woman," said Mr. Less, without apparent sarcasm.

"If we don't do the spell now," said Chantel, "the wall

is going to collapse from the weight of all this water. It's already been weakened, and—"

A guard interrupted. "You had better not do a spell without the permission of the king."

"He already forbade the sorceresses to try it again," said Bowser. "Because they've done so much damage already. And it kept raining and the floods kept rising. He's got some of them trying to open the city gates now."

"They can't do that! If they open the gates, all the water will rush out and people in the harbor will drown!" Chantel thought of the kind woman and her daughter.

"Perhaps you'd care to come and tell him that yourself?" said the clerk.

The sky was growing lighter still. The sun would rise very soon.

"No. I'm going to do the spell. It didn't work before because—"

A huge stone, flung by the Sunbiters' catapult, came sailing overhead. It crashed down into the water, causing an enormous wave. The boats and rafts pitched and rolled. Some capsized; Chantel heard the cries of people tumbling into the water.

"It didn't work because I wasn't helping!" Chantel shouted. There was no time for maidenly modesty. "I have to help with any great working because I'm the dragon-bound sorceress now."

"How very interesting. When did—"

"Mr. Less, there's no time!" said Chantel. "Excuse me, but I have to go *now!*"

There was a rasp as several sentinels drew their swords.

"No!" said Bowser.

The dragon arched his neck, and Chantel could feel fire rumbling inside him.

"No!" Chantel told him. "I would *not!* Not Bowser!"

"Where is the king?" Franklin called suddenly.

"His Majesty is in the upper tower of the Hall. His Majesty must be kept safe," said Mr. Less in neutral tones.

"With some of the sorceresses to protect him," said Bowser bitterly.

"I think you'll find," said Mr. Less, "that he is protect-ing the sorceresses. Yes, I'm almost certain that's the case."

"Lightning, go on, please," Chantel murmured. "It's almost dawn."

And the dragon swam on. Chantel looked back to see the boat bobbing dangerously in their wake.

<hr />

The top of the wall, behind the parapet, was thronged with soldiers, both men and boys. There were a few sorceresses casting small spells—they had probably been forbidden to use bigger ones, Chantel supposed.

Chantel did an abnegation spell on herself, and turned quickly to do one on Franklin. She was surprised to see that he had a crossbow in his hand. It occurred to her suddenly that he was a Sunbiter, inside Lightning Pass, and armed.

Then again, she told herself, he was Franklin. He was on her side . . . right?

"Didn't they take that from you?"

"I hid it at the school."

They climbed off the dragon. Soldiers stared at Lightning. People jostled past. The water splashed at their feet, cold waves that lapped over the wall-walk and wet their shoes.

Franklin lowered his crossbow and, rather to Chantel's surprise, took her hand. "Listen, um," he said.

There's not time for this, Chantel thought. She could see the crack in Dimswitch. Water was seeping through it. The wall was weakening. It was tired. She could hear the excited voices of the Sunbiters below. It was nearly dawn.

But Franklin was still hanging on to her hand. "If things turn out . . . well, I mean . . . that is, if anything happens that, um, isn't exactly what you're expecting . . . just remember what you have in your pocket, okay?"

"I have a lot of things in my pocket," said Chantel.

She squeezed his hand, let it go, and turned her attention to Dimswitch.

The sorceresses were levitating rocks and letting them fall on the enemy. Paving stones, rubble from broken buildings, even gravestones. The soldiers were raining down arrows and boiling water. Through a crenel in the parapet she could see ranks of Sunbiters standing, just out of range, with crossbows aimed. They'd built new siege engines, too.

A ray of the rising sun caught the red-horned helmet of Karl the Bloody.

Chantel couldn't see the men who were scraping and hammering and prying at the wall. But she could hear them, the sound of iron screeching against stone. She sensed the weight of water pushing at Seven Buttons. The wall groaned. It was battered and ancient and almost ready to give up.

Well, she was here to strengthen it. She raised a light-globe and waved it to Anna, on the rooftop, the signal that it was time to begin.

Across the water, Chantel could just make out the figures of the other girls starting the new spell.

No bells or trumpets sounded in the beseiged city now to announce the dawn. Instead, bleary-eyed soldiers did battle.

Chantel kicked off her shoes. She cast down powdered snake oil leaves washed with the mist of May morning. She drew the seventh and fourteenth signs with her feet. She drew three new signs the girls had invented. Then she spoke the words that she'd heard Miss Ellicott use.

"Derval sabad ijee. Dwilmay kadapee pasmines choose maul."

And she touched the wall to make it whole.

Nothing happened. The wall felt just as weary and hopeless as before. Down below, iron scraped relentlessly at stone.

Well, they'd known when they made their new spell that those old words might not work. They'd made a list of things that Queen Haywith had said.

Chantel tried the queen's vow. "'By the power of the dragon, I swear to protect the city of Lightning Pass and its people from any force, within or without, that may harm it.'"

Still the wall felt exhausted.

Chantel went through the whole list of words of Queen Haywith that they'd gleaned from different books. None of them seemed to be the right ones.

So maybe the sorceresses were right when they said you couldn't make new spells. Chantel slumped in despair.

Wait. She didn't need words from books. She'd actually spoken to Haywith herself.

She tried to think of some words that she knew Haywith had really spoken. But amid the crowding guards, and the screech of the Marauders' tools on the stones, and the lapping of the water behind her, it was hard to think.

Only one thing the queen kept saying came to her mind.

"'Too small!'" said Chantel.

And Queen Haywith was standing beside her. "Do you summon me now, for a third time?"

"Yes," said Chantel.

"Are you certain?" said the queen.

"Yes," said Chantel. "The situation is desperate."

"And do you trust me?"

"Yes."

"Very well," said the queen. "What comes next in the spell?"

"I already touched the wall," said Chantel. "That was supposed to make it whole."

"Are you sure?" said the queen.

"Well, no," said Chantel. "It was in the rhyme that Miss Ellicott hid in our heads. But the old spell wasn't complete. We've made a new one actually."

"Things tend to get garbled over the centuries anyway," said Queen Haywith.

A volley of arrows came thwipping over the wall. Chantel ducked, and heard cries and splashes all around her.

"There is an ancient belief," said the queen, "that wholeness comes from brokenness."

"Well, we *have* brokenness. The wall is cracked. See?" Chantel pointed, still crouching. "Right here. It was cracked after the sorceresses tried to do the spell. And the Marauders are about to break through!"

"Hm." The queen touched the wall, right where the crack was fused.

Chantel reached out and touched the wall in the same place, her hand beside Queen Haywith's.

And there was a mighty rumbling, and the wall beneath them collapsed.

25

The Circle

Rocks cascaded down. Water crashed out of the city in an unstoppable torrent. Soldiers fell from the wall, screaming, and vanished in the deluge. Chantel fell, too, and was dragged down into the maelstrom. This was chaos. The water rushed, and things rushed with it. Some of the things were heavy and hurt to be crunched against—rocks and timber. Other things were alive . . . or had been very recently. Chantel tumbled and bumped and bashed along, not knowing if she was right side up or upside down. She kept colliding with things. More and more of her was pain.

Then she hit something heavy and reptilian.

"Take hold of the dragon, Chantel," said Queen Haywith. "If you want to live."

"Of course I want to live," said Chantel, but she wasn't

saying it with her mouth, and she wasn't entirely sure she was still alive. The queen pulled Chantel up onto Lightning's back.

Things were still slamming into them, and the flood dragged them along, and Chantel wanted to live. And so she . . . did something. She was never sure afterward quite what.

And then they were floating in a quiet, green place, Lightning, Chantel, and the queen. Nothing banged into them. Breathing didn't seem to be a problem anymore.

"Am I dead now?" said Chantel.

"Wrong question," said the queen.

"Well, here's another one!" said Chantel, furious. She swung around so violently to face the queen that she fell right off the dragon.

This didn't seem to matter. She floated easily in the green glow. That didn't make her any less angry.

"Why didn't you tell me this would be the price of the third summoning?"

"I didn't know," said the queen with infuriating calm. "It—"

"You tricked me! I summoned you to help! Not to destroy the wall! I know you don't like the wall, but that was just *sneaky!*"

The queen frowned, and stepped off the dragon. "I will ignore your insulting manner, Chantel, on the grounds that you are upset by recent events." She sat down on the greenness and floated, with one knee up, and an arm resting on it. "The fact is, Chantel, that you did not want the wall either."

"I did too!" Chantel stood bolt upright on nothing, which seemed to be an easy thing to do here, and clenched her fists. "Why else would we have gone to all the trouble to make those spells?"

"You wanted to protect your people," said the queen, floating imperturbably past Chantel and then circling her as if caught in the eddy of a green stream. "But you thought the best way to do that was to take the wall down."

"How do you know what I thought!"

"I don't. Tell me."

Chantel looked away. Lightning had drifted on and was lying belly up, kicking his legs idly.

"I wanted the patriarchs and the king to give the Sunbiters what they asked for," Chantel said. "And I wanted to see the Roughlands again. And for other people to see them. And maybe I did think that I'd like to go to High Roundpot and the Stormy Isles some day. But that doesn't mean."

She let it go at that. They floated on, through an infinite gentle green glow. It was as endless as the sky.

"This much water can't have come out through Dimswitch," said Chantel. "And anyway it wouldn't be so clean, or so—"

"You seem to have summoned a brief interlude from

lost time," said the queen. "Very nicely done."

"Are the girls all right?" said Chantel. "And those men on the wall, and the sorceresses, and—"

"It's very likely that there's going to be a certain amount of not being all right," said Queen Haywith. "I'm sorry."

The haggard faces of all the people on the wall seemed to float in Chantel's mind. "It's *my* fault, then."

And Franklin . . . where had Franklin been?

"The situation existed," said the queen. "You were among those who chose to act. There is no time for the luxury of guilt. Things are going to happen very quickly now, and it may be possible for you to forestall complete disaster."

"Forestall it?" said Chantel. "It's already—"

"Are you prepared to act?"

"I already did, and look what happened!"

The queen repeated her question.

"I—I guess so," said Chantel. "But what do I have to do?"

"You will know that only when the moment arrives," said the queen. "As we all do. However, if you are willing to act, you may be able to summon someone to help you. Some*ones*, I should say."

"Who—"

"They have been watching you for some time," said the queen. "And they are called the Circle of the Mages of the Dragon. Is that enough? It may be all I'm permitted to say.

I'm not in it yet, you see. I won't be until I die."

"Oh, great," said Chantel. "What?"

"Can you see the way to summon them? It may be a sort of fold or a tucked corner of reality."

Chantel looked at the gentle green all around. There were no folds or tucks. "Can't you just tell me?"

"No," said Queen Haywith. "Because I cannot see it. Summoning is your talent, not mine. The important thing is that you have made up your mind to act. Remember not to think too small, because the time to come will call for large thinking."

"Will you stay with me?" said Chantel.

"No," said the queen. "Trust yourself."

And not particularly suddenly, but quite definitely, Chantel was alone. She couldn't see Lightning anymore either.

Owl's bowels! Tucks in reality, indeed! And meanwhile who knew what was going on in the city? All that water . . . all those people . . . no matter what Chantel did now, there was no way to stop that deadly rush of water.

She looked up, and saw that there was after all a little snag in the upper corner of the green silence, like a folded-over edge of Now.

She reached for it with her mind, and tugged.

And now?

      And now the girl approaches.

Oh?

        So soon?

           Did one of us help her?

I very much suspect that one of us

                  did.

      Is there a problem with that?

There should be no help.

      If there is no help, then what is our
purpose?

      Our purpose is simply to be.

        I very much doubt that that is
        anybody's purpose.

Never mind that. The girl, Chantel,
approaches. What is our plan?

    A plan. We ought to have   had   a plan.

    We ought to have

           discussed this.

It is too late.

          She is here.

Chantel found herself walking through the catacombs, with skulls staring down at her.

There was a blast of cold air, and a smell like a flooded grave, and the fiend appeared before her, green and glowing. She didn't back away. She didn't expect it to attack, and it didn't. It glided ahead of her, leading the way.

Soon they reached the round chamber in the caves beneath the city, the one with a painting on the wall. She knew the chamber was not actually *in* the catacombs, but then, she wasn't sure she was, either. Was she in the space between this world and the next? The place where the restless dead roamed?

The fiend vanished.

The chamber was full of people. They filled the circle of benches. And Chantel was standing in the middle, with all of them staring at her. She turned around and around, looking them over.

"So," said one of them. "This is the girl Chantel."

"She wears the dragon robe already." This was said with a sniff, by a hawk-nosed woman who, Chantel saw, was also wearing a dragon robe. About a third of the people were.

And most of them were elderly. Because, Chantel realized with a chill that went all the way down to her feet, all of them were dead. Queen Haywith had said so.

"Are you all mages of the dragon?" she asked.

"We ask the questions," said a man with an enormous cloud of hair. He wore red robes.

"We have been watching you for some time," said another man.

"You can't be a mage," said Chantel. "Men can't do magic."

"They could in the past." It was a light-skinned girl who spoke, one not much older than Chantel. Chantel realized with a start that the girl's purple robe was the one Chantel herself was wearing. There was a slight burn mark on the hem, and a hanging thread on the embroidered dragon's right front claw. Chantel looked down at the exact same burn mark and thread on her own robe.

This was deeply weird.

"Things in your time have become very unbalanced. That's why the men have lost their magic," the girl said.

The man in the red robe frowned at her. "We don't *know* that to be the case. It is merely a theory we have discussed."

"This is beside the point," the hawk-nosed woman interjected. "We have the girl before us. What do we think? Shall we evaluate her?" Without waiting for an answer, she went on. "She doubts what she is told. That is often wise, but just as often a waste of time."

"She has courage. But she is afraid of making choices. And of being wrong."

"I never said that!" said Chantel.

"She is loyal. But confused in her loyalties."

"I am not!" said Chantel. "Confused."

"She is often painfully polite, but she has learned to speak her mind. And like many young people, she does that rudely. My concern is whether she will grow in wisdom."

"What difference does that make?" said Chantel. "My city is being attacked!"

The man with the big cloud of hair glanced at her. "It is all of our city." He turned to the others. "Her power is Summoning. We have no one strong in that power. When she dies, she will bring that to our circle."

"I'm not going to die!" said Chantel.

There was a soft murmur of laughter around the circle.

"Oh, yes," said the hawk-nosed woman. "You are."

"However, it may not happen for some time," said a woman who had not spoken before.

Chantel looked at her in surprise. The woman was old. Her face had settled into kindly wrinkles. Her dragon robe was thrown on any old how, and not fastened in the front. She was wearing men's clothes underneath, and useful-looking boots that Chantel could have sworn were caked with swamp muck.

"Queen Haywith?" said Chantel. "The Swamp Lady?"

"We have met before, haven't we?" said the queen.

"About five minutes ago," said Chantel.

"I'm sorry," said the queen.

Chantel didn't know what that meant, but the queen turned away and addressed the circle of mages.

"This dissection of Chantel's character is pointless," she said. "Nor is it necessary for us to evaluate her. She has already tested herself by summoning us."

"She didn't summon us."

"We were here."

"Then she summoned herself *to* us. The point is," said Queen Haywith, "that her summoning skills are very strong. We know we must act. The threat to the city is real. The walls have been breached, and the enemy is entering the city."

"They are?" said Chantel.

"What did you expect?" said the man in red.

"Bringing down the walls like that!"

"She didn't bring down the walls, she only opened the gates as they were meant to be."

"But there are no gates anymore. You fools filled them in, in your time."

"There were never meant to be gates. There was never meant to be a wall."

"There must be a wall. The wall keeps the city safe."

"Someone else here was involved in bringing down the wall." This was said with a fulminating glance at Queen Haywith.

"I have to get back right *now!*" said Chantel.

"You must be tested first," said the hawk-nosed woman.

"Chantel doesn't need to be tested," said the queen. "She needs to do battle. She needs to save our city."

"That is the test, then."

"But we must help her," said the queen. "And we know her greatest strength is—"

"Summoning," several people murmured.

Queen Haywith nodded. "Therefore, I suggest we allow her to summon our power."

"But she's just a girl!"

"I was just a girl when I died defending Lightning Pass," said the girl who was wearing Chantel's robe. "And since then, Lightning's never been able to manifest himself again. Until now."

"Because no one would let the snake into their head," Chantel told her distractedly. "They were too shamefast and biddable."

"Silence!" said the hawk-nosed woman. "You can give us your opinion when you're dead."

"Well, *I'm* willing to give her *my* power." The girl who had died defending the city turned to Chantel. "Summon it when you need it."

"Thank you," said Chantel.

She would've liked to know who the girl was and how she'd died, but there was no *time*. Anything could be happening.

"We haven't decided—" said the hawk-nosed woman.

"When you summon our power," said a man with a thin gray mustache, "your own spells will be stronger."

"Great," said Chantel. It was taking all her deportment not to actually hop with impatience. "Thank you."

"What other spells can you do?" asked the hawk-nosed woman, in a nice leisurely tone, as if nobody's friends were stuck on any rooftops in front of attacking armies.

"There's no *time!*" said Chantel.

"There has to be," said Queen Haywith. "We must be prepared to do the spells too, when you summon. Tell us quickly."

"Oh," said Chantel. "Um, okay, levitation. Light-globes." Would there be a use for that? "Ice. Adhesion. Wards. Shrinking. Making plants grow. Kindling fire. Abnegation. Inversion."

"Ah, inversion." A man chuckled. "That's a good one. Do you remember the time—"

He broke off when Chantel shot him an absolutely frantic Look.

"Very well," said the hawk-nosed woman. "You may summon our power for all of these things, when your need is great. But only then."

"You will also need to summon courage," said Queen Haywith. "But that, of course, is your own."

"Thank you," said Chantel. "Really. And I need to get back right now. So can you please send me?"

"Us? Send you back?"

"We can't send you."

"Silly girl."

"Summon the city."

26

In Which Some Things Change, After All

It wasn't too difficult. It was a bit like summoning Lightning, and asking him to bring his city with him.

Chantel emerged into a blast of cold wind. She was
high in the air, on Lightning's back. She ached abominably.
That was from being caught in the deluge. Every part of
her was bruised, possibly even her hair. But there was no
time to think of herself as she surveyed the destruction
below.

All six of the seven buttons had collapsed. The rest
of the wall, and the front gate, had held firm. The water
level in the city was much lower now, and the first terrible
flood was over, but the wreckage of it lay in wide alluvia
outside the tumble-down gaps in the walls. Slabs of wall,

and rocks, and smashed wood, and . . . bodies. It looked like a lot of Sunbiters had been killed when the buttons came down. And a lot of Lightning Pass soldiers. Frantically, Chantel looked around for the people she knew. Bowser, was Bowser all right? He'd been in that boat. And Anna, and the other girls on the rooftop, and . . . and Franklin . . .

Too small.

Chantel had a whole city to fight for.

Lightning flew lower. The invaders were pouring through Dimswitch. Chantel did not see the red-horned helmet of Karl the Bloody. No, there it was, lying on the ground beside a heap of bodies . . .

A couple of sorceresses clambered through the rubble in the gap that had been Dimswitch, slipping and sliding on wet rock, struggling to raise a ward. One of them was Miss Ellicott. Chantel saw her furiously making ward signs with both thumbs as she climbed. Chantel urged Lightning on, but before she could get any closer, the invaders closed in. Chantel saw Miss Ellicott's tall form just once more, over a crowd of soldiers' heads, and then the battle intervened.

And Chantel couldn't decide what to *do*. It was already too late. The Sunbiters were in the city and there were far too many of them, and she couldn't ask Lightning to breathe fire because there were Lightning Pass people mixed in with them, and . . .

Right. So the first thing was to stop any more from getting in.

Ice.

Chantel did the ice spell, and she summoned the power of the Circle of Mages. Some of the power came easily, from people who had been used to giving. And some of it Chantel really had to struggle to get ahold of. Once she had it, though, she didn't need anything else to do the spell. No ingredients, no signs. She just thought

ice

and it happened.

Ice covered the rocks, and the Sunbiters slipped, slid and fell. The water flowing out of the city froze. It froze around boats, and around the legs of people sloshing through the flood.

This was not ideal, but it would do for now.

Everyone who tried to cross the gap slipped and fell. Dimswitch was a sea of waving arms and legs.

Chantel summoned more of the Circle of Mages' power. The battle in the lower city needed her attention, fast.

It was a boiling mass of raging humans, and it poured from Dimswitch up through the square called Traitor's Neck, and all the way to the square in front of the Hall of Patriarchs. With the remaining water in the lower city turned to ice, the enemy had stopped moving forward.

There was steel and blood. The steel, she could do

something about. Chantel drew on the Mages' power hard, and thought

shrink

And the people below her were clutching weapons the size of toothpicks.

For a moment, the fighting stopped. The whole crowd was stilled and astonished.

Then they began punching, kicking, and trying to strangle each other.

Chantel thought

inversion

Everyone in the battle was suddenly seeing everything upside down, and they couldn't figure out which way to swing their fists. The trouble was some people adjusted to the change quickly, and—

"Frozen legs," Lightning remarked laconically.

What—oh! Chantel had forgotten that most of these people were standing with their legs encased in ice. Others had climbed out of boats and were sliding atop the ice, which made them taller than the frozen people and capable of doing serious damage to them. The people who'd been standing in the now-shallow water were in danger of losing their legs to frostbite. Chantel had to take the ice away.

While she was doing that, huge rocks began flying into the melee from above.

The invaders' catapults! Chantel had forgotten about

them. And the first few rocks landed before she could remember which spells to use. Shrinking, levitation—she did both furiously, and the rocks began rising as softly as autumn leaves, caught in an updraft. Meanwhile she and Lightning flew over Seven Buttons and set fire to the Marauders' catapults.

Just as the last one was erupting in dragonflame, Chantel heard the clash of weapons from behind her. Lightning wheeled and flew back over the city. With Chantel's back turned, the shrunken weapons had regained their former size. The battle was on again.

"Lightning, what do I do?" Chantel yelled.

The dragon seemed to think about this for an unconscionably long time. Meanwhile people were killing each other.

At last he turned his head in midflight and suggested, "Tell them to stop?"

Why would they listen to me? Chantel almost asked.

Wrong question, she chided herself. "All right. Land on top of the tower on the Hall of . . . of Whoever, please," she said.

Dragons have a sense of the dramatic. Lightning swept low over the fighting throng, so low that his claws rattled against the invaders' helmets and his wings swept the surviving recruits' floppy gray hats off their heads. Then he swooped upward sharply—Chantel nearly slid off his back—and landed atop the tower.

Chantel looked out over the battling throng. She cupped her hands to her mouth and yelled more loudly than she had ever yelled in her life.

"EVERYBODY STOP FIGHTING RIGHT NOW! OR THE DRAGON WILL FRY YOU!"

And for emphasis, Lightning sent an orange jet of fire blasting out over the throng. And Chantel summoned the Circle's power to control the flames, and made the fire longer, and turned it into a great loop, and then used it to write in the sky

Stop Fighting

And it worked. At least for the moment. They stopped. They stared. Every face in the square was turned up to the tower, to Chantel and Lightning. Amid the crowd Chantel saw Sunbiters and sentinels, new recruits and sorceresses and the ordinary people of Lightning Pass.

"GOOD!" Chantel yelled. "NOW—"

But a voice boomed from the tower window below her. "Don't listen to the sorceress! Fight on, men of Lightning Pass! Defeat the Marauders within your gates!"

It was the king. And he went on and on, and his voice became noticeably richer, and louder, and more important-seeming . . . because some surviving sorceress, Chantel realized, was putting a Gleam spell on him, and making him ten feet tall.

"Lightning," said Chantel, between clenched teeth. "Now, to save lives, I would . . . I would . . . will you please . . ."

"Fight on, for your country!" proclaimed the king, in rolling, golden tones. "Fight on, for your honor! For what is right! Drive back the Maraud—URK!"

And as Chantel looked over the battlement, the king, not ten feet tall but only ordinary sized, tumbled from the window with a crossbow bolt through his neck. He splashed into the shallow floodwaters.

There was a long, long moment in which everyone took in what had just happened. And it seemed to go on and on, but it wouldn't really, Chantel realized. And when it was over, the fighting was going to break out worse than before, and a lot more people were going to die . . .

"Lighting, what do I do?" said Chantel.

But she already knew. She didn't even need him to say, as he did . . .

"Pockets?"

Chantel reached into the pocket of her robe. She had a lot of things in her pockets, but only one had a hope of stopping this war. Chantel took out the circlet of gold, and she held it in her hand.

We did not tell her to do this, did we?

Of course not.

But we knew she would.

We did not know.

We hoped.

Chantel looked down at the streets and squares. The fighting was just about to begin again. Men were hefting swords and axes. People who were alive were about to die.

And Queen Haywith was right, the dragon had changed Chantel. She was a dragonbound sorceress, and she had a crown in her hand.

And she put it on her head.

And she clambered onto the dragon's back and said, "Go, Lightning," and he fell from the tower and spread his wings over the square, and landed with a splash, sending up sheets of water over the battle scene.

Chantel stood up on the dragon's back. And every eye in the square was turned to her—Sunbiters and Lightning Pass people.

"The fighting must stop now," said Chantel. "There will be no more."

She looked out over the flood. There were many people, besides the king, who were lying motionless in the murky water. So she really meant this next part.

"If the fighting does not stop now, then the dragon will scour the battleground with flame, and no one will escape."

Lightning would do it, because she would do it, if she had to.

"Lay down your arms," said Chantel.

And then, slowly, they did. And swords sank, and

crossbows floated, and the battle was over.

"Who shot the king?" someone asked.

Probably somebody who was very good with a cross-bow, Chantel thought. And wanted to save lives.

But she chose her words carefully. She would always have to, from now on.

"I don't know," she said. "Everyone, please start look-ing through the water. We may be able to save some of the wounded."

⁂

Chantel was exhausted. She and Lightning had stood guard all through the day and the following night to make sure the fighting didn't start up again, as the wounded were gathered up and treated and the dead were laid out.

Someone had set up some sort of fancy chair on a dais for Chantel, there on the steps of the Hall of . . . Who-ever. Chantel sank gratefully into it. Tired as she was, she kept up her deportment. Queens needed it.

Many people, as weary as Chantel, were sitting on the steps, talking to each other about what would happen next. This talking was probably good, Chantel thought. She was much too tired to listen to it.

The Sunbiters had to leave the city. Chantel had given orders. But they were to have time. They were still tending their wounded, still gathering their dead. Their chieftain moved among them, his red-horned helmet gleaming in the moonlight as he stooped to tend a wounded man . . .

. . . which went to show, Chantel thought foggily, that there was some kindness even in Karl the Bloody. But wasn't Karl the Bloody dead? Hadn't she seen the red-horned helmet lying on the icy rocks, just about the time she'd last seen Miss Ellicott?

"Miss Ellicott?" she said aloud.

"No, it's me."

Anna stood before her.

Ridiculously, Anna tried to curtsey, but Chantel scrambled down and stopped her.

"The girls?" she asked.

"They're all right," said Anna. "And Bowser, Bowser's all right, but, but—"

Chantel felt a wave of dread.

"But Miss Ellicott's not, Chantel. They found her a few hours ago."

"I saw her fall," said Chantel. And when Miss Ellicott fell, what was left? The old world was gone.

What was left was for Chantel to do her duty.

"She died nobly," said Chantel. "Defending Dimswitch after it fell."

"Yes, Your Majesty," said Anna, and Chantel drew back and looked at her to see if she was being sarcastic. "Most of the patriarchs are dead too. But not Sir Wolfgang," Anna added.

It figured. There always had to be a Sir Wolfgang, to tell you how the world looked from his point of view, as if it was the only point of view that mattered.

"Where is everyone?" Chantel asked.

"The girls and Miss Flivvers are down in the dragon's lair," said Anna. "Miss Flivvers really doesn't like it much. But I thought we shouldn't go back to the school till we were sure where things . . . well, actually, the girls don't want to go back at all. They prefer the cave. And—and I really think you should get some sleep, Chantel."

"Queen Haywith lived to grow old," said Chantel, swaying on her feet.

"Are you all right?" said Anna.

Chantel was exhausted. But she had to watch what was going on in the city. She couldn't take her eyes off things for a moment. True, Lightning was watching everyone, but Lightning was a dragon, and he tended to miss some nuances. She turned to tell Anna this, and the flagstones came up to meet her. She was asleep before they did.

A lot happened in the days after that. The invaders withdrew from the city (which, after all, was remarkably full of dragon) and the new queen made certain decrees about the port fees and the road tolls, which the Sunbiters found satisfactory.

With the lower fees, more ships landed in the port,

and soon there was more to eat in Lightning Pass. But the queen was most particular about shipments of serum for spotted swamp fever, which she insisted had to be landed without charge and without delay, and then carried up the toll roads as quickly as possible.

Meanwhile, there was that extra food stored in the castle subcellars. The new queen appointed a kind woman and her daughter from the harbor district to be in charge of distributing it.

Chantel supposed that later she would have to have a council or something with whom she would discuss such matters, but for now, she needed to get things done, and it was easiest to just do them.

She didn't like the castle at all; it was too far away from things in general, and so she held court in the building that she was trying to get everyone to call the Hall of the People. She sat in a carved chair at a table that had once had nine chairs around it. And people came to see her. It seemed to her that at least half of these people were Sir Wolfgang. She had to keep sending him away.

A man who looked like death, only with a lot of bruises and a badly torn black robe, came and asked her for a job.

"I'm the royal summoner," he said. "You'll need me. When you want someone, I'll bring 'em."

Chantel thanked him politely and told him she could do her own summoning.

She saw the surviving sorceresses. They thought they should be put in charge of Miss Ellicott's School for Magical Maidens. Miss Flivvers thought *she* ought to be.

Chantel thought Anna should be.

"What the school should be," said Anna, "is a place for finding out about magic, for re-learning what's been forgotten and for discovering new things."

"And I suppose it will still just be for girls," said Bowser.

He was using crutches, because he'd broken a leg in the battle. He had a scar on his face. He hadn't done too badly at soldiering in the end. But he still just wanted to be a magician.

"In the Ago," said Chantel, "when there were queens, women and girls were not the only ones who could do magic."

Bowser brightened slightly.

"There were mages," said Chantel. "Women and also men. Sorceresses and sorcerers."

"Then we'll have boys in the school," said Anna. "We'll let—well, I suppose we'll let in everybody who wants to learn. Even Leila, I suppose."

"Did Leila survive?" said Chantel.

"Of course," said Anna. "People like Leila do. And I think we should still call the school Miss Ellicott's."

Chantel agreed. In memory of a woman who had been brave, but not brave enough to be who she was meant to be.

So the sign on the door was changed, with some scratchings out and writings in, and now it said

MISS ELLICOTT'S SCHOOL FOR the MAGICALly
~~MAIDENS~~ Minded
SPELLS, POTIONS, WARDS, SUMMONINGS
AND ~~DEPORTMENT~~
the making of new magic
TAUGHT ~~TO DESERVING SURPLUS FEMALES~~

The girls, however, decided they wanted to stay in the caves, and Bowser liked it down there too, and Anna and the queen agreed there was room there for many more students. Provided they weren't afraid of dragons.

Anna interviewed the sorceresses to decide which ones to hire as teachers, and one of the questions she asked was whether they were willing to try new magic, and another was how they felt about caves.

As for Miss Flivvers, she was not at all interested in caves. She found them simply shocking. So she was sent back to the house on Fate's Turning. It was arranged that students would visit her to learn reading, writing, and as much deportment as they needed to get by. And Anna and Chantel agreed between them that they'd just keep an eye on her and make sure she didn't get out of hand and start teaching anybody to be shamefast and biddable.

All of these decisions and discussions were constantly interrupted by Sir Wolfgang, who kept demanding audiences with the queen and was very hard to get rid of.

One day Mr. Less, the clerk, came to see the queen. He had come through the war pretty well—he had his arm in a sling, and a bandage around his head, but his mustache was as curly as ever. He wanted a job.

"I'm the only one who understands the filing system, Your Majesty," he explained.

"Yes, that's good, Mr. Less," said Chantel. "But you might also be the only one who cares about it."

"Have you thought about how you're going to pay for all these changes you're making, Your Majesty?"

Chantel had, actually. "Well, there are port fees—"

"You just lowered them."

"And taxes—"

"How do you intend to collect those?"

Chantel looked at him doubtfully. He was right, of course. The things she wanted to do for Lightning Pass would cost money, and she had learned nothing about money at Miss Ellicott's School. In fact, she realized, she needed someone to teach her, and quickly.

She wasn't sure she quite approved of Mr. Less. He had to do with the patriarchs. But they were gone now, and—

Sir Wolfgang burst into the room. "What's this I hear about schools in caves?"

"I don't know," said Chantel, truthfully.

"Look, gir—er, Your Majesty, I don't think you're capable of appreciating the kind of minds that designed this city's educational system!"

"That's true," said Chantel, in the neutral tone she'd learned to adopt with Sir Wolfgang.

"And I heard some nonsense about lower port fees, and I'll have you know—"

The queen held up a hand, so regally that Sir Wolfgang was momentarily stilled. "Sir Wolfgang, this is my clerk, Mr. Less. If you'll go along with him to his office, he will listen to all of your concerns, and take notes, and ah"—she shot the clerk a look—"file them."

The clerk bowed. "Certainly, Your Majesty."

And Sir Wolfgang, sure that he'd just been passed on to someone with more authority, went off with the clerk, complaining happily.

The queen turned to receive some people from the harbor district who wanted something. Everybody wanted something.

And then one day a messenger came from the Sunbiter tribe and said that their chieftain would like an audience with the new queen.

The queen was seeing everybody—it felt as if she'd done nothing for months but see everybody, though it had really only been a week. So the chieftain in the red-horned helmet was ushered into her presence.

The chieftain did not bring attendants, and he did not toss his helmet over his shoulder. He set it on the floor, and he bowed, and bent over the queen's hand, which Chantel privately thought was a bit much.

But she was so glad to see Franklin alive that she didn't care.

"What happened?" she asked him.

"Karl the Bloody was killed in the flood when the walls burst," said Franklin.

That much, Chantel had known. "And you were the heir. And you were there."

"Someone had to be."

"This isn't what you wanted," she said.

Franklin looked around the room, which, despite Chantel's best efforts, had begun to acquire a certain air of royalty. "Not what you wanted either, is it?"

Chantel thought about this. "It's all right. For me. But for you—"

Franklin shrugged. "It was the best way to save lives."

To save lives. Yes.

"It was a good shot," said Chantel.

A shadow passed over Franklin's face. "They're never good shots."

"I . . . I was going to do it," said Chantel. "When he told the people to start fighting again. I . . . I was working up to it. I was telling Lightning."

But she hadn't had to.

"Yes. And Karl the Bloody died when the wall came down," said Franklin.

So he hadn't had to.

Neither of them was going to thank the other. You couldn't, really. And neither of them was where they wanted to be, exactly. But they were where their people needed them.

Chantel swallowed. "Some day . . . we'll go to High Roundpot. And the Stormy Isles."

And if this were a story, and someone else were writing clever things for Franklin to say, he would have replied, "To the ends of the earth, Your Majesty."

But instead he looked startled and said, "Sure."

For now, though, they both had work to do.

High Roundpot would just have to wait.

⟨⊙⊙⟩

Chantel and the dragon flew through the sky. They soared over the city, and over the camps where the Sunbiters were packing up, heading back to their mountain homes.

They flew over a harbor thronged with ships—ships from High Roundpot and the Stormy Isles, and from everywhere else in the world. Every berth was full. White sails dotted the sea all the way to the far horizon. The city gates were thrown wide. The sailors were eager to see the no-longer-closed city, and the city people poured freely into the harbor neighborhood. Teams of workers were clearing the rubble from the ruins of the other six buttons, and people were walking out into the Roughlands, and marveling at the vast open spaces. With any luck, Chantel thought, they would all meet people different from themselves.

As for Chantel, she asked Lightning to put her down on a rock in the ocean. And he did, and went off to gambol between the waves and the sky. Chantel watched him.

He would come when she called him. But right now, after so many royal audiences, she just needed some time alone. She wasn't afraid of the rock anymore. The waves only crashed on one side of it, and not all the time. And if the tide rose, well, she knew how to swim.

The rock had been here a long time, unafraid to let the tides of change wash over it. And the city, Chantel thought, would learn.